UNWRITTEN RULES

JORDAN MARIE

UNWRITTEN RULES

USA TODAY BESTSELLING AUTHOR

JORDAN MARIE

By:

Jordan Marie

BLURB:

Marcum

I'm done with women.

At my age I'm not going to change, and women can't handle the man I am.

When I met Toi, she intrigued me.

But she's way too young for me.

Still, I can't help feeling protective of her.

I took her as payment for a debt owed.

I didn't do it for me. I did it for her.

She needs someone to watch over her ... keep her safe.

That's all this is.

That's all it can ever be.

And then ... we kissed.

That one kiss changes everything.

I can keep her safe from the world.

But, who's going to keep her safe from me?

Welcome back to the world of Filthy, Florida Alphas. If you're looking for a hard, fast ride with a man on the wrong side of the law, but with a heart as big as Texas and other things even bigger... (nudge, nudge, wink, wink) you're in for a treat! So, hang on tight, grab a fan and enjoy the ride.

DEDICATION

I find inspiration in the unexpected. At the recent signing in West Virginia I met a beautiful lady named Toi. I adored the name. I knew I had to use the name. At first my intention was to give her to Devil. The Devil, after all, needed a Toi! But, Marcum—as he often does, lately—yelled. He demanded Toi. So, to the beautiful lady named Toi I met at the Rebels and Readers Event... Sorry?
To my readers who keep demanding I come back to my MC stories, and write what is in my heart, rather than what the market demands. Thank you for keeping me honest, and able to enjoy the voices in my head. I thought the Baylee stories were dead, but you kept asking—so here he is. I hope you love Marcum.
Xoxo
J

❧ 1 ❧

TOI

I HEAR THEM IN THE DISTANCE. THE WRACKING OF THE PIPES can't be misunderstood. My father finally messed with the wrong people and soon the devil will be here, demanding his due. In this case the devil is a tall, tatted biker named Marcum. He's been here before. For some reason he's given my father at least two chances to get his shit together. He didn't. I could have told him he wouldn't.

I guess this is dear old Dad's third strike. I should wake him up. He's passed out on the stained, broken, worn out, red futon in the back room. I know because that's usually my bed. When I came home from my shift at Jenny's—the local diner where I cook—that's where I found him.

I should wake him up. I should warn him. I suppose that's what a decent daughter would do. Then again, Dad's never been decent to me, not in all of the years I've known him. So, I'm having trouble drumming up the energy to care what happens to him. That probably makes me a bad person, but hell, being good never did shit for me. If life has taught me one thing, it's save yourself. No one else is going to. Marcum runs the Steel Vipers. They're a one percent MC club here in Florida that no one fucks with. No one, except my father. Which again, is proof that my father is a moron. One percent basically means they don't give a fuck about rules and laws. They're their own entity. A smart person would steer far away from them. My father has never been smart.

I run through the house grabbing my overnight bag and begin stuffing what clothes I can find in it. I've got to get out of here. I know enough about Marcum and his thugs to know they leave no witnesses. Maybe I'm a bitch and risking great cosmic issues of epic proportion, but my father made his own bed and I've been on the receiving side of his fists often enough that I don't really give a damn. I've only stayed here this long because of my grandmother. She died last week. She had been living in a local nursing home facility. I always said that when something happened to her I would kiss Crescent City goodbye. But I'm still here, trying to come up with money to move.

The most I've accomplished is trying to live on my own. That didn't work, my father found ways to spread his shit to my new place, so it was just easier to stay here.

The roar of the bikes is getting closer. I took too long trying to get my crap. My hands are shaking as I grab my keys off my dresser. I can hear them pull into the drive. I'll come back for my car. I can't risk going out there. I run through the back of the house, even as a fist is banging against the front door—almost hard enough to make it collapse. I gasp, and then bite my lip painfully to stop the noise. I'm sure it's impossible for them to hear me, but I don't want to chance it. I bite so hard I can taste the bitter, coppery tang of blood in my mouth. I ignore it and then go straight for the small bathroom at the back of the house, right off the kitchen. I close the door quickly, which dulls the yells of Marcum demanding my father open the door. My hands are shaking as I close the lid on the commode and then climb on top of it. I push on the small window, pulling it up. I would have preferred a bigger window, but this is the only one in the house that doesn't have a screen. Once I get it pushed up, I throw my bag out first. I hear it land on the ground, but luckily it's quiet enough I doubt it will alert the others. Next, I heft myself up and swing one leg over the ledge and then contort my body to the outside while I slowly slide down the back of the house.

"Look what we got here boys!" a man calls out, just as I feel his large hands capture my hips, locking me in his arms and making me his prisoner. My heart somersaults in my chest as fear wraps around me. I was stupid to grab my stuff first.

What in the hell was I thinking?

"Is that Weasel's kid?" another asks.

"She don't look much like a kid to me. She'll make a good addition to the club talent," I hear from another one. I'm afraid to look at him. My hands are on the shoulders of a very tall man, who probably isn't much older than I am. He's got dark hair which is cut unevenly and sticking up in different directions on one side of his head, but done so in a jagged enough pattern that it looks good. He's covered in ink; I can see it on his neck and on his thick arms that stick through the leather club cut he's wearing. His eyes are brown and where I expected hate and anger, I see none. I don't even see the look of interest in my body. I can literally feel those looks from the other two men standing close to us, but not from him. I almost feel...safe. I start to calm down. Maybe this won't be as bad as I feared. Most things aren't... *Right?* Your mind always creates worst case scenarios. Maybe this is one of those cases. Maybe this guy will be my savior.

Then he speaks.

"String, go get Marcum, tell him we have a present for him," the guy says.

That spark of hope I felt dies right there and panic quickly takes its place.

Crap! It looks like karma found me early.

3

❧ 2 ❧

MARCUM

I WALK IN THE HOUSE, SURPRISED. I EXPECTED THE PLACE TO look and smell like a dump. That'd be the way I pictured Weasel living. It doesn't. Instead it smells nice... almost reminding me of the ocean. It's clean. Fuck, you could probably eat off the floors. Few things these days have the power to surprise me, but for some reason this does.

"The fucker's bike is here. Spread out and find him!" I growl the order, ready to get him and get back home. I'm getting too old for this damn shit. I'm starting to feel my fucking age too. I have since Cherry left me. I really thought she was it. I cared about her. We were good together and she had been in the club long enough, she knew my lifestyle and I didn't have to hear bitching about it, or about the number of kids I had.

Women get so twisted over the kids. I have eight kids. Why that's such a fucking big deal I don't know. A woman shouldn't worry about where I stuck my dick before her, just as long as she's the only one getting it when I'm with her. But they get so fucking pissy. I love my kids. And despite the rough start Max, my oldest son, and I had—I'm a damn good father. I take pride in it. I'm at least much better than my old man ever was.

"Hey, Marcum dude, Moth is outside. He's got a package you might want to check out."

"A package?"

"Unless I'm wrong, it's Weasel's old lady."

"That bitch flew the coop years ago. Right?" Splinter asks.

"Yeah. I heard she packed up and left her daughter behind and everything," Dirty replies.

"Tell Moth to bring her to me," I growl, walking into the tiny kitchen. I grab the handle of a mop bucket that was stacked neatly beside the cabinets. I fill it up quickly with cold water out of the old sink. Then cart it to the small futon I saw through the crack in a door off the living room. I pour the water over Weasel and watch as he sits up, yelling and trying to force the water from his face, nose and eyes.

"What the fuck?"

"That's exactly what I asked when the money you stole from me wasn't back in my account this morning. You and I had an understanding, Weasel. Did you think I'd forget?"

"I... Listen, Marcum... Man, I was getting the money back to you, I swear."

"Really? Because, motherfucker, it looked like your sorry ass was passed out," I growl.

"I was just resting, man. I was out all last night calling in markers to get your money back!"

"Then where is it?" I ask, having no doubt that the dumbass doesn't have my money. I've given him two chances, two chances too many. I only did that because Splinter said he had a daughter at home. Children need their father, but fuck this. The girl will be better off without Weasel in her life. I have eight kids. What the hell is one more? She'll probably thank me when it's all said and done.

"I don't have it yet," he mutters and I can't resist punching him hard in the nose. There's a certain amount of pleasure that comes when he stumbles back against the futon, falling down. Even more satisfaction when blood begins spewing from his face. He should embrace the pain, because in a little bit he'll feel nothing... *ever again.*

"I gave you two chances, Weasel. You've been skimming from our club for six months. Did you really think I wouldn't discover that shit? You're a dumbass," I tell him, leaning against the wall.

"I'm serious, man! I'll have it all with interest. It may just take a few more days. I'm working on something—*something big.*"

I look over at Splinter and he tosses me a bat. This is why the dude is my enforcer. He carries the fun and he knows me. Then I take a swing and slam the bat into Weasel's stomach. The fucker curls immediately, crying out. I need to make him stand next time —just so I can watch him fall down. In fact...

"Drag him up," I order and Splinter pulls the fucker up by his hair. I'm about to take another swing when Moth walks in. He's packing a woman on his shoulder. Her upper body is draped down his back so I can't see her. But her lower body is pressed to his front so that her ass is right there, staring at me. It's not a small ass either. It's lush and encased in worn, tight jeans. The denim is so faded they're pale blue to white in color. It's the kind of ass a man can grab and hold onto. A thick, lush ass that you could spank and enjoy the change in color, all while sinking inside of it until your balls bottom out against her.

It, however, is *not* the ass of a little girl.

Not by a long shot.

Motherfucker.

𝕊 3 𝕊
TOI

THE MAN CARRIES ME BACK INTO THE HOUSE LIKE A SACK OF potatoes. I don't make a sound or protest. I want to—but I don't. It's a learned reflex. There was a time when my father's beatings were horrible. I was younger then; there was no getting away from them and no leaving. He punched me in the throat, repeatedly bruising the vocal chords and doing damage there. That was ten years ago. I haven't spoken a word that anyone could hear since.

At first it was because I couldn't. Now I can, though my voice sounds different and it's hard to even make a whisper. I've kept that to myself, partly because I can't be sure my father wouldn't try again to make the damage more permanent, and partly because I've learned the quieter I am, the less attention people pay me, and there's a certain amount of safety in that.

Now as the man carrying me puts me down and I face Marcum and the others, being quiet is easier than ever, because whatever words I might utter are drowned by the fear inside of me. I wring my hands together nervously and look Marcum in the eye.

I see a moment of surprise move across his face, but it quickly fades. Which is a shame, because it's replaced by an intense look that unnerves me—probably because it is solely focused on me.

I've seen Marcum in town. He's even come into the diner while I worked, but I work in the back and he never saw me. I've always been more than a little fascinated by him—and a lot scared. He's larger than life. People tend to talk more around me than normal, because they feel secure in knowing I can never tell their secrets—since I supposedly can't talk. Yet, hardly anyone talks about Marcum, he gets that much respect—*or fear.* Still, I've seen him and though he has to be older than me—maybe by a lot—there's something about him that intrigues me. He reminds me of Kris Kristofferson in looks, or maybe even Sam Elliot like he was in the movie *Roadhouse.* Tall, lanky, but still built, long hair that looks unkempt, but still manages to be sexy. A face that has seen miles, but somehow remains appealing. Lines and scars that tell a story all on their own. There are moments when he smiles or laughs with his men and those lines around his lips and eyes crinkle and I like it... I can't even say why I like it—but I do.

Right now, however, his face scares me. This entire scene scares me. It feels as if he's studying me. In my experience when a man looks at you that hard and for that long, good things don't follow.

"What's your name?" he asks, and my first instinct is to answer him. I almost feel compelled to do it... but I fight the instinct. His voice is dark and gravelly; it sounds like he smokes six packs a day and has for more years than I've been on the Earth. He probably has... I bite my lip, giving myself pain to concentrate on, rather than his intense stare. Silence fills the room. "I asked you a question, sweet thing," he adds, and again I bite down the urge to answer.

"You can ask the bitch until the cows come home and her answer would be the same. She can't talk," my father explains and I can't stop the hateful look I give him—especially since he's the reason my voice is the way it is.

"You don't like him much, do you?" Marcum questions, and too late I notice that his gaze never left my face. He sees the hate I didn't bother to hide.

"She's an ungrateful little bitch is what she is!" my father starts.

He takes a step toward me, and I can't stop the automatic reflex to step back, to get away from him. I hate that I do it, but it's an instinct that has been born over years of abuse. Just because he hasn't touched me since I got old enough to hit back doesn't mean my body has forgotten the years before. Years when I was helpless to defend myself.

Marcum's men grab my father before he can make it to me. I hold my body still, to keep from jumping back anyway.

"Why can't she talk?" Marcum says, and I can't help but think it's not good that I've captured his attention. He stands in front of me, his hand drifting up to touch my hair. My breath stalls in my throat. His hand is huge and there are these silver rings on them that have skulls. His hand is also inked along the inside of the palm. When it spreads open I can see a tattoo of a skull with fiery red eyes.

"An accident." My father shrugs, like it's no big thing—and maybe to him it's not. I don't bother controlling my reaction to his words. I grab the first thing I find, which is a ceramic statue of a dragonfly sitting on a shelf where I'm standing. I grab it quickly and hurl it at my father. It crashes into his face. The men holding him duck as it bounces off of him and then crashes to the floor. "You bitch!" my father screams and lunges at me again. He almost gets to me right before Marcum's men grab him tighter. I spit at him, because I can, because I hate him and because I figure I'm going to die today and when I do, I at least want the satisfaction of letting everyone know how much I hate my own father.

"Why do I get the feeling I'm not getting the whole story here?" Marcum asks, pulling my attention back to him. I look up at him, my breathing hard because of my anger.

"Let me go and I'll teach her some manners," my father growls.

Marcum laughs, but it's not a sound filled with joy. This laughter is dark, tainted... and it sends chills down my back. This is a man you shouldn't get close to—a man you should run from. Which I would gladly do, if I could get free.

"You're going nowhere, Weasel. In case you haven't figured that out," Marcum says. "Tie him up in the back, then burn it down," Marcum orders.

I blink. He orders my father's death so easily it takes my breath away. I knew it was coming and the man means nothing to me—not after everything he has put me through, yet somewhere still in the back of my mind is the thought that I should plead for my father's life...

If I don't, does that make me as bad as the rest of them?

"You can't do that! You have to give me a chance here!" my father begs. I could tell Marcum it doesn't matter how much my father begs, he'll never make things right. My father is great at leaving people in the lurch... He's great at hurting people. It's kind of his specialty.

Marcum walks to my father, bends down and picks up the statue of the dragonfly that I threw earlier. It's broken in two pieces, the actual base broken away from the statue itself. He drops the base back to the ground and holds the dragonfly, staring at it. His large hand nearly swallows up the piece. It was an old keepsake of my grandmother's. I hate that I broke it, but I lashed out without thinking.

"What do you think, Dragonfly? Should I give him another chance?" he asks. At first I think he's asking the statue, but when I look up his eyes are trained on me. I want to scream no, but I can't bring myself to sign my father's death warrant when it comes down to it. Before I was leaving my father to Marcum, but I wasn't actually sticking around to see what happened. This feels different and I can't find myself cruel enough to help make the decision to kill him. So, even though I know better, I nod my head yes.

"Marcum—" one of his own men starts to interrupt, but Marcum cuts him off.

"Your daughter thinks you're worth sparing," Marcum says, looking over at my father. "I wonder if she thinks you will actually pay me back, Weasel."

"Of course she does! She knows I'll pay you, Marcum. It's just going to take a few days until my markers I called pay me back!"

"Well, Dragonfly? Will your old man pay me back?" His gaze focuses on me again. I start to shake my head yes, but he stops me. "Don't lie to me now. I expect your father to lie. I'd like to think I can trust you—at least a little more than your old man."

I rub my lips together. I want to say yes, but I don't want to lie to Marcum. Lying to a man like him can be dangerous for the health. I spare one last glance at my father and read the warning in his eyes. I turn to look at Marcum and shake my head no.

I hear my father yelling and calling me names, but I tune it out, my face never leaving Marcum.

"She's a lying cunt!" my father screams and my brain registers that, because some words can't be ignored.

"You should watch your mouth. She's saving your life," Marcum warns.

My attention goes back to him as I hear my father question, "She is?"

"She's buying you time, Weasel. Time for you to get my money."

"I'll get it! I promise! I'll get it."

"I don't trust you. That's why I'm taking collateral."

"Collateral?"

"Something of yours to keep until you pay me back."

"But, Marcum, I don't have anything, man. If I did, I wouldn't—"

"I'm taking your daughter," he says and I shake my head back and forth in denial, which just makes Marcum smile. It's a smile I don't like.

"Load up, boys," Marcum says, grabbing my hand and pulling me along behind him. "Remember, Weasel. If you don't pay me back, there won't be a rock big enough for you to hide under."

I try to pull away from Marcum, but his grip on my wrist is like iron. No matter how hard I pull, I can't get away. I glance off to the side, looking for help. There's none to be found. The guy who carried me earlier has my bag thrown over his shoulder and he actually winks at me. I stop walking abruptly when I slide into

Marcum's back. He gets on his bike and looks up at me expectantly. It's only then I realize he's let go of my hand. I start to turn and run, but the man with my bag is standing right in front of me, not letting me move.

"Sorry, honey," the guy says, and my gaze slowly raises to his smiling face.

"Hop on, Dragonfly, time to go to your new home," Marcum says, and I want to scream no. Instead, I stand there looking at him and then I get on his bike.

I don't have a choice.

❦ 4 ❦

MARCUM

"YOU GET OUR GUEST LOCKED IN HER ROOM?"

"Yeah, and put Ghost guarding the door," Moth answers.

"Good enough." I nod, taking a drink of my Scotch.

"What are you doing taking her? That's not something we usually do, man."

I rub the side of my face, scratching my skin through my beard. I think over it all and I still don't have an answer. Moth is right. I hadn't planned on taking the girl. I still can't figure out why I did. I bring my hands down to my lap and twist the insignia ring there, still thinking things over.

"There was something in her eyes," I mutter, being honest. That's still not all of it. Fuck if I know what it is about her that made me want to take her. She's going to be trouble. Usually you bring a girl into the club for one reason and one reason only. That means the boys are going to want to sample the goods and I can't let that happen.

"You know the men—"

"She's off limits."

"Are you claiming her? Because that's the only way they'll listen. We're not fucking boy scouts here, Marcum."

"Fuck you," I grumble, rubbing the back of my neck. I'm feeling older than the damn hills.

"Seriously, man..." Moth starts, before stopping and looking at me for direction. The problem is I don't know what to tell him, because I have no fucking idea what I'm doing with the girl.

"I'm not claiming her ... *but* she is under my protection."

"That's not going to go over well."

"I don't really give a fuck. Something tells me that girl has a story to tell. I find I want to hear it," I tell him, and I'm pretty sure I'm being mostly honest.

"That's going to be kind of hard since the bitch can't say a word," Moth laughs.

"That just makes it more interesting," I smirk, taking my drink and getting up. The boys are in a partying mood and I haven't been that way since Cherry left. I may not have loved her, but I was settled. I thought she was okay with my life and my club. Then she had to go throw a shit-fit because of the way I handled Jenna. For some reason she wanted to go all moral on me over that crap.

People aren't left breathing when they fuck with me and mine. They fuck with my kids that's even more true. Did it bother me that Jenna was a woman? She knew the score. She bought her fucking ticket. Cherry couldn't accept that and I got tired of her bitching and moaning.

I walk back to my room nursing my drink and taking a bottle with me. It's a sad day when a bottle of Scotch is more comforting than a woman's body.

What the fuck has happened to me?

5

TOI

"MOTH SAYS YOU REFUSE TO TRY AND COMMUNICATE WITH ANY of us," Marcum says. He strides through the door like a king on a throne—which I guess here, that's what he is. I turn to look at him, and I doubt I keep the anger out of my face. I resent being here. I probably got fired from my job. This makes the third day I've been here at the Saints club and that's three days I've not reported to work. Marcum probably doesn't understand how hard it is to find a job in this small town. I doubt he has any idea how hard it is for someone who doesn't speak, and I doubt he's ever worried about money in his life. Still, he's cost me a lot by holding me here. I didn't like him or his club before, now I really don't like him. He tosses me a pad of paper and a pen.

"You can write, can't you? You're not too stupid to do that?" he grumbles, sitting across from the bed. I shouldn't be on the bed. It feels weird with Marcum in the room, even if I am fully dressed and the bed is made. My fingers move nervously over the blanket and I grab the pen I had failed to catch. In reply, I grunt at him. This fails to impress him. I know that because he completely ignores me and fires his first question. "What's your name?"

I sigh heavily. He crosses his arms at his chest and waits, his face full of warnings that I probably should take note of. We stare at each other like that for a few minutes. His face is set in concrete. I'm stubborn, but somehow it seems to ooze out of his pores. I curse him, though only in my head—sometimes not talking has its advantages.

Toi. I write.

"Toi? How the fuck do you pronounce that?"

His response pisses me off. I roughly pull the notebook back and write, knowing he can't miss my irritation.

Gee. Let me just sound it out for you!!!!

I can't verbalize my anger so I make sure to put extra explanation points at the end of the sentence. Marcum reads it, and I expected it to anger him, which admittedly is stupid—but, for some reason I wanted to piss him off. Instead, he laughs.

"You've got some fire in you, Dragonfly. I like that," he says. He called me Dragonfly at the house, and it makes me feel funny when he says it. I don't know why. I almost think... I like it.

My name is Toi like T. O. Y.

My response makes him smirk. I have the strangest urge to stick my tongue out at him. I resist, although just barely.

"Can you talk at all?"

He asks the question I really don't want to answer. I could lie to him, but there's really not a point.

It hurts.

"Do it," he orders, and for some reason I just *knew* he would say that.

It hurts!!!! I write again, adding explanation points and stabbing my pen at the paper to make noise, trying to get my point across.

"Life hurts, Dragonfly. Do it."

Fuck you.

"I never would have thought you were afraid of a little pain." He sighs like he's disappointed.

"Fu...ck you!" I squeak out, then cough. It feels like broken glass being rubbed against my vocal chords, and it hurts like hell to get the words out. You also can barely hear them, but I manage it. Marcum looks at me strangely, saying nothing.

"How did you lose your voice?" he asks, studying me and I get the feeling he might see something I don't really want him to.

Accident.

"Like a car wreck?" he asks, and I shrug my shoulders, not about to answer that.

When do I get to leave?

"Probably never," he says with a shrug, like what he said isn't supposed to bother me at all.

My mouth drops open, unable to believe what he just said.

But I have a job! A life!

"Do you have a boyfriend?" he asks, watching me closely.

If I said yes?

"It wouldn't matter. Just mildly curious," he shrugs.

I have responsibilities!

"So do I, and you just became one of them. Clean yourself up and when you get ready, knock on the door. Ghost will bring you to me. I have some people I want you to meet."

I'm not becoming a club whore! I write as panic tears through me. Everyone in Crescent knows about the club and the stable of women the men keep. My heart is slamming against my chest. The Saints even run a club where men can go and pay for a woman. Prostitution is supposed to be illegal, but Marcum and his boys own the law around here. Hell... they are the law.

"Good to know. Now go clean up. Right now you look like hell," Marcum says and then gets up and leaves, dismissing me. I stare at the closed door and try to swallow down my fear of what comes next.

I don't succeed.

❧ 6 ❧

MARCUM

"Here you go, Marcum," Ghost announces when he walks into my office with an obviously reluctant Toi.

Toi... the name makes me shake my head. Her parents didn't do her any favors. A name like that gives a man ideas. It offers something. There was a time *I* would have wanted to take up that offer. I'm too damn old now. Toi might have her father's blood, but something about her tells me she's a good woman. She needs a man to take care of her and get her settled. I've got some good men, but with her disability she'd get run over and forgotten. She's got some grit to her, but she can't make it known.

I have no idea why I feel so protective over her, but I do for some reason. She calls to a part of me I thought was dead. The part that was bred into me by my old man before this life. A man —a real man—takes care of a woman, cherishes her because they are special in a world full of ordinary.

I've always loved women. I have since I was old enough to get my dick wet. Hell, way before I should, even. But never in all my years, have I met a woman who calls to me and reminds me of what Pop used to preach to me. He had this list of rules, all of them unwritten. He'd just pull them out of his head, but they were rules we would follow. No one dared ignore Pop's laws. He would have taken Toi under his wing.

I miss him. Fuck, the older I get, the more I remind myself of him and maybe that's what all this is about. Hell if I know.

"Thanks, man. Remind Moth there's church tonight when I get back from Max and Tess's."

"Will do," Moth says, leaving the room. He almost slams the door as he exits, and the loud noise makes Toi jump. She's much too timid to survive in my world. Only the strong survive in my world. That's my unwritten rule number one. It's served me well. The only problems that I've had is when someone I thought was strong turned out not to be... *Cherry*.

"You look better," I tell Toi, looking her over. I'm mostly lying. I doubt she's done anything. Maybe brushed her hair and pulled it back in a ponytail. She might have washed her face. That's the only real change, but I don't really give a damn so I'll let her have her small victory. Her lips spread into a smile and her eyes light.

She's a pretty thing. Long, sandy blonde hair with blue eyes, and I still have trouble taking my eyes off her body. She has a body definitely made for sin. When she's smiling like this, she triggers something in the man I am. It's like a challenge and I want to answer the call. Which is stupid, so I tamp down the urge with regret—and that's annoying.

"I don't suppose when you look like you do, much could help it anyways," I tell her, lying out my ass and just trying to cover up the fact that this young—too young—slip of a girl makes me want to show her I'm a man. God, maybe I am too old for this shit.

Her face shows shock, and then anger, but I can tell my remark bothers her, and I feel like an ass for saying it. I don't deal well with guilt, I've never really felt much of it in life—except maybe when it came to my boy, Max. So the fact that Toi makes me feel guilty pisses me off more.

"Bastard," she hisses and then coughs. Her voice is so soft and raw that I can barely make the word out, but it is there and for some reason the sound of it and the anger in it makes me happy.

"Always have been. Let's get a move on. I need to show you what your new role is here at the club," I tell her, moving from my desk.

Toi grabs my arm and shakes her head back and forth in a *no* motion.

"Well, if you don't want the position I've made for you, the boys have been wanting new talent." I shrug, getting my message across. I know she's worried about me making her free pussy for the club. Normally, that's exactly what she'd be. I'm growing soft in my old age. That's the only explanation.

She grunts in reply, but she follows me as I walk out of the room, so I take it. I walk down the hall from my office. It's a part of the place that's separated from the men's quarters, the kitchen and the common areas. It's my half. The part where none of the others go—without permission. I may be the president of the club, but I fucking like my privacy. We pass my private room and then a bath and finally the room my kids used to play in. There's a door to a fenced and protected area in the back where they can go outside on nice days. They're getting older; even the twins are in school now. They probably deserve better than what I give them.

"Daddy!" Desi yells, running to me. She might be in school but she's still Daddy's girl. I bend down to scoop her up in my arms.

"Where you been?" her brother, Harley asks, much more reserved. His arms are crossed, and he looks much older than his seven years.

"Got someone I want you guys to meet," I tell them, ignoring Harley's question. He's pouting at me because I wouldn't take him with me when I left earlier. Kid has entirely too much attitude. He may be the death of me.

"Who is it?" Desi asks, her little arms wrapped around my neck, molding her little body into my side. Her brother may make me want to pull out my fucking hair, but Desi warms a part inside of me that was cold before her birth. I love them both more than I could ever tell them.

"Does it matter? They'll leave too," Harley answers, and I

frown. He hasn't taken Cherry's absence that great. Hell, honestly, the fact that my kids miss her has probably made everything worse. I probably would have forgotten her by now if not for that. That's a fucked-up thing to admit, but it is true.

"Mind your manners, Harley," I growl. He gives me a look that I swear I've seen mirrored on Max's face a million times ... maybe even on my own face. "Toi, come over here please," I order, shooting her a look. Until this moment, I didn't realize that she was standing by the door and hadn't followed me farther into the room.

"Toi?" my kids say in unison and I grin. Her gaze locks on mine, and her eyes flash with annoyance. It's strange, but I seem to read her thoughts clear as day. Girl would be useless in a poker game.

"She's going to take care of you when you get home from school and make sure your homework and things are done," I announce and watch Toi's eyes go round in surprise and not a small amount of irritation.

"How long will she last?" Harley mutters, looking Toi over. Toi's back goes straight.

"As long as I want her to." I shrug and the fire that flashes in Toi's eyes can't be mistaken at this point and for some reason my smile stretches across my face, working muscles that haven't been used in years. I even fight the urge to laugh.

7

TOI

HE CAN'T SERIOUSLY WANT ME TO BE A NANNY TO HIS KIDS? *CAN he?* He doesn't even know me! How can he trust his kids with a complete stranger? One look at the smile on his face and I know he means it. I want to scream at him. How does he expect me to get his kids to respond to me? I can't talk to them. I suddenly have the urge to cry in frustration, but I resist—barely.

"What's wrong with her?" his little boy asks, and God help me, he sounds just as surly and grumpy as his dad.

"Is she broken?" the little girl asks, walking to me and reaching for my hand. I fight the urge to pull it away. She's sweet, but I feel like I'm on display and that's never a feeling I've been comfortable with. If she only knew how broken I am. Then again, no child should ever know that feeling. I watch as her small hand encompasses mine.

"There's nothing wrong with her." Marcum exhales loudly, rubbing the side of his neck with his hand. For a minute my eyes get lost staring at that hand. It's covered in ink, and I mean there's not a speck of skin on his hand that isn't marked in some fashion, and he has on these rings...skulls and insignias, large and heavy silver. I've never been around a man who wears rings, unless it's my boss at the diner. Then again, all he wears is a wedding ring—nothing like this. Marcum's hands should make you afraid. They're so big, it's not a stretch of the imagination to think he could physically rip someone's head off ... or at least choke the life out of them.

Of course he's probably done that.

"Toi? Are you listening?" Marcum's voice growls, interrupting my thoughts. I breathe heavily to indicate my frustration. Marcum either ignores the sound or doesn't care. I'm betting on it being the latter.

When I look at him he's holding out a notebook and a pencil. I frown.

What? I mouth, not bothering to say the word. I add in a motion with my hands that indicates a question and just because his kids are here I don't flip him off—*which is what I really want to do*.

This time it is Marcum who breathes out his irritation, and his is much more effective.

"I was telling my kids that you had an accident and have trouble speaking so you'll communicate like this," he grumbles, waving the notebook and pencil.

I take it from him, but I do it not understanding. His kids are young—probably too young for an old coot like him to have. Can they even read? *Does he really think this can work?* I stare down at the notebook, unsure of what to do.

"Tell my kids hi," he huffs, clearly at the end of his patience. I don't think Marcum has much patience.

It takes me a minute to get the notebook open, but I write on it and hold it out.

Hi.

"I'm Desi! And this is my brother, Harley!" the little girl says, her voice high-pitched and excited.

I blink. I've never been around kids. She's beautiful and her energy is infectious, but I feel way out of my depth.

"Is she stupid?" Harley asks and hand to God, his voice in that moment sounds just like Marcum.

My eyes go to him in shock. I've heard shit like that before, but not from a piss ant who has yet to grow into a man. He's going to be trouble. If I take this job—and it's not like I have a lot of choice —I'm going to have to try and contain that pint-sized, alpha-in-training, mini-Marcum and that's really not going to be easy.

Marcum takes the palm of his hand and slaps the back of mini-Marcum's head. I blink. That seems harsh, but then, I don't have kids. So, what do I know?

"Shit, Dad! What was that for?" he asks.

Okay, I know that little kids shouldn't say shit... right?

Marcum must agree, because he slaps him on the back of the head again.

"Show some respect and what the fuck did I tell you about using grown-up words?" Marcum asks and my mouth drops open. *Does he not realize he just said fuck?* Hello pot, meet kettle and all that jazz.

"Hi," Harley says, reluctantly, rubbing the back of his head.

"I'll leave you guys to get acquainted," Marcum says. "Be nice," he orders with a warning look to Harley.

"We will!" Desi chirps. "We'll introduce her to the others."

"Good." He kisses the top of Desi's head and then does the same to Harley. My heart flutters watching it. I've never seen a parent be good to a child before... weird but true. And also, it hits me just how much Harley and Marcum are alike. Of course it helps that Harley is wearing a leather jacket, white T-shirt and jeans, which is almost exactly what Marcum is wearing. It's just that Marcum is wearing a leather cut instead of a jacket, and it has patches on it proclaiming him not only a member of the Saints, but also the president of them.

He walks around me to leave and I don't think, I just reach out and grab his arm. Marcum stops and looks over his shoulder at me.

Others? I mouth my question and for some reason he grins and my gaze is frozen on his face—specifically his mouth.

"Yeah, Dragonfly. I have more than two kids. You're in charge of all of them."

I huff and hold up my finger, indicating he should wait a minute. Then I write in my notebook.

I don't know how to care for kids!

"You'll learn," Marcum answers as he reads the page I hold up. Then he shrugs. "Unless you've decided you'd rather become a club—"

I clap my hand over his mouth—harder than I needed to—and let my eyes shoot imaginary daggers at him. I look back at the kids and then to him, trying to relay the message. I'm not sure it does any good, because he just laughs and leaves the room.

I stare at the closed door for a minute. Then I stare down at a smiling Desi and an obviously unhappy Harley.

Shit.

8
MARCUM

I WALK AWAY FROM THE CHILDREN'S ROOM SMILING AND MY LIPS still feeling the weight of Toi's hand on them. She's got more spirit than I gave her credit for. Each time I catch a glimpse of it, I want to see more. Maybe I should try and find a man to watch over her. Ghost is taken with her, I can see it on his face. He's relatively new. He came in after Blaze left the brotherhood. Blaze was a fuckwad, but there are days I miss the asshole. He transferred out to another chapter a year ago. His old lady, Jinxy, left the club not long after that. Those two should have never got together. Jinxy is a good woman, but Blaze isn't the kind of man who can keep it in his pants with only one woman. Hell, I was the same way when I was younger. Which probably explains why I have so many kids.

I briefly wonder what Toi's reaction will be when she discovers how many kids I have, but I shrug it off. Really, four of my kids aren't even there; they've moved out to families of their own, like Max, or they're away in college. I miss them. I may be an asshole, but I'm a decent father—or at least I've always tried to be.

"Where you headed, Marcum?" Topper asks, coming around the corner, hugging his old lady, Babs, close. Those two couldn't be any more different in looks and in personality, but for some reason they just work. Topper is tall, skinny as a rail and kind of goofy looking in general. Babs is hot as fuck and curvy in all the right places. Topper is a good man, though, probably one of my best besides Moth.

"Heading to Dawg's," I tell him, giving my son Max's road name. "Tess is cooking dinner, and I'm going to spend some time with Maddie. I'll be back in time for church."

"Want me to go and watch your back?" he asks. He's always worried about me going places alone. I wave him off.

"You just want some of Tess's fried chicken."

"She's a damn fine cook," Topper laughs.

"I can cook," Babs grumbles.

"Babe, I love you, but more for your ass than your food," Topper answers, and from the look on Babs' face he might be in trouble.

"Later," I tell them, leaving them to it.

"Later, old man," Topper says, and he's probably older than me, so I flip him off as I leave.

"Look what the cat dragged in," Max says, opening the door. He's smiling. It's the kind of smile that puts an ease in my soul. I've spent a lot of years worrying about Max. I thought I lost him and I wasn't sure he'd make it once he got out of prison. I owe Tess a lot—for a lot of things—but none more important than the peace she brought to my boy.

I hug him tight and he returns the hug without thought. There was a time in my life that wasn't the case.

"Hey Maxwell, where's my pretty little grandkid at?" I ask when he steps back to let me in the room.

"I just got her down for a nap, and you will not wake her this time." This comes from Tess, who walks in the room smiling. She comes over to me and hugs me, as close as she can because her stomach is stretched with my soon-to-be second granddaughter.

"Tess, honey, how are you?" I ask softly next to her ear as I hold her a little longer. She's a good woman. A woman I respect and as much my daughter in my heart as if she had been born of my blood.

"Tired and fat," she laughs, pulling away and holding her stomach. "But really happy," she adds, looking up at my son, who wraps his arm around her and pulls her into him. It's not a show of ownership. Not really. It has more to do with the fact that the man literally wants her in his arms all the time. I cared for Cherry, but until I saw these two together, I didn't think what they share truly existed.

Fuck... maybe it doesn't except for Max. With everything he's been through, the man upstairs must have decided he needed a reward.

"You're beautiful, Kitten," Max grumbles, kissing her temple, making Tess's smile broaden. "You two grab a beer and go out on the deck. It's going to be a bit before dinner is ready."

"Damn Maxwell, too bad you found her first," I joke with a wink at Tess.

"Don't even joke about that shit. I'd hate to have to kill my own father," Max grumbles, grabbing us some beers out of the fridge and kissing Tess quickly before leading me outside.

I twist open my beer and take a big pull from it as I drop my ass in a chair. I kick my legs up on the banister and watch the waves of the ocean crash into the shore. The club owned this house, but when all the trouble came down with Max, and Tess was pregnant, I made it into a home for her and Maddie. It's a good place, a peaceful one, and now that Max is back with his family, it is exactly what they need.

Max mirrors me, propping his legs up on the deck railing, but he looks at me.

"You okay, old man?" he asks, as if he can sense I have shit on my mind.

"I'm always good," I mutter and for the most part that's true.

"Okay then, what's on your mind?" Max asks—like a damn dog with a bone.

"I'm fucking old, boy."

"You're only as old as you feel," he spouts off.

"Well then fuck, I have years on the damn dirt."

"Oh, give me a break. What's got you all fucked up over age?"

"What else?" I answer, taking another drink.

"Who is she?"

"No one. A damn girl I took in payment."

"Jesus Christ, Marcum! Payment?"

"Her dad owes the club. He couldn't pay and until he does..."

"You'll what? Use his girl? Christ."

"Stop getting all sanctimonious on me, Maxwell. Your past is not exactly warm milk and nursery rhymes."

"You can't use her if she's innocent."

"That's not even why I did it," I sigh, feeling uneasy again. "And I'm not using her. She's watching over my kids, mostly the twins."

Max is quiet for a minute. My boy is sharp, like his old man. I know this is not the end of it.

"Why did you do it then?"

"She needs protection," I grumble—which is partially true, but that's not the full reason I took her. Hell, I don't fully know the reason.

"From her old man?"

"Probably. She can't talk. Had some kind of accident that injured her. I'd lay money on the fact her father was behind the accident."

"You left him breathing?"

"I couldn't kill him in front of her."

"You like her."

"She's a baby."

"How much of a baby?"

"Probably Tess's age. I don't know."

"So you like her."

"I told you son, I'm too fucking old."

"She like you?" he asks, completely ignoring my answer.

"She can't stand me," I growl. "Keeps thinking I'm going to turn her into some club whore."

"I like her already."

"You really are a fucking pain in my ass, Maxwell."

"When do I get to meet my step-mother?"

"Fucking asshole. I don't—"

"What's her name?" he interrupts me.

"Toi," I grumble and Max straight out laughs.

"God, this just gets better and better. I'll tell you one thing, old man," he laughs.

"What?" I growl, draining my beer.

"You're never boring," he laughs, and I have to resist the urge to hit him over the head with my empty beer. That'd probably piss Tess off, and I actually like her.

"Fucking prick," I grumble and do my best to ignore his laughter.

❦ 9 ❦

TOI

"I'M NOT DOING IT."

I stare at Harley, annoyance filling me. I've been here two weeks, and though Desi and I have become close, Harley fights me at every turn. I scratch my forearm. It's a nervous habit, and honestly I've done it so much since Marcum brought me here that I'm scratching it raw. This morning after round one with Harley, it started bleeding. This will make the fifth time I've sparred with the little brat today, and if I ever manage to get him in bed so I can finally call it a day, I'm going to have a stiff drink and a long cry.

You will.

I write, and then for extra emphasis I hit my pen against the notebook.

"You're not the boss of me," he yells, like the spoiled brat he is.

It doesn't help that Marcum has been gone for the last three days. I don't know where he is. He didn't bother to tell me he was leaving. I learned he was gone through Ghost. Even his children didn't know he was leaving and apparently that's a common prac-tice—which makes me sad. It's not unexpected, however. I haven't seen anything in my life to show me that a man can be a caring parent, and Marcum being who he is, surely wouldn't be. Still, when I've watched him with his kids, there was a moment that I had hope that I was wrong.

"That's exactly what she is when I'm not here," Marcum states matter-of-factly from the door.

A chill runs down my spine when I hear his voice and I can feel goosebumps rise on my neck and arms. I resist the urge to hug my arms close to my body. For some reason I can't explain, Marcum's voice does strange things to me. Maybe it's fear, but if it is, it's unlike any fear I've ever experienced before.

I turn slowly and look at him. He's not changed, not really. It's only been three days I suppose, but there's something different about his appearance. He looks...haggard. Definitely more haggard, as if he has gone without sleep for days on end. Probably partying hard. Ghost hasn't made a secret about the club and the way of life each of the men live. He's even said things about Marcum and the amount of women that have been in and out of his life. I cringe thinking about it.

"She's not my mother!" Harley yells, stomping his feet and trying to go toe-to-toe with Marcum. It's a war that probably won't go well for the little man—it hasn't for me so far.

"If she was, you'd be in trouble, wouldn't you, since the bi—"

"Marcum!" I cry and it hurts to say his name. My voice comes out quiet, but you can hear the distress and at least it is loud enough to stop him from talking. His eyes hold mine, and there's some kind of emotion in them that I can't name.

"Since your mother hasn't bothered to even check on you in five years," he finishes, as his gaze holds mine while he finishes his statement. Then he looks at Harley. "Show some respect if a woman cares for you."

"She doesn't care for me. She'll leave just like Cherry!" Harley answers.

I want to argue. I've only been here a couple of weeks though. It's not my place to interfere. I know how Harley feels. Marcum thinks he's holding me as leverage over my father. I'm not stupid. There's no way my father is going to do anything to get me back.

Unless I miss my guess—and I doubt very seriously that I have—my father is probably as far away as he can get from the state of Florida.

Marcum walks to Harley, bends down on his knees, and puts his hands on each of Harley's shoulders. Then he looks at me.

"Leave us," he orders. I look at him, and then at Harley—who for all his bravery has tears in his eyes. I swallow down the urge to argue. I don't know Harley, and he doesn't like me. It doesn't make sense that I want to comfort the little boy—but I do.

Instead, I turn and walk to the door. Standing there waiting is Ghost, and I give him a smile. At least someone around here makes me feel welcome.

❧ 10 ❧

MARCUM

"SON, YOU'RE GOING TO HAVE TO STOP JUDGING EVERYONE BY your mother," I start, but that sounds damn inadequate.

Which is exactly how I feel.

Sitting here on the floor, on my knees, staring up at this tiny boy with tears and a world of sadness in his eyes... I am at a complete fucking loss as to how to deal with him. Harley and Desi might be twins, but they are as different as night and day. Desi has a lightness and a joy about her that fills a room and makes you smile. Harley, however, has always been the more cautious of the two. The one to question everything, and the one who feels things so deeply it cuts him.

I let my thumb brush against his small cheek, watching him struggle to keep his tears at bay. He tries to be me, too much really, for his age.

"Everyone leaves," he answers. "Desi and I don't need anyone else. I'm big now. I can take care of Desi."

"It's my job to take care of you and Desi, son."

"You're gone. When you aren't here, I take care of Desi. You told me that, Dad. We don't need that woman. We're fine on our own."

34

"You need someone here to watch over you when I'm not here."

"The men are here. I'm big now, too," he argues again.

Jesus. I'm getting too damn old. I have no idea how to tackle this shit.

"Well I like her! I want to keep her! Can we keep Toi, Daddy? Can we?" Desi argues, finally speaking up. She had been watching everything intently and staying quiet, which is unlike her. Seems she has finally decided to speak up.

"Desi just likes her because she plays dolls with her."

"She doesn't play with you, Harley?" I ask, knowing the answer, but trying to draw my son out.

"I don't play dolls," he grumbles. "I'm a boy."

"Toi tried to play video games with him, Dad."

"She did?" I ask Desi, but I'm looking at Harley.

"She's just here because you're making her. She doesn't care about us," Harley grumbles.

"She's here to teach you. I didn't ask her to play with you guys and spend time with you."

"She's just doing it to make you happy," he argues. My son is a tough nut, much like his old man. In my world, no one does anything for free. He's probably right. Toi doesn't know my kids and chances are she's doing everything with my kids to survive. That's the ultimate motivation for anything a man or woman does. *To keep breathing.* Still, I don't like that he's this cynical at his age. At seven he should be laughing and enjoying life, until he's faced with the truth about the world and people.

"Harley threw his game controller at Toi," Desi whispers. Harley shoots her a mean look and Desi squirms. This is new. Desi and Harley are as thick as thieves. They always have been. They band together always and hold each other's secrets over everything else. Desi has to already be attached to Toi, deeply. How did that happen in a couple weeks? I'm not sure I like it, which is crazy and I have no explanation, but it's true.

"Did you?" I ask Harley.

He shrugs, remaining as stoic as a seven-year-old can, and for my son, that's damn formidable.

"He threw his controller and hit her in the mouth and stomped out," Desi adds and maybe it's time to talk to her about not ratting her brother out quite so strongly. Though, shit, I do want to know this crap. Fuck, when did raising kids become so motherfucking complicated?

"If that's the way things are son, then go to your room," I order Harley. He looks at me, his eyes defiant. "Go. And there will be no more X-box until you apologize to Toi," I add walking over to the stand in the corner of the room with the kid's system on it. I start disconnecting it, wondering exactly how I'm going to handle Harley. I have to find a way to reach my boy, but in the meantime, I can't let him take his anger out on Toi.

"I hate her. I'll never apologize," he cries, and I look over my shoulder at him.

"Then you'll never play your games again," I tell him plainly.

"I hate you too! You're always gone! I wish you'd just stay gone!" he cries and flees the room. Desi looks toward the door a little lost. Harley's never had this bad an outburst before. I knew it was coming though. It's been coming for a while. Cherry had gotten close to my kids. They loved her. Her leaving hit them a lot harder than it did me—*which is fucking sad*.

"He'll be okay," Desi whispers, and I nod, trying to reassure her. I give her a tight smile.

"Yeah, he'll be fine, princess. He'll be fine."

I wish to hell I believed that right now.

꧁ 11 ꧂

TOI

"You okay, blue eyes?" Ghost asks. I'm sitting outside on the doorstep. Ghost is standing against the building watching me and smoking a cigarette. I've never been a fan of smoking, but for some reason Ghost smoking close to me I find reassuring. He's been really nice to me. One of the small bright spots in my new world.

I nod my head yes, but I avoid his eyes.

"What's up?"

"Harley." I mouth the word, barely making a noise. I rub my throat. I hate the way it makes me feel like I'm weak.

"Don't let him get you down. The kid talks tough, but you'll break through to him," he says, and I want to scream that I won't. I don't know anything about kids, especially kids that are angry at the world. Hell, I'm angry at the world. How am I supposed to make things better for them?

I don't respond, but I look at Ghost, and I'm pretty sure my thoughts are plain for him to see. They must be, because he laughs and sits down beside me once he snuffs out his cigarette. I scoot over on the step to make room for him. It feels weird having a man sit this close to me. It actually makes me nervous; even though

Ghost has been good to me, I haven't been here that long. I don't really know him, and I don't trust people. I hug my knees, letting my fingers bite into the fabric of my pants, until I reach the point that I can feel the sting of pain on my legs.

"You're something, Toi," he says as I pull my eyes to his face. He's leaned in close, and I might be inexperienced, but I'm not that young either. I see the intent on his face.

Ghost wants to kiss me. I'm not sure how I feel about that. I have been kissed before. Before I lost my voice, I went on dates, I had boyfriends—*kind of.* Ghost is really cute, but he is part of this club. He's part of Marcum's crew and... *Marcum confuses me.*

"Ghost," I whisper, and it's a definite whisper, since that's all I can manage. It's so soft I wouldn't be surprised if he couldn't hear me.

"You have courage, honey. You manage to make yourself known more than any woman I've seen, and you do it with very little communication. I admire you," he says, and those words warm something inside of me.

I mean, they're nice. I don't think anyone has ever told me they admired me before. Again, I'm not naïve, so I know he may only be saying it to get me to sleep with him. But, still it's nice. I lean a little closer to him. What harm could one little kiss be?

"Ghost, Topper needs you in the garage," Marcum says from behind us.

I tense up immediately. I hear Ghost whisper a muted curse under his breath, and I resist the urge to smile. He likes me. For some reason, that makes me feel special, and I'm not even sure why. But, I like it.

"Marcum, when did you get back?" Ghost asks as he gets up. He reaches his hand down to me, and I place mine into it as he pulls me up.

"Just a bit ago. Go see what Topper needs," Marcum answers, his voice tight. He's obviously still upset over Harley.

"Topper didn't call my cell," Ghost responds, staring at

Marcum. Marcum doesn't answer; instead they stare at each other intensely. "That's strange, don't you think?" Ghost adds.

"Not my problem," Marcum responds.

"I'll take Toi back to her room then and head over there."

Ghost puts his hand at my back. I'm staring at Marcum, and it's clear he's upset. I have to wonder what Harley told him. If he's upset at the way I've been trying to teach them and spend time with them, then it's on him. It's not like I have experience with kids. He knows that. He didn't give me much of a choice in this situation. I've done the best I could!

"Leave Toi here. I need to talk to her about Harley."

"You need to talk to your son."

"I did. Not that it's any of your business."

Marcum crosses his arms and stands looking at Ghost as if he is daring him to say one more word. If I was Ghost, I wouldn't. Anger seems to be radiating off of Marcum now, and I get the feeling he's just looking for a fight.

I don't think I'd take the bait.

12

MARCUM

WHEN I SEE GHOST ABOUT TO KISS TOI, I'M FILLED WITH annoyance. I'm not sure why; I just know I don't like it. He's been interested since he first saw the girl, and she needs someone to protect her. Having them get together would be the perfect answer to a lot of issues. I should be happy about it.

I should.

"I could wait and take Toi back to her room," Ghost responds, and it takes work not to knock his ass down and stomp him under my foot. I like the motherfucker, but he's playing on my last damn nerve right now.

"You could go to the fucking garage like I told you to," I growl.

Ghost jerks his head around to look at me. He's usually pretty stoic, but I can see the surprise that lights up his face. I don't blame him. I'm pretty fucking relaxed unless it's club business, and I never get into it with the men when there's a damn chick involved. I don't know what the fuck is going on with me, but I'm not backing down here. I stare at Ghost without blinking, daring him to push me on this. I almost wish he would. I need an excuse to slam my fist into his face.

"I'll see you later, blue eyes," he tells Toi. I watch as his finger

40

travels down the side of her face, and she murmurs the word bye to him. I frown watching the display. Ghost looks at me. "I'll just go to the garage like I was *ordered* to do," he says, and walks off.

"You sleeping with him?" I ask Toi once Ghost has gone. Her eyes dilate with my question and shock is evident on her face. It's quickly replaced by anger. I see the moment it sparks in her gaze, and I like it. She can hardly talk and she's had a shit life up until now, but it's done nothing to quell the spirit inside of her. She's got grit. She sure as fuck didn't get that from Weasel. I'm not sure where it came from, but I find myself hoping she never loses it.

She grunts, but doesn't reply. I know it hurts her, but like always I find I push her to go further.

"Answer me."

"Not your business," she whispers, making the words short so that they don't make a real sentence, but I understand them. Which I can appreciate. What I don't like is the fact that she didn't really give me an answer.

"I thought you didn't want to become a club whore?"

Her soft gasp makes me want to smile for some reason.

"Asshole," she roughly whispers.

"Just saying if I knew you were open to that, I would have given you the first go around. I usually sample the talent before I let the boys have it," I tell her with a smirk, pushing her because I can. I like when I get a glimpse of her fire. I expect her to sass me. For some reason, I even like that. What I don't expect is for her to draw her hand back and slap me hard across the face—which is exactly what she does.

"Do you have that kind of fire in bed?" I mock her and she hauls her hand back to slap me again. I grab her wrist before she can connect.

"I don't think so," I growl and her hand jerks in my hold as she tries to pull free. If she were able to right now, she would be screaming at me. For some reason, I wish she could.

"Let me go." Her strained whisper is full of anger and fury.

Hell, her blue eyes practically glow with emotion and her face is flushed. She really is quite beautiful when she's fired up like this.

"Did you fuck Ghost?" She jerks her hand to try and slap me again. The intent is clearly broadcasted on her face. "You managed to slap me once, Dragonfly. You don't want to do it again. Trust me on that," I tell her, my voice low.

She narrows her eyes at me, frustration and anger warring clearly on her face.

"No," she whispers, finally answering my question.

"Good. See that you don't. If you want to be a club whore, you don't need to be around my kids."

"You're an—" She pauses to get her breath, "—asshole."

"You have no idea," I grin. Fuck, I know I'm an asshole. I'm good at it. She'll get used to it. It's not like she has much of a choice. I let go of her hand, and she jerks it back against her body. She goes to walk around me, and for some reason, I watch her ass as she walks away.

In my head, I hear Maxwell laughing.

Fuck.

❧ 13 ❧

TOI

HE'S INFURIATING! HE'S AN ASSHOLE AND AN IDIOT ALL ROLLED into one! He's a pig! I march down the hall to the room I've been staying in, still rubbing my wrist where he grabbed me. There will probably be bruises there tomorrow—not that Marcum will care. How is it his business if I sleep with Ghost?

Or anyone for that matter!

I've had it with the men in my life ruining everything for me. While Marcum was gone, I began to kind of like this place. Having him back brought reality back like a bucket of cold water. I need to start thinking about breaking out of here. I don't know how I'm going to do it, but I have to. If there's one thing I know, it's that my father is never going to give Marcum money.

In my life, there's been one recurring theme. There's no prince to ride in and save the day for me. If I'm going to survive or get out of this, I have to save myself. I just wish I knew how.

I make it back to my room, but I know Marcum is following. I can hear his heavy footsteps behind me. I don't bother looking back and I don't try to talk further. It wouldn't stop him, so there's really no point. That doesn't stop me from trying to close the door before he gets inside, however. Too bad it doesn't work.

I march straight over to the bed and grab the pen and paper I've kept there and write quickly.

Do you mind? I came here to be alone.

"This is my club, Dragonfly. There's no place here you can go to be alone. If I want to see you, I will."

Then let me go.

I don't know what I expect his reply to be, but his laughter wasn't it.

"I'd probably be better off if I did, but I'm not going to, Toi. Turns out I don't seem to get wiser with age."

I have no idea what that means.

"Stay away from Ghost," he says out of the blue and I can't help looking confused.

Why?

"He's not for you." Marcum shrugs his shoulder, looking uncomfortable. I can't help feeling hurt and it takes all of my courage not to look down in shame.

You think I'm not good enough for Ghost. I don't make it a question. It's a statement. This is a familiar song and dance. I've heard all about my failures from my father. Surprise hits Marcum's face. I can see as it spreads over his features. Did he think I wouldn't call him on the fact that he's being an asshole? I'm sick of people who treat me as less. I've taken it for far too long. *I want to leave!!!* I write on the pad, holding it in front of me and shaking it, like that could make the words come off as the scream I wish I could make.

"I need you, Toi. So you will stay," he says, walking to the door.

"No!" I respond, ignoring the tightness in my throat.

"I like your fire, Toi. I find I like it too much. You might want to cap that shit before we both prove my son right," Marcum growls.

His words make zero sense.

"What?" I ask, and even though I'm barely whispering, I know Marcum can hear me.

"I need to stay away from you," he says strangely. He takes a

44

step toward me. Ironically, I have to stop myself from stepping backwards to get away from *him*.

"Let me go," I respond, barely hearing my own voice.

"Strangest thing happened to me the last couple of days, Dragonfly," he answers, so close I feel his breath on my skin. His large hand reaches out and his thumb brushes against my neck.

"What?"

"I thought of you."

"Don't... understand," I strain the words, my heart beating harder. The look on his face makes me feel strange and again, I don't understand exactly why. I swallow. Is he going to kiss me? Why would he? *Why am I wondering what it would feel like?*

"I don't either, Dragonfly. I don't either," he says, dropping his hand and stepping back. Then, without another word, he walks away, leaving me to stare after him.

Feeling lost.

❧ 14 ❧

MARCUM

"HEY MARCUM! DIDN'T KNOW YOU WERE JOINING THE PARTY tonight," Topper calls as I down another shot. He sits down in the chair across from me, pulling Babs down astride him.

"You're looking good tonight, Babs," I tell her, just drunk enough to ignore Topper and enjoy that Bab's curves are popping out of the barely-there mini-dress she's wearing. *Shit.* If her dress shifts just a little to the right her tit is going to pop out. Not that I haven't seen Babs' tits before. I have. It's just I usually have another chick's to play with. I've been without a woman for six months. After Cherry left, I got my dick wet a few times, but I kind of lost interest.

I may not have been in love with her, but I respected her. It was as much of a relationship as I've ever had. I was settled, and as fucked-up as it sounds, I liked coming home to a woman, knowing some other man's dick hadn't been keeping her warm for me. I liked the life we were building. I thought we understood each other.

And maybe that's exactly what's wrong with me now.

I've been too long without a woman, and it's got me looking at

Toi in ways I shouldn't. She's a kid. A defenseless kid—and the last thing I should be thinking about is getting between her legs. This is Maxwell's fault. He put the damn thought in my head. I just need to get lost in a different woman and everything will be back to normal.

"You hear me man?" Topper asks, and until that moment, I didn't realize I had completely tuned everyone out. I jerk my head up to look at him. It's then I notice he's uncovered Babs' tit and is palming it in his hand, basically milking the DDD morsel.

Yeah. I really fucking need to get laid.

"What's up?" I ask motioning for a Proby to bring me another drink.

"I asked if you had heard from Weasel?"

"Nah. Not that I expected to."

"What are you going to do with the girl?"

"Who knows," I growl, and down my shot in one gulp once it's refilled. I lift the glass and the guy fills it again.

"Ghost is sweet on her," Babs says, taking a break from nibbling on Topper's neck.

"She's only been here for a few weeks."

"Doesn't matter. He wants her."

"He's always looking for a new place to stick his dick," I answer. I'm lying out of my ass. Ghost has had his turn with the club talent, but he's more reserved than any of us. Truth be told, he's a good man. I was thinking about giving him the greenlight with Toi...until... *Maxwell.*

This is all my son's fault. He put this damn thought in my head about Toi.

About having Toi.

"This is his fault."

"Whose fault? What are you talking about, Marcum?" Topper asks.

"Maxwell! This is his fucking fault. Smartass boy. He's trying to fuck with his old man."

"Marcum, old man, you aren't making a lot of sense here," Topper mumbles.

"You sure ain't, honey," Babs adds.

"You got damn nice tits, Babs," I compliment her.

"Thank you, honey." Babs laughs.

"How much have you had to drink, man?" Topper asks, and I shrug. I haven't been counting the shots or the drinks. I've been here since I left Toi and its dark outside now. I can see that through the window. That means it has to have been more than a few hours.

"Maxwell needs to learn you can't fuck with me. Everyone knows that," I complain. "Everyone but my own flesh and blood."

"Dawg respects you, old man."

"He doesn't yet! He keeps wanting me to fuck her, but I'm not about to fuck her!" I mutter. I drink down another shot and motion for another one.

"Marcum, honey, maybe you should slow down the drinking."

"Maybe I need to drink more."

Topper reaches over and grabs the empty bottle the Proby left when he filled my last shot, warning me it was the last of the stock. He looks at it and whistles through his teeth in a long, annoying call.

"Fucking hell, Marcum. Devil Springs Vodka? Did you drink this whole bottle?" he asks, waving it in front of me like a damn moron.

I don't know if I've had the whole bottle. I drank whiskey, somewhere along the line he made a flaming shot, and eventually I just started downing whatever he gave me. I can hold my liquor pretty good, but even I can admit I'm drunk off my ass at this point. It doesn't matter. Topper is just trying to distract me. He's always taken up for Max and he wants to keep me busy so I don't go kick my son's ass.

"I'm going to Max's!"

"What the hell are you going to do there? Shit, I bet you can't even walk."

"I'm going to tell him he's an asshole," I growl. I stand up, holding onto the table for a moment. I am a little dizzy. Topper might be right and I'm a little drunk. "Still sober enough to kick my oldest son's ass," I mutter, beginning to walk out.

"Not sober enough to drive. Ghost, take Marcum out to Dawg's," Topper hollers.

"The fuck he will. This is Ghost's fault too. I ought to kick his ass."

"What the hell did I do?" Ghost asks, as if the fucker didn't know.

"She's not going to be my stepmother!" I growl.

"Marcum man, I think maybe you need to sleep that shit off."

"Max's stepmother," I mutter, knowing I got it all wrong. "Fuck it. I have to go talk with Max."

"I'll take you man, I got a feeling this is something I want to see," Ghost says. I look at him and then haul off and hit him. He's playing some fucking games because his head keeps moving but I manage to catch him. I pulled my punch, I guess, because he keeps standing. "What the hell was that for?"

"I don't like the way you look," I growl.

"I'll make note," he says.

"See you at Dawg's," Topper says, carrying Babs out of the room.

"Why can't I ride with you?"

"Taking my bike, and no offense, man, but I'd rather have Babs riding bitch than you."

"You're a fucking asshole."

"Have been for years," he says, laughing.

"I need to clean out the club and start all over. You assholes are stinking up the place," I growl to Ghost, walking toward his truck.

There must be a hole in the asphalt outside, because I almost fall in the parking lot. Ghost reaches out to catch me, but I knock him away, managing to stand on my own.

"Marcum—"

"I'm not that fucking old. I don't need you helping me walk. Next thing I know you'll be asking to wipe my ass."

"Trust me, Marcum, man. That's one thing I'll never ask."

"See that you don't," I mutter, my head feeling woozy.

I get in his truck, and he slams the door shut for me. Bastard probably thinks I'm too fucking old to shut it myself.

I need to hit him harder next time.

🌾 15 🌾

TOI

I LOOK OUT THE WINDOW AND SEE EVERYONE LEAVING. MY GAZE zeros in on Ghost and Marcum. I watched them walk to the truck, I even watched Marcum stumble and then hit Ghost. He's obviously drunk. Maybe he was drunk when he was here earlier. That would explain a lot. All I know is that now is the perfect time to leave. I may never get another chance like this.

The minute the taillights disappear, I move around the room packing my things. I don't have much, so that definitely doesn't take a long time. I'm about to go to the door when there's a knock. My heart kicks in my chest and a cool flush of heat hits me. Panic —that's what it is. I look at my bag as I hear another knock. I stuff it under my bed, pulling the comforter down so that it's lopsided, but manages to hide the bag.

I open the door, not sure of what I will find. Marcum and Ghost are gone and that's usually the only two I see. Besides, if it was either one of them they would have just walked in. I'm surprised when I see Desi there.

Hi.

I mouth the word, knowing I don't need to speak it for her to understand. She's in her pajamas and holding a worn teddy bear, but it's the tears running down her face that melt my heart. I gather her up in my arms, kick the door shut and carry her to the bed.

"Harley hates me," she sobs.

I swallow, because I know this will be painful, but some things are worth the pain. Desi already owns a piece of my heart. Hell, Harley does too—*even if he despises me.*

"He doesn't hate you."

My voice is rusty, but I know I *can* talk like this, and Desi needs my voice right now. I'll pay for it tomorrow. The doctors have warned me not to strain my voice, but right now I feel I don't have a choice. I've spent years trying to conserve what vocal use I have. I had dreamed of having surgery on my vocal chords. I need to face the truth, though. It's been years since my injury and I've barely managed to save money, let alone enough for surgery.

I have to stop dreaming.

"He does. I told Dad on him and he got mad."

"He'll get over it, honey."

"You don't understand, Toi. I've never told on Harley before. Never!"

"Desi..."

"But he was being mean to you and I was afraid he would make you leave. I don't want you to go, Toi."

"Baby..."

"I love you, Toi," she cries and if your heart could break in one moment that would do it. No one has ever told me they loved me before.

In a lot of ways, I wish it hadn't been this little girl telling me now. I could ignore a lot of things, but I could never ignore Desi—or even Harley, for that matter. I hold her close whispering soft nonsense, trying to comfort her in ways I've always wanted someone to comfort me, but never had.

Slowly her sobs ease and she falls asleep in my arms. I should take her to her room, but I like the feel of her in my arms. I close my eyes.

How am I supposed to leave with Desi's cries in my heart? Will she hate me if I leave? Will I be another person who hurts her like the long list of people in my life? Can I live with myself if I am?

Tonight I have no answers. Which means instead of escaping the club, I'm holding a little girl close and falling a little more in love with her.

❧ 16 ❧

MARCUM

"Maxwell! Get your sorry ass out here!" I yell, as I stumble my way to his house.

"Marcum, man, maybe you should go home and sleep this off," Ghost says, following behind me like a damn dog. I hear Topper and Babs pull up on his bike, too. Motherfuckers. All of them. I'm surrounded by fucking assholes.

"Fuck off," I growl at Ghost. "Maxwell damn it! Get out here!"

I stagger to the door and he still hasn't got the nerve up to open it. He's smarter than I give him credit for. He should be scared to tangle with his old man. I might have some mileage on me, but I won't be fucked with.

Damn boy still isn't here and I have to take a piss. I unzip my pants and take out my dick.

"Jesus, Marcum. I don't want to see that shit," Ghost and Topper yell.

"I don't mind," Babs says and I wink at her while I drain my dick.

"Thanks, darlin'," I tell her.

"Anytime," Babs laughs as Topper swats her on the ass.

"What the fuck is going on here?" Max questions with a roar

when he opens the door. I'm still pissing. I guess all that alcohol had to go somewhere. "Jesus Christ old man, what in the hell are you doing?"

"You and I need to have an understanding Maxwell."

"One where you take a piss on Tess's flowerbed at midnight?"

"Just watering them. See, I'm not fucking old, the old prostate works just fucking fine."

"Fucking hell," Max mutters from behind his hand. "Top why in the hell are you letting him out in this shape?"

"You know your old man. Not an asshole alive can stop him when he gets something in his head."

"In case you assholes were wondering, I can still fucking hear too," I tell them, shaking my dick dry. I turn to see Babs looking at my dick. "It still works just fine too," I tell her with a grin.

"Marcum, dude, don't make me kill you," Topper says, pulling Babs to him.

"You could try." I shrug.

"Oh stop it both of you. You know I'm not going anywhere, you old fart. But a girl can be taken and still look. Jesus, I'm not dead and he's packing a monster," Babs laughs.

"She's got a point there." That comes from Tess, and that's something that I don't want. My daughter-in-law should never see my dick. I zip up my pants quickly.

"Tess, darlin', you just forget you saw any of this."

"I'll try. What's going on with you, Dad?" she asks softly and she doesn't call me Dad often, but when she does, I find I like it.

"He's here to get killed if he keeps flashing you his fucking cock."

"That! That right there! I'm sick of this Maxwell! Tess is a daughter to me! I don't think of her like that! You're wrong for even thinking that shit."

"Marcum, you aren't making a bit of sense."

"To be fair, he wasn't at the club either," Topper adds and I flip him off.

"Or in the truck," Ghost responds.

"Fuck you, fuck all of you," I growl. "Sorry for the language, Tess."

She grins. "It's okay."

"This is Maxwell's fault," I grumble.

"It usually is," Tess answers, and Max frowns at her. She reaches up and kisses him and the sight makes my heart hurt. Max deserves this. He went through hell. He totally deserves it...

Or at least he did before he tried to fuck with me.

"You put shit in my head and I can't work around it!" I growl.

"Uh... I think I'll go make some coffee. I'm thinking we're going to need it. You guys staying?" she asks the others.

"Wouldn't miss a minute of this, honey," Topper says.

"Same here," Ghost adds, "But, I'd rather have a beer."

"I'll be in the house when you guys move this in. Dad, I love you, but if you could be just a little quieter so Maddie sleeps, I'd appreciate it."

"You got it darlin'," I yell.

Tess winces.

"Think you're beating a dead horse there, Kitten," Max says, pulling her close and kissing her temple.

"Be gentle," she whispers, and I don't know what she's talking about, but it's sweet. Yeah, Maxwell deserves this—*if he wasn't such a fucking prick.*

"All right, old man. Why don't you come inside and let's hash this out?" Max responds when she disappears back in the house.

I blink because fuck... I think there might be two of them.

Maybe I am a little too drunk...

🎋 17 🎋

MAX

"I'M NOT COMING IN," MARCUM GROWLS. "YOU AND I ARE going to have this out, Maxwell."

I step outside, closing the door, trying to keep what noise I can out—just so Maddie can sleep. I've learned that my father doesn't let things go easily. I've rarely seen him drunk. I don't think I've *ever* seen him this drunk, so I figure he's definitely not going to be cooperative.

"Fine. Would you like to tell me exactly what we're having out?"

"Don't play stupid, boy! You know what you did! You messed with my fucking head and that shit is messing with my dick!"

"Jesus Christ," I mumble rubbing the side of my face. I need more sleep to deal with this. "What in the hell did you let the son of a bitch drink, Top?"

"Vodka... Devil's blend. Not sure how much, Dawg. God's truth it could have been the whole damned bottle."

"Fuck, he'd be dead," I argue, but from looking at the shape Marcum is in, I can't completely dismiss what Top says.

"I could always handle my liquor," Marcum brags. If the old

57

man could get a look at himself right now, he might think twice about making that boast.

"Fine. Then tell me what's going on, Marcum. It's late and I was in bed with my wife and I want to go back there."

"You fucked with my head and it's fucking with my—"

"Dick. Yeah, I got that the first time, old man. I just have no fucking idea what you're talking about."

"Toi!" he growls. The others have been talking and laughing to that point; now everyone goes quiet. For me, suddenly everything clicks into place and I start to relax.

"How is my stepmother?"

"That shit right there! That's it! She's a kid! I can't fuck her!"

"Sure you can."

"She's too damn young!"

"Do it to the tune of the Hokey Pokey. Put your dick right in, pull your dick right out. Shove it back in and move it all about," I finish, and I hear Topper and Babs laughing, *barely*—because I'm laughing harder.

"Fucking prick. I didn't beat you as a kid, that's my biggest regret," he growls.

"I'm just saying—"

"You're saying too much."

"What's the real problem here, old man?" I ask, when he drops to the ground looking miserable.

"I keep thinking about her."

"Why is that wrong?"

"I'm too old for her and she's... Fuck, I think she's innocent."

"Jesus. How old is she? Is she like sixteen?"

"No! Christ, I'm not that fucked up," he grumbles.

"Is she legal?"

"She's legal." This comes from Ghost. I turn to look at him, because there's a tone in his voice I can understand immediately. He's sweet on this girl.

"Did you fuck her?" Marcum asks, getting up and except for a slight wobble, it's like he's not drunk. It's almost as if his anger is burning through.

"If I did, then it's none of your business. I won't stand by and let you use her," Ghost says and it's been awhile since I've been in the life, but it takes guts for a man to stand up to Marcum like that.

"I'm not going to use her," he growls.

"Then what are you going to do with her?" Ghost asks.

"Protect her," Marcum mutters.

"Even from yourself?" Ghost asks, right before he walks away.

Ghost starts his truck up and leaves. The four of us are standing there and Marcum looks up at me, and I don't believe I've ever seen the man more torn up. I *know* he hasn't been in this shape over a woman before. Christ. Tess was right the other night when she told me my father was going to fall hard. I think he already has.

"See what you've done, Maxwell?" Marcum asks me. I don't get why he's blaming me, but who knows with him. He's never been in love before, and I remember from my days on the run with Tess that when a woman gets under your skin, she fucks up all your thoughts. "Motherfucker," Marcum grumbles, walking toward the door.

Topper waves in the background, taking Babs with him toward his bike. I nod my head slightly in acknowledgment. Guess Marcum is my responsibility tonight.

"Later," I mutter, standing back so Marcum can come inside. Marcum just stands there looking at me, completely lost. It's not a look I like, so I react the one way I know will get his anger going. "Toi and Marcum sitting in a tree. K-I-S-S-I-N-G," I smirk. Just as expected, my father comes walking towards me and before I can blink, he buries his fist into my stomach.

"Smartass motherfucker," he growls, walking on in and leaving me gasping for breath.

He might be drunk off his ass, but he can still hit. I find I don't care. It was more than worth it.

❧ 18 ❧

TOI

"WHAT THE FUCK?"

I awake with a jerk. My eyes open to find Marcum standing over my bed—*a very upset and scary looking Marcum*. I sit up quickly. Fear, shock and annoyance all war with one another, as they always seem to do when Marcum is around. When I glance at the bedside table, the clock says it's almost 10:30.

Shit, I overslept. Still, it's not any reason for him to look like he's about ready to kill me.

"I overslept." The words are raw—even more so than usual. I talked too much with Desi last night. That's when memories of the night before come back to me and I look around the bed to find Desi. She's sound asleep, curled up to my side. I smile down at her at once. And hug her gently, then I lean down to kiss the top of her head. I slide off the bed, looking sternly up at Marcum. "Outside, now," I mouth.

He stands there staring, but when I walk around him he follows me to the door. I grab the pen and paper off my bedside table and, once we get out in the hall, I gently close the door.

"What the fuck is Desi doing in bed with you?" Marcum

growls. His question surprises me. I knew he was upset, but why that should bother him, I don't understand.

She was upset.

I write angrily and don't bother trying to keep the anger off my face. It's clear that Marcum and I are going to be enemies. I should have left last night, but I just couldn't after Desi came to my room. I'm not sure I can now.

"About what?"

I sigh loudly, and even though that hurts, I want him to know how impossibly annoying I find him.

Her and Harley had a fight. She needed comfort.

"She needs to sleep in her own bed. Do you have any idea the hell you've put me through?"

I don't see how. You're being crazy.

"Crazy? Fuck, Dragonfly. How do you think it felt when Harley reported to one of the men that his sister was missing? Or how I felt once I had my men comb the entire club and not find her?"

I take a step back. I can kind of understand what he's saying now, but still, he's being an ass. I'm at a loss on how to reply, so I don't.

"You talked in your room. Your voice was louder," he says.

So?

"If you can talk like that, you need to do it more often."

I was told not to.

"Who the hell told you that?"

A doctor.

"Who?"

It's not any of your business.

"What the fuck? Haven't you got it yet, Toi? Anything to do with you is my business now."

"Why?"

"Because I own you."

I shake my head no, rather hysterically, I'm my own person. No one will ever own me.

"But I do, and you better get used to it, Dragonfly," he says.

There's something about the look in his eyes that scares me. I open the door and back away from him. When I close it, I can hear him laughing behind it.

"You sure got a way with women, old man," the voice says.

"Fuck off, Maxwell," Marcum growls.

A minute later I hear them walking away and I'm glad. I look over at Desi and my breath freezes in my chest. I need to get out of here. I just wish I knew how without hurting the little girl lying in my bed.

The little girl who owns a piece of my heart.

19

MARCUM

"THAT IS NOT THE WAY TO WIN OVER MY STEPMOTHER DAD," Max laughs.

"Fuck you, Maxwell," I demand, marching into my office. Max comes in after me, closing the door behind him.

"With an attitude like that, I'm never going to have a new mommy."

"If you don't shut the fuck up, Tess is going to be a widow."

"You're awful grouchy this morning. What's wrong Marcum, feeling a bit hungover?" Max laughs.

"Can you quit being a fucking dick, and while you're at it stop screaming? They can hear you three rooms over."

"It's not as much fun though."

"Asshole."

"Okay, okay. All jokes aside, if you do like this woman, you're not doing yourself any favors here."

"She's not a damn woman, she's a girl. Too damn fucking young and innocent for me."

"Not to play devil's advocate here or anything, but it may be out of your hands soon."

"What are you talking about now?"

"Ghost likes her. I could tell. If you don't make a move that man will, and soon."

"He'd be a good man for her," I respond, refusing to look at him. Instead, I sift through papers on my desk that I don't give a fuck about.

"Damn, old man, I never figured you for a man who'd be too afraid to make a move."

"Shut your mouth, Maxwell. You don't know what you're talking about."

"Explain it to me."

"I'm fucking tired of talking about it."

"Hey Marcum!" Dusty says, opening the door.

"What's up?"

"Saved by the bell," Max whispers.

"Fuck off."

"Two things. First, Ride's woman is here to look at Toi."

"Take her to Toi's room. I'll be there in a bit."

"You aren't going to like the other news," Dusty stalls.

"Just spit it out."

"Weasel's outside wanting in."

"Fuck!"

"Told you that you wouldn't like it."

"Bring him in. Keep him contained in the pit room. I'll be there after I see to Toi."

"If he demands to see his daughter?"

"You keep that fucker away from Toi. He doesn't get near her. He doesn't breathe the same fucking air as her."

"Got it, man. Got it," Dusty says. He closes the door, and I look up to find Max watching me closely—too fucking close.

"What?"

"You're awful protective over a woman you're willing to give to another man without a fight."

"I told you she's not a woman, she's a gir—"

"Yeah, whatever, Marcum. You know the answer to that," he says getting up.

"What the fuck are you talking about now?"

"If she's not a woman yet, maybe you need to make her one," Max says leaving the room.

Fucking prick.

❦ 20 ❦

TOI

"HEY, TOI, HONEY, YOU GOT COMPANY."

I look up from the floor. Desi and I are on the floor playing Go Fish. I showed her this game a day or so ago when I found the deck in the nursery, and it has become her favorite thing ever. I would hate it, but every minute I spend with Desi, I fall deeper in love with her. I just wish I knew how to reach Harley. When Dusty opens the door, I feel a nervous flutter in the pit of my stomach. It reminds me that I don't need to reach Harley—I need to plan a way out of here.

"Dusty! We're playing Go Fish! You wanna come play?" Desi cries excitedly.

"Are you short stuff? Maybe I will after the doctor looks at Toi."

"Doctor?" Desi and I say this together, and I think we're both panicked.

"Marcum wants your voice checked out," Dusty answers.

My hand goes to my throat, touching it on reflex.

"Toi's voice is broken," Desi says.

"It sure is, but Ride's friend thinks she can fix it," Dusty says, stepping aside. Ride, who is a member of the club, comes in.

Following him is a really tall woman with long black hair. Ride has to be way over six foot. If I was guessing, six and a half, and this woman is just a couple of inches shorter than him. She's beautiful too, coal black hair, soft ivory complexion, slim with a little curve and those jeans she's wearing hug her body. I don't think I'm horribly ugly. I'm decent. My ass is definitely too big, but it doesn't matter how much I diet—it never goes away. I also will never be smooth and ooze femininity like this lady does. Most days I'm lucky if I don't trip over my own feet.

I shake my head no, standing up. Desi comes to stand in front of me, and it's so cute because I think she's trying to protect me.

"It's just an exam," the woman says, and her voice is even beautiful.

"My Toi don't like doctors," Desi says, grabbing my hand, and if I wasn't so annoyed I'd giggle.

"She needs to see her." This comes from Marcum, and suddenly my rather large room feels way too small. He sucks all of the air out of the room.

"Daddy, Toi don't like doctors," Desi whines, arguing and still standing in front of me as if she's defending me from the world. *Is it any wonder I can't make myself leave?*

"Remember that time you fell and hurt your wrist?" Marcum asks, getting down on his knees in front of Desi. His large, ink covered hand gently holds his daughter's face, and my heart squeezes. How can he be such an asshole, but yet be so tender with his daughter? The softness he gives his kids makes me ache. I've never seen a man do that, and Marcum seems like the last man on the planet who would do that—*yet he does, so easily.*

"Yeah, you made me go to the hospital," Desi mumbles, and the accusing look she gives her father is sweet and funny at the same time.

"And it made it better, right?"

"They used a needle on me," she mumbles, clearly not willing to concede the point.

JORDAN MARIE

"But they made you feel better, right?" Marcum keeps pushing, and I can see him smile, though his lips are hidden by his beard.

"The needle hurt," Desi grumbles.

"Well the doctor isn't going to use any needles on Toi."

"She's not?"

"Not a one," Marcum confirms.

"You're not?" Desi asks the woman, obviously wanting to make that clear.

"Not a one." The woman smiles.

"Dusty, you take Desi back to her room, and you stay with her and Harley. Ride, you get with Ghost and lock our guest down," Marcum orders.

"What about his demands?"

"Keep him contained."

"Got it man," Ride answers. He kisses the doctor on the cheek before he leaves. "See you soon gypsy," he says, and he squeezes her hip in a familiar move that only a lover would do.

She smiles at him and, in that moment, I doubt she realizes anyone else is in the room. I find myself envious of her, but I don't have time for that. Desi hugs me and then leaves the room with Dusty. I cross my hands at my chest and look directly at Marcum.

"No."

"You don't have a choice, Dragonfly. I'm getting your throat looked at. I like your voice. I want to hear more of it."

For some reason hearing that he likes my voice gives me a funny feeling. I ignore it. It's not a good idea to get distracted around Marcum.

"No," I answer again and he stands up, softness leaving his face as he looks at me. Now, his face is filled with annoyance. I'm okay with that, because I'm annoyed too.

"I'm not asking, Toi. I'm telling you that you're going to let Kasha look at you."

Kasha. Jesus. It's not enough she looks like a movie star; she has to have an exotic name too.

Those feelings of inadequacy just keep growing.

68

I huff and go to the bed to get my notebook and pen. I ignore how lacking I feel when I stand so close to the doctor. Will Marcum notice how useless I am next to her? *Why do I care?*

When I turn back around, Marcum yanks the notebook out of my hand.

"Use your damn voice, Toi! Quit relying on a crutch."

His harsh voice and the way he yells at me in front of the doctor, when I already feel so much less, wounds something inside of me. I hate myself even more because I know the exact moment Marcum can see the tears gather in my eyes.

"Get out!" I yell, and it's probably the loudest my voice has been since my father hurt me.

"Damn it, Toi!"

"Get out!" I cry, and my voice cracks and I hate him—but I hate myself even more in that moment.

"Fucking hell, woman! I'm just trying to—"

"I think maybe it's best if you leave. I'll see to Toi," the doctor breaks in. Marcum starts to argue, but looks at me. I see the disgust on his face. That's one look I'm really familiar with.

"Fine," he growls and stomps out, and I'm glad even if that does leave me alone with a doctor who I didn't want to see in the first place.

21

MARCUM

"Where in the fuck is my money?" I demand. I barrel into the room letting my anger fuel me. I grab Weasel by the collar of the dingy beige T-shirt he's wearing and slam him against the wall. The motherfucker has the nerve to walk into my club and demand anything from me? I'm going to cut his nuts off one small piece at a time.

Weasel's head bangs against the wall, and he throws his hands up as if in surrender. His bloodshot eyes widen with fear, and they should. I'm going to kill him. He's the reason Toi is under my roof, torturing me—for that alone he should die.

"I don't have it!" he cries.

"Well, motherfucker, you should have tried running because you won't walk out of here alive," I growl.

"Marcum you're choking him, we can't hear him beg if you do that," String says.

"I don't want to hear anything the fucker has to say."

"I think I'd let him talk. He was saying something really interesting before you came in here," Dusty responds.

I know my men well enough to know that I'm not going to like what the motherfucker has to say. But there's a reason they brought it up so I ease up on my grip before I completely crush his larynx. I haul him to a chair that's in the center of the room and all but throw him into it.

"You've got two minutes to talk. I'll warn you now, Weasel, if I don't like what I hear, you won't live to see another minute go by."

"I don't have the money right now—"

"Motherfucker—"

"Wait! I have it under control."

"Shit dude you don't have nothing under control." This comes from Ride and I couldn't agree more. Still, something about the look on Dusty's face makes me decide to let Weasel finish.

"You're running out of time," I warn him when he doesn't finish.

"I made a deal with the Garcias."

That stops me cold. I know the Garcias. They're part of the Cuban crime family that we've had to deal with from time to time. They have a big pipeline that runs through Miami and occasionally they push their shit up my way. I don't like it, but they keep out of my way and I sure as fuck keep out of theirs. My club has a reputation and no one fucks with us and lives, but I'm not stupid. It doesn't matter how big you are, if you tangle with the wrong people, you can fall. Don't get me wrong. I can handle the Garcias, but I'm not getting into a my-dick-is-bigger-than-yours contest with them. I have reach, but their reach is possibly bigger. The men in this room pledged their lives to me and the club. In return, I'd like to fucking keep them breathing.

"You've been talking to the Garcias?" I ask, highly doubting they'd give this piss-ant the time of day.

"Yeah, man. I'm in tight with them."

"I just bet," Ride mutters.

"The only way the Garcias would give you the time of day is if you were doing something for them. You laundering money for them too, Weasel?" String asks.

Me...I'm remaining silent. This entire thing stinks. The fact that Toi's father has any dealings with the Garcias is bad fucking news. I got her out of this fucker's reach just in time—even if she doesn't appreciate it.

"Nah, man, they got a man for that. I help them find local talent."

"Local talent?" I ask, but fuck I know. I feel like cold steel is being poured down my back. Jesus fucking Christ, does this asshole not know who he's dealing with? Of course that's a stupid question since he thought he could fuck with my club and still live.

"Yeah. I help find them some girls here and there. They trust my judgment," Weasel says, and he might be trying to act like the big man on campus, but I can hear the panic in his voice and it's good he's panicking. He needs to panic. If this is going where I think it is, he's ensuring his death is going to be fucking painful.

"What the fuck does this have to do with my money, Weasel?"

"They've agreed to give me the money to pay you. I just need out of here."

"Then why the fuck did you show up? You had to know without my money, you were signing your own death warrant."

"It's dangerous dealing with the Garcias. I wanted to see my daughter one last time in case things went south."

"Motherfucker, it's dangerous dealing with us!" I growl, and I hit him full force with my fist. His head jerks back blood spouting from his lip.

"I just want to say goodbye to Toi in case this goes south. Surely you can understand that Marcum. You have kids!"

"I didn't see much fatherly concern about her before. Fuck, to me it looked like she couldn't stand the sight of you," Ghost answers. He had been silent until now. I glance up at him, and I see the concern on his face. I can't discount it. I feel it too. I can't help but think that Weasel is making a play here, but I can't really figure it out. Toi hates this man. Even if I let her in to talk to him, it's not going to gain him anything. Unless he urges her to give me whatever I want and pay his bill with her body. It won't work, but I wouldn't mind her warming up to me a little more...

Fuck, this girl is playing with my head.

I scratch the side of my beard, tired of dealing with all of it. Maybe after I kill this fucker, I'll find a woman and get laid. Maybe that will keep Toi from haunting me.

"I made a lot of mistakes," Weasel says, and I snort.

"Fucking A boys, Weasel finally has something right."

The others laugh with me and Weasel shifts uneasily in his seat.

"But I made the most with Toi. I just want to talk to her and then I'll go see the Garcias and I'll do what I need to do to get your money," he says as he looks up at me, pleading.

I should just end the fucker now, but in my head I can still see Toi's tears. Will she shed tears for this motherfucker? Will she hate me if I don't allow her to at least have last words with the asshole? The only thing I know for sure is that he's a short timer. If the Garcias don't end him, I have to. Whatever it is I'm feeling for Toi is bothering me. Do I really want her father's blood on my hands? *Would that be just one more thing Toi holds against me?*

"Please, Marcum. Father to father here, will you let me talk to Toi before I go to the Garcias?"

"Ride? See if Kasha is done with Toi and then bring her here."

"Shit, you can't let her around this asshole!" Ghost growls.

"He's a walking dead man. If Toi wants to say goodbye to him, I'm not going to rob her of that. Would you, Ghost?" I ask him. This fucker is as much under Toi's spell as I am. He and I are going to have problems if I can't clear my head of her.

And I'm starting to think I can't.

𝔖 22 𝔖

TOI

"WHY DO I GET THE FEELING YOU'VE HEARD EVERYTHING I'M about to tell you before?" Kasha asks, her face resigned. She holds out the notebook and pen for me and I look at it like it is the enemy.

Because I have.

"How long has it been since you received the injury?" she asks.

I hate those words. I hate the way they make my stomach coil up in distaste.

Years.

"You realize that your chances to have your voice repaired lessens with time? This is something that needed seeing to immediately."

I don't respond. She's right, but then look at her. *She's perfect.* She'd never understand the problems of not having money or insurance. She would never understand the life I've lived in general.

"It's going to be like that, is it?" she asks and I shrug, avoiding looking in her eyes. She sighs, not bothering to hide the fact that she's put out with me. "Fine. I'm going to prescribe some medicine for you to take twice a day and there are some exercises you can do that will help."

No medicine is going to give me my voice back.

I don't know if she thinks I'm naïve or what, but if there was an easy cure, I would have begged, stolen, or borrowed to get it already.

"You're right. There is a surgery, but it has been so long now I'm not sure it would help. Still this medicine will relax your vocal chords and keep them from being under so much strain. The exercises will keep the damaged chords a little more viable. Ultimately, surgery is the best choice."

No insurance.

She stops and looks at me strangely. I feel like she's searching for something from me.

"Honey, you do realize Marcum has claimed you as his? The last thing you need to worry about is money. He will pay for it. The biggest worry you have is if it will even work at this point. You could permanently paralyze the chords too, that's always a worry. But then, you don't exactly have much use of them now. Still, it's something you two need to discuss.

"Claimed?" I croak.

"Claimed. He's a little old for you, honey, but I'm not here to judge. You're a smart cookie. As sugar daddies go, I'd say Marcum is one of the best. You sure won't have to worry about anything as long as he's around. And you'll have the club's protection when he's not."

I stand up somewhere in her speech. My mind is whirling around and around. She thinks Marcum has claimed me? I barely get time to register that before she accuses me of using him. She's taller than me and probably better than me in every way one could measure. I shouldn't have pride, but ironically I do and she's stepping all over it.

"Which is good, because let's face it. If an enemy doesn't get him he's probably not going to be around much longer. You're a practical girl. I can respect that."

My breath almost stops in my lungs. Marcum brought this woman into his club; it's clear he trusts her and it just feels wrong that she repays him this way. I've not had anyone to show me loyalty in my life, and because of that maybe seeing it so blatantly pisses me off. I slap her, mostly to stop her talking, though I might hit her harder than I normally would have because I'm angry.

I'm tired of not having any control. I'm tired of being here, I'm tired of living a life where I'm forced to be put in these situations.

I'm freaking tired!

She stops talking and stops to look at me. Her eyes are wide with surprise. I figure she'll either kill me in a fight or with her perfection, but I'll at least try and make a good show of it. I prepare myself for it, knowing she will strike back... *how could she not?*

"You bitch!" she growls, but before she can hit me the door opens.

Kasha must not care because she grabs me by the hair and yanks my head. Which seems really weak. In her perfection, I expected her to deliver a cinematic punch that would knock me out. I try to jerk away. Unfortunately, I do it just as she tries to deliver a slap to the side of my face. I miss the majority of that, but I move at just a good enough angle her large diamond ring catches the bottom of my cheek and cuts it. I stomp on her foot and I might have done worse, but before I can, Ride comes over and separates us.

"What the fuck is going on?" he yells, and I figure this is where I'll get worse. I had a chance against Kasha even if she is a freaking Amazon. When Ride hits me I probably won't get up easily. Let's face it, I never did well going toe to toe against my father.

"Marcum's latest little pet hit me," she yells and just because she called me a pet—like I was a dog—I reach for her hair and grab it hard before Ride can stop me. I'm rewarded by taking some of her hair with me when he pulls me farther away. Kasha tries to strike back, but Ride ends it.

"Don't move, Kasha. I'll be back. Marcum wants Toi downstairs," he growls, and he does it in such a way, she immediately minds him. I can't blame her. I'm more than a little scared of him too.

So scared I leave—even when he's taking me to Marcum and I'd rather claw Kasha's eyes out.

23

MARCUM

THE ROOM IS PRETTY SILENT ONCE RIDE LEAVES. WEASEL TRIED to say a few things, but it was pretty clear we were ignoring him and thankfully he stopped talking. I'm second guessing myself. I shouldn't let Toi anywhere near this fucker, but I don't want to do anything she will hate me for later.

Because apparently I care what she thinks about me.

Or at least I think I do. This might all go away if I strangle Max and I just might—if I can find a way to do it without pissing my girls off.

"Here you go, Marcum," Ride says coming in, almost pulling Toi with him. She looks around the room. There's a frantic look on her face, but that's not what bothers me. I walk to her instantly and it might be my imagination, but when I cup the side of her face she seems to calm.

There's a thin line of blood trickling from a scratch on her face.

"What the fuck happened to her?" I growl at Ride, using the pad of my thumb to wipe the blood away.

"Her and Kasha seemed to be having a difference in opinion," Ride answers, surprising me.

"Were you that set against seeing a doctor, Dragonfly?" I

whisper against her ear, where only she can hear me. A fine shiver runs through her body. I feel it immediately and it hits me like ninety proof whiskey, drunk straight down.

Is she attracted to me?

A question I shouldn't even be concerned about, and yet I find myself thinking about it when I should be dealing with the fucker sitting in a chair across from us.

"Toi! I've missed you," he says, almost as if on cue. Toi's body tightens in my hands instantly. There's nothing soft about her now and I mourn the loss. It's yet another thing to hate Weasel for.

"He's just here to say goodbye. He won't hurt you, Toi. I won't let him have the chance to do that," I promise her, and I don't stop myself from kissing her cheek, taking the blood there and using my lips to erase it. Her coppery taste hits me, the metallic flavor sinking inside of me in a way that I know I'll never forget this moment. She pulls away from me confused, and I let her go because she's not the only one wondering what in the hell I'm doing.

I walk her over to a chair across from Weasel. There's a large table between them, but I still worry he's too damn close to her. Her eyes look hard, but she doesn't blink at him, instead choosing to hold his gaze the entire time—*almost warily*.

"I'd like to talk to my daughter alone," Weasel says, as if he has the right to demand anything of me.

"Too fucking bad," I smirk.

Toi looks up at me and then to her father.

"I need to say goodbye to my little girl. There are things I need to tell her. You know as well as I do if this deal with the Garcias falls through, I won't get to see Toi again."

Toi studies him and then she surprises me. She puts her hand on my arm, squeezing it.

"It's okay," she whispers.

I study her face. Not long ago she was upset with me and I was being an asshole over Desi. Now she's touching me. I like that she's touching me. I'm liking it a lot and even though I know I shouldn't, I want her to keep touching me.

That one stupid, fucking bone-headed reason is why I direct the men out of the room. I might as well let her hand my balls to me. "You got five minutes, Weasel," I growl, ignoring the disapproving look on Ghost's face. He can go fuck himself. He's not going to get the chance to claim Toi as his—and it's pretty damn clear he wants to.

Maybe I need to find a mission to send the asshole on. It might be good to get him away from Toi for a few days.

Maybe even a few weeks.

❧ 24 ❧
TOI

I NEED MARCUM GONE. I JUST NEED A FEW MINUTES TO BREATHE away from him. When he held me a minute ago, whispering to me... he was almost tender. My body reacted to him in a way I wasn't expecting. I don't understand it. We don't even like each other. Why, when he kissed my face, did it feel like I had electricity running through every nerve ending in my body?

The last thing I want is to be alone with my father, but if it gives me a minute away from Marcum and the strange way I just reacted to him—then I'll do it. Once the men file out, Marcum is the last one.

"Toi," he calls out and I look over at him, even though I don't want to. He holds my gaze in his and I couldn't look away if I wanted to. "Five minutes and I'll be back," he says, and I can't figure out if he's being protective or warning me. I'm left feeling even more confused.

"You tangling with Marcum now? Shit, I wouldn't have thought you had it in you. If I'd known that I wouldn't have tried to save myself by dealing with the Garcias, I'd let you protect your old man by spreading your legs. Tell me, are you Marcum's private play toy, or are you seeing to it the whole club gets a piece?"

It's been a long time since his words had the power to hurt me. Still, these are so vile, they make my stomach turn. I look at him, and not for the first time I wonder how he can be my father. I feel nothing when I look at him—except distaste. Still, I don't respond to him. He's not worth the pain or the effort it takes to talk.

"You get in a fight with one of Marcum's regulars?" he asks, motioning toward my face. I touch the spot on reflex. It was burning before Marcum touched it. "You might be smarter than I gave you credit for," he continues. He leans back in his chair, watching me. "You might have some of me in you after all," he says, with a sleazy smile. It takes great effort to stop myself from showing my disgust on my face. If he sees how revolting I find him, he might lash out. My hand goes to my throat.

I've learned the hard way to avoid those outbursts.

"I AM SORRY ABOUT THAT YOU KNOW," HE SAYS, MOTIONING TO my throat. "You just do this stupid shit to get me upset. It's your fault really."

I bite my lip, resisting the urge to try and scream. The beating that all but stole my voice from me happened because my alarm clock went off to wake me up for work that morning. He only heard it because he had picked the lock to my bedroom and was standing over my bed staring at me. The look in his eyes when I woke up is one that still scares me. There are times I wake up in the middle of the night, reliving that morning. The fact that I have that much fear inside of me, makes me feel.... *ashamed.*

"Still," he continues, as if he's being perfectly logical—*as if he's not a monster*—"I feel bad about everything. I want to make it up to you."

I can't keep the disgust out of my gaze this time. I don't even try. There's nothing he could do that could possibly make this up to me.

Nothing.

I don't reply.

"It's my fault Marcum and his gang have their hands on you and you have to know Toi, there's no way I'm going to be able to pay him back."

I swallow down the bile. I knew. I also knew he didn't care what that meant when it came to me. Would Marcum move me away from Desi, Harley and the other kids to become a club whore then? I'm not stupid about the way the world works, and specifically the world Marcum and his men live in. I was stupid to hesitate. Nothing good ever lasts and Desi and Harley and my connection with them...is definitely good.

I have to leave, before everything is taken from me.

"A friend of mine used to live here—until they discovered just what kind of man Marcum really was."

I tune him out. The irony of my father disliking anyone for the person they truly are—is not lost on me.

"They gave me this," he says and he reaches under the band of his wristwatch and hands me a key. It's mostly a key. The sides have been cut so it makes it rectangular and small in shape... a shape easily concealed. It sits on the table, the tarnished silver shining.

I clear my throat.

"What is it?"

"The key to the back door out of this place. I'm going to tell you where it is and you will use this key to escape tomorrow. There are two guards out front, but I have a diversion planned for them. I'll distract them while you get free. My friend will meet you and drive you to the nearest greyhound station with a ticket out of here, and enough money to get you settled."

"Why?" I ask, not sure I trust him, but seeing a glimmer of a chance to finally live my own life.

"I figure I owe you. Consider this my gift and one that makes us even."

I stare down at the key and then back at my father. I'm not sure I should trust him, but I literally have nothing to lose.

I reluctantly reach down and capture the key. When my father smiles at me, I suddenly feel like I've made a deal with the devil and I'm really terrified of what he's going to require in payment.

"My friend tells me almost every evening after eight, Marcum visits with his two youngest brats. While he's doing that, you follow my instructions and you'll be a free woman."

"What instructions?" I ask, even though I'm not sure I should —especially when my father looks like he just won the lottery.

Shit.

25

MARCUM

"MOTHERFUCKER! WE NEED TO MOVE IN NOW AND SHUT THIS down!" Ghost yells, completely losing his cool.

I just keep staring at the monitor. An unreasonable sense of betrayal rises in my gut as I watch Toi's hand wrap around a key. It's useless. I change that lock often and the door is electronically wired. Still, very few people besides me and my closest men know that. Which makes me wonder exactly who Weasel's so-called friend is. Are they still in my club? It's possible, but when I find them, they won't be breathing air any longer.

Toi taking the key isn't exactly a surprise. She owes me or the club nothing, but it still feels as if a dull knife has been plunged into me. I'm not sure how I'm going to deal with it. But the feeling in my gut says I'm going to let her go. I'm too damn old for her, I've been fighting this unreasonable appeal she has. If she's that unhappy here, then I need to let her go. I brought her in to protect her. Today her father signed his death warrant for a second time. He was dying before—now he just made sure it will be bloody.

"No."

Ghost, Ride and a few of the others stop immediately. All look at me in surprise, but it's Ghost who almost comes unglued.

"What in the fuck do you mean, no?"

"I mean, we shut nothing down. We act like we don't know what in the fuck is going on."

"What in the hell for?"

"So I can find out who in the fuck is betraying me and so I can make sure Weasel's final breath is filled with pain."

"What about Toi?"

That question wasn't asked by Ghost. Surprisingly, it is Train that asks it. I look at him, and I see it. He knows I'm fighting myself where she's involved. That doesn't surprise me, but I don't entirely like it either. I sigh, leaning against the wall, and wishing I was anywhere else right now. A million things run through my mind, but the two main ones are that Toi leaving will hurt Desi and Harley and that's on me. When I put her in charge of them, I didn't expect her to get to them. She's under their skin. They care about her.

Just like she's under my skin...

No matter how much I fight it.

"Marcum? What about Toi?" Ride pushes me again with his question. It's a question I don't want to answer.

"If she wants to go, we let her go."

"Fuck, no!" Ghost growls.

"This was never about keeping her prisoner. She needed protection from her father. If that little meeting in there is any indication—she needed it a fuck of a lot sooner. No matter what happens Weasel is dead. Toi will be safe."

"Christ," Ghost mutters.

"Be glad, man," I tell him, scratching my beard. I need to get back in there. Weasel's been alone with her too much. But I also need to make this point.

"Glad? How do you fucking figure that?"

"If she stayed, man... If she stayed, she would never be yours," I tell him finally. It's time to lay my cards on the table with Ghost.

"You don't know that."

"I know I want her. No matter how much I shouldn't or wish I didn't, I want her."

"She might not want you." He shrugs.

"I wouldn't give up, but even if she didn't..." I trail off.

"Finish it," he says, even though he knows me well enough there's no point in him asking. Still, I'll lay it out for him—if that's what he wants.

"I'd never allow it to be anyone but me," I tell him plainly.

He stares at me and for a minute I think he might call me out. Instead, he leaves. I watch his back as he goes through the door.

And that right there is why I'd win.

If it's for Toi... I'd never walk away.

Never.

I look at Toi on the monitor. It's for the fucking best I let her go. It doesn't mean I have to like it, however. I turn to leave the room and get her away from Weasel.

"It's time to get this started," I growl to the other men.

It's time to let her go.

❧ 26 ❧

TOI

"YOU GOING TO TELL ME WHAT BROUGHT YOU AND KASHA TO the point of fighting?" Marcum asks as he walks me back from talking to my father. He's standing beside me and his hand is on my lower back. It feels nice, and that weird electrical current seems to move through me again.

Marcum excites me.

What I don't understand is why, or what caused the change. Was it because of the tenderness he showed me when I was brought to my father? The small kiss he placed on my cheek? I touch the spot before I can manage to stop myself.

"You kissed me," I tell him, and I'm whispering so softly that I would be surprised if Marcum heard me. I'm half wishing he doesn't.

He's silent as we finish our walk down the hall to my room. When he opens the door to my room, I go inside expecting him to leave. He doesn't; instead he comes in with me. I back away from him a few steps.

Does he know about the key in my pocket? Why do I feel guilty about having it?

"Is there something you want to tell me, Toi?"

I shake my head no, feeling panicked. My hand goes down in my pants pocket to find the key. If he finds it, what will he do? People don't really cross Marcum and keep breathing.

"Are you sure?"

I bite my lip as he walks toward me. I take another step, but I back into the nightstand. I'm afraid to take my eyes off of Marcum.

"Careful, Dragonfly. It'd be a shame to injure these beauties," he whispers, moving his thumb over my bottom lip, brushing it softly, forcing me to release it. "You have beautiful lips, you shouldn't bite them," he adds, and his words cause my stomach to feel funny. When I take in the look on his face—*the look in his eyes*, I feel moistness gather along the inside of my thighs. I gasp in surprise.

"Wha... what .... you... doing?" My question comes out a broken rush of air, words missing and little more than a breath in volume.

"Do you know, Toi, that I've been imagining kissing you for the last few weeks?"

I shake my head back and forth in denial.

"That small touch on your cheek was not a kiss. It wasn't even close."

"It wasn't?"

"When I kiss you, Dragonfly, you will definitely know it."

"I..."

"It wouldn't be smart to kiss you now," he says, and I get the feeling that he's talking to himself.

"It wouldn't?" I'm still barely whispering, but then, so is Marcum and his voice has a hoarseness mixed in with the soft tone that seems to make my body vibrate.

"Definitely not, because I can't keep you," he whispers. "I'm way too old for you."

"Yeah," I murmur, but I'm not sure what I'm answering.

"But you know what they say about older men, don't you, Dragonfly?"

"What?"

"They've learned all the ways to make a woman purr," he answers, leaning in even closer. Our lips are barely separated now. I can feel his warm breath against my skin. I should be scared. I should be saying no. *I should be moving away from him.*

Instead, when his fingers tenderly caress against the throbbing artery in my neck, I moan. I want his kiss.

I want Marcum to kiss me.

That's the last thought I have before he presses his lips to mine. It's a gentle kiss, and entirely innocent. But the things it does to me are far from innocent. I feel alive. Shivers move through my body instantaneously and they warm and excite me. I press into him, needing a deeper connection—hoping against hope he takes me in his arms. He doesn't; the only touch he gives me is the hand on my neck, and the soft pressure of his lips against mine. He doesn't even move his lips, but I can taste him, and the minute I do my tongue comes out without permission and licks against his lips. I hoped his would do the same, that the kiss would grow, but it doesn't. Instead, Marcum pulls away.

"I can't kiss you like I want, Dragonfly, because you're not mine to keep."

He steps back from me then. I touch my fingers to my lips, missing him so bad it hurts.

"But if you were, Dragonfly... if you ever decided I was your man... Nothing would ever keep me from you," he literally growls, right before leaving the room.

I don't move. I'm not even sure I'm breathing. I just stand there looking at the empty space where he used to be...and wondering what would truly happen if I told Marcum he could be my man...

🦋 27 🦋

MARCUM

"You sure about this man?" Topper asks as we watch Toi leave Desi and Harley's room.

"Don't have a choice," I mutter. Desi and Harley are at the back of the room with Babs while she distracts them.

"You like her," he says, stating the obvious.

"Quit beating a dead horse. So I like her. I've liked other women before. Let's get, before she gets too far ahead of us," I growl. I'm hurting, in a way I didn't expect. I don't need Topper rubbing salt in my wounds. I look over at my children. They're going to miss Toi almost as much as I am. Harley included, even if he is struggling right now. "Hey kids, Uncle Topper has something he wants to show me. We'll be back a bit later."

"Okay, Dad!" Desi hollers. Harley just looks at me. He hasn't said much since our talk. I'd be lying if I said I wasn't worried about how he will react to Toi being gone.

"You know as well as I do Marcum that your reactions with Toi have been different than with any other woman you've been around."

"Bullshit," I deny immediately. "She's like every other woman."

I arguing, but I know she's not. Toi is special. The feelings she evokes in me are different.

"It's bad enough you're fucking lying to yourself, but now you're lying to me. Man I've been with you from the beginning."

"So?"

"I've seen you deal with women. It's always sex. Most of the time it's *just* sex. Cherry was different. She's the first woman I've seen you around where you seemed genuinely happy."

"Fuck off, Topper. I'm always happy."

"Yeah, you're a barrel of laughs," he mutters, and I flip him off.

"Just let it be. Cherry might have been a little different, but she ended the same. She left and it's all water under the damn bridge now."

"To be fair, man, there's not a lot of women out there that would be okay with the fact you killed—"

"She was part of the club, Topper. It's not like she didn't know what happens."

"True, but you had never sought vengeance on a woman before."

"Jenna was a fucking bitch who deserved death. She crossed me, she crossed my club, but most of all, she endangered Tess and Maddie. Not to mention the fact she fucked up Maxwell's life."

"Still, have you told any of them that you ended Jenna?"

"Wasn't their concern."

"Right. So you expected Cherry to accept what you're afraid your own family can't."

"Babs doesn't have a problem with what you do for the club," I mutter, scratching my beard.

"Babs is a special woman. She's been in this life as long as I have, and knows that anyone in this life better not cross the wrong people. She doesn't ask for details, but she would never condemn me either."

"Fine. Let's say you're right. Toi is young and never been in this life. Do you see her accepting anything that a woman like Cherry couldn't?" Topper doesn't say anything, even though I wish he would—but he'd be lying and we both know it. "And there's my answer asshole. So like I said, let it go. Nothing is changing who I am and who Toi is. Nothing is changing the fact that I'm way too fucking old for her, I live the life I'm in—one I happen to like. She would have to accept it and there's no way that's going to happen. If nothing else Cherry taught me that. It's a no-win situation, any way you look at it."

"You could..."

"Change? Fuck that shit. I am who I am and I'm not about to change now. Shit I don't even want to."

"I was going to say that you could lie to her. Keep the truth about what we do hidden."

"Lies always have a way of floating to the top. You know that. It's better this way," I tell him and I wish I could believe my own words.

Nothing about letting Toi go feels right. I went around and around it in my head last night. Every answer ends up the same. She's too young, inexperienced and sweet to touch. No matter how much I'm fucking dying to touch her. Shit. Last night I passed up sex with one of the club girls, only to end up coming in my hand to visions of Toi riding me and those fucking tits of hers bouncing as she used my cock hard and fast. Shit, even now I can see it in my head and my cock jerks in my pants.

I want her. I'm not sure I've ever wanted a woman more. Which means I'm screwed, because I can't have her. I won't allow myself to pull an innocent into my world. Even if being without her means I have the world's worst case of blue balls.

"Zip it up," I whisper as we start walking down toward the secret stairway that leads to the cellar. Sound echoes from here out and I don't want Toi to know I'm following her. I already have men stationed around the area outside, but I couldn't bring myself to let her go unguarded even through the passage.

Topper nods and we walk as quietly as we can toward the stairwell. I can hear Toi's footsteps, hurried and erratic. I hate that she's worried. I hate that she doesn't trust me. Mostly I hate every fucking thing about this.

Every. Fucking. Thing.

❦ 28 ❦

TOI

I'M CLOSE TO A PANIC. I CAN ADMIT IT FREELY. MY HEART IS beating so hard it wouldn't surprise me if it's not bruising my chest.

And guilt...

That's something I wasn't expecting. When Marcum came into the kids' room, I was swamped with a feeling of guilt. It's crazy and I shouldn't feel like I'm letting him down, but it's there. I'm even halfway convinced I saw hurt in his eyes. Which is crazy. Being this close to Marcum, being inside the club is coloring the way I view them. That's the only sane explanation. I knew on the outside what the club was like. I heard firsthand of how they ran things, and what Marcum does when people lie to him, or cross the club. It was easy to live in fear of them then.

Now, I've seen how Marcum interacts with his children—even if he does have enough to field an entire football team. I've seen how his men are around the kids, and how they treat each other. Although it's not anything I've ever experienced, I have imagined families and the closeness that I witness here at the Saints is definitely what I would call a family. From day one, they've treated me like one of them too, which is remarkable to me. Especially since every one of them knows I'm Weasel's daughter. I expected the worst when Marcum brought me here and though I've not been here a long time—each day is better than the one before.

Even today.

Harley was nicer to me today—guarded, but nicer.

What happens if I'm making a mistake by trusting my father?

I wish I knew all the answers to these question that are constantly swirling in my brain. The sad truth is, I don't. I have a feeling I'm running away now, and not to escape being held against my will—but because I'm afraid of what might happen with Marcum if I stay. I dreamed about his kiss all night last night. I woke up once in the middle of the night, dreaming of him touching me, only to find I was touching myself. I got out of bed and took a very cold shower at four in the morning. It didn't help much, but it did help. Getting away from Marcum is probably a great idea... *if it didn't leave me so sad.*

I finally make it to the stairwell. I'm so nervous that there were a couple of times I could have sworn I heard someone following me. I looked around but didn't see anything. I put my hand on the door and open it with a frown. It's just a closet. My father said it was a secret stairway, but...that's when I see it.

On the back wall there's a crack, like big enough to put my hand through—which is exactly what I do. The wall swings back when I push and it reveals a dark corridor with stairs. I take my cellphone from my back pants-pocket and turn on the flashlight app. Pale light floods the stairs and though I'm still nervous, I push it aside. I've gone too far to turn back now.

I don't trust my father. I don't buy that he's doing this for me either. My best case scenario is that he's doing this to show Marcum he's not in control. My father is stupid, and he loves getting the last word in. If he could take something away from Marcum before he runs for his life, he would. I don't even want to think about the worst case scenario. I'm planning in phases. Phase one is escaping. Phase two is eluding my father and whatever hare-brained scheme he's come up with. I figure I've been doing that my whole life, it can't be that hard. Phase three will be the hardest one...

Trying to forget how Marcum makes me feel.

✢ 29 ✢

MARCUM

TOPPER AND I ARE QUIET AS WE FOLLOW TOI THROUGH THE small stairway. The girl really is shit at taking care of herself. I don't know how she survived with her father as long as she did. She has no idea we're practically on her heels. She didn't get wise when she opened the closet and found the door mostly opened. If we hadn't done that, I doubt she would have ever found it. Now that we're at the doorway, I wait to see what she does. For a minute she looks behind her. I can't see her face clearly because it is shadowed, but I'm pretty sure she looks more sad than frightened. As she pushes the key into the dummy lock, I know it's sadness that fills me.

If only I had met Toi sooner... of course she still would have been too young. Maybe somewhere in an alternate universe we would have worked, but nowhere in this world would the two of us ever have been possible and she will never know how much I regret that.

She gasps when the door opens. How surprised would she be to know that I had the lock doctored? You can literally put any key in there and it would release. Hell, you could even put a nail file in it. I'll need to fix that shit quick.

Topper and I push against the wall to remain out of sight as she opens the door and light begins to filter in. She takes a cautious step outside and she should be cautious. I'm not sure what's out there yet; we've kept things silent while Top and I followed Toi down. They know to stay hidden—unless Toi is walking into a fucking free for all. I don't want her hurt, and I don't trust Weasel not to have something up his sleeve. I know without a shadow of a doubt he's not helping his daughter out from only the kindness in his heart. The cold truth is that Weasel doesn't give a fuck about Toi. If he did he would have never hurt her, and he sure wouldn't have got her mixed up with me and my club. So, if he's helping her escape it's to benefit him—of that I'm sure. I'm also positive Toi knows that, and maybe that's what bothers me the most. Her going through with this is clear proof that she's desperate to leave me. If that isn't enough to make a man's gut burn, I don't know what is.

I shake off my thoughts and Top and I silently move further down. When we get to the door we look out and Toi is standing in front of an empty field.

I frown. Maybe whoever is behind this shit with Weasel saw my men move into position before dawn this morning. I doubt it, my men are damn good at reconnaissance, but I suppose anything is possible. I know her father said she had to walk to the old dirt road at the edge of our property, but I figured if the fucker was going to pull anything, it would be here.

Guess he's smarter than I gave him credit for.

I have more men in place on the old stretch of road. If that's how this is going to play out, then it is. I watch as Toi walks away.

I guess I better get used to that view. When she disappears into the trees I know that Ride and Ghost have her in their sight. So I motion to Top and we speed back up the stairs to go to our bikes.

Adrenaline feeds through my body, because I know the time for confrontation is close. I just hope I did the right thing in letting it play out like this. If Toi gets hurt because I didn't protect her enough, I'll never forgive myself.

❦ 30 ❦

TOI

I'VE NEVER REALLY HAD A HOME BEFORE AND AS STRANGE AS IT sounds—even to me—Marcum and his club felt like a home. That's the overwhelming feeling I experience as I leave them behind. I do need to go, though; there's no getting around that. I know it. To stay would be insane. Marcum's moods shift with the wind. And now...with my attraction to him in the mix—it's really just too dangerous for me to stay.

I don't think I could handle seeing him with one of the club women. Not after having felt his gentle touch. I've dreamed about him. I've kissed him—even if it was mostly chaste. I couldn't handle not having that and watching another woman get it in place of me.

Then there is the club itself. I've lived most of my life with a dangerous man. I don't need to be living in a clubhouse full of them. I need to get away, to start over far away from everyone here in Crescent City. Even as I say that, I know. I have to leave Florida all together. That's the only way to see peace from my father... and to not risk running into Marcum again.

The longer I walk, the sadder I get. I rub the sides of my arms. I keep getting the feeling someone is watching me. When I look around, I don't see anyone and again I just mark it down to nerves. As I near the old road I can hear a vehicle running. This is almost over. Once I get away and put Florida—*and Marcum*—behind me, everything will be better.

When I make it through to the clearing there's an older woman sitting behind the wheel of a red convertible. She's really pretty. Her red hair falls in waves with just enough curl that it looks beautiful. She's got long slim fingers that have red painted nails that match her lipstick. She's looking around nervously and then she spots me. She studies me for a minute and then smiles.

"You must be Weasel's girl Toi," she says.

I swallow, but nod my head.

"Well, come on. We need to get going if we're going to make it to the Greyhound station in time."

A sense of disbelief hits me. I expected a double cross. I came prepared to fight for my life and there's nothing...

Could it be possible that my father didn't lie?

My legs are frozen in place for a moment, so great is my shock. Then when I do start walking it's to hear the ringing of motorcycle pipes. I can't hear the woman, but I can read her lips when she yells.

"Shit! Hurry!"

I stumble, but I'm at the car door when a hand slaps against it, stopping me. I turn around to see Ghost standing there. He followed me. There's no other explanation.

"I don't think so, Toi."

I might have tried to respond, but the motorcycles arrive that we heard and there's Marcum and he's looking right at me. Fear flutters through me at the look on his face. I think it might all be directed at me, but it's not. I know that absolutely when he stops by the car and looks at the other woman.

He knows her.

I don't know why that surprises me, but it does.

"Well, I sure as fuck didn't expect this," Marcum growls. He looks over at Topper. "Don't let her leave," he orders, his voice low.

Then he walks around the car to me. Ghost moves away and there in front of me is the man I desperately needed to leave. The man I didn't want to leave. The man whose anger I can almost reach out and touch right now.

"I have some shit to handle here, Dragonfly," he says, and as mad as he is... his voice is softer when he talks to me. "I know what you had planned."

"I didn't—" I try to reply, not sure of what I will say, but feeling like I should say something.

"Let me deal with this, Toi. I'll help you leave when I'm done, you have my word," he says and his words hurt me. Why they do, I don't know. I should be glad he's giving in like this. It should make me happy. But the pain is so intense that I have to fight to keep from crying. Then he turns around, motions Topper and Ride. They walk over in the clearing away from the car and Ghost joins them. My legs are weak, so now that I can, I open the door and slide in it. If I don't sit, I'm going to fall down. I look up and find Ghost's eyes on me. Marcum is looking this way too, but he's not looking at me. He's looking at the other woman.

"Fuck, I have to try and salvage this. If you got my ass caught..." she grumbles at me, and I look over at her. I have no idea what I'm going to say to her, because I don't know this woman. She doesn't give me the chance, however. She hops out of the car and hurries over to where Marcum and his men are.

"Marcum, honey, what's going on here?" she asks, putting her hand on his back. I've never been jealous. Mostly, I've never had something to be jealous over. Marcum most assuredly is not mine, and yet the sight of her hand on him makes jealousy burn deep inside of me. I don't like it. I can't even tell you the reasons I don't. I just know that in this moment I'd gladly scratch her eyeballs out.

"Cherry, back the fuck away. I'm talking to my men and then you and I will discuss how you're helping Weasel betray me."

Cherry.

I may not know her, but I definitely know that name. Butter-flies seem to take flight in my stomach. I heard his kids talk about

Cherry and how much they missed her and how much their daddy loved her. I would have been glad never to see her.

She's beautiful. More Marcum's age, but she carries it really freaking well. Her hair is beautiful and maybe her best feature. It's rich in color and tones that are either all natural or costs a fortune to get touched up every month. Sadly, there's not a sign of gray in it. She's tiny. Her body is sleek and athletic, with perky breasts that are either natural or the woman has a hell of a knack for picking out bras. I feel mousey compared to her and my ass suddenly feels like it's five sizes bigger.

I make myself look away. I have to. I can't handle the sight of them talking together. That's when I see it. A flash of metal reflecting in the slowly dying sun. I blink a few times, trying to figure out what it is. That's when I see the barrel of a gun sticking out from the tree line, and my own father holding it. He's got his hand on the trigger and it's trained on... *Marcum.*

I want to scream. I try a few times. But my voice isn't loud enough to carry over the raised voices of Cherry and Marcum. I could blow the horn but I'm not sure Marcum would move. More than likely, he will turn to face me and make an even broader target for my father to hit. I make a split second decision and slide over the console of the car and get in the driver's seat. I yank the car into drive, and then I floor it. The car's back tires squeal and I fight the wheel to keep it from fishtailing.

I thought I could hear someone screaming my name, but probably not. Between the screaming of the car's tires and the thumping of my own heart—I doubt I could hear anything. My father sees me and he pulls the gun away from Marcum—and aims it at me. I have the gas pedal on the floor and I'm aiming directly at my father. I don't know what kind of person I am, but I don't feel remorse for what I'm about to do. I'm just scared I won't do it in time to save Marcum.

I can't let him die....

I can't let my father kill Marcum.

❧ 31 ❧

MARCUM

"TOI!" GHOST SCREAMS, GETTING MY ATTENTION. I TURN TO SEE the car speeding past us, cutting into the field. My heart flies up into my throat. She's headed straight for those damn trees. She's not going slow either, if she hits the trees like that... I take off running. I don't have a hope in fuck of reaching her, but I can't just stand there and do nothing.

Once I turn, I see him. Toi's father is standing there with a rifle in his hand and he's got his sites on me. He turns quickly though when he hears the car and the screaming. He aims the gun at Toi and my heart squeezes painfully in my chest. I'm terrified he's going to shoot her, but at the last second he decides to run. He doesn't make it a foot from where he was standing before the car hits him with a thud. His body slows the car down as she plows him over, but it still hits against the trees with a force so hard my breath nearly stops. I watch as Toi's body is pushed upward with the impact. Then she's at a stop. The car is still running, the engine revved up as if Toi is still giving it gas and now the horn is blaring loudly as Toi's head is slammed against it.

She's not moving.

I yank on the door, it doesn't want to open because the fender has been mangled and it's holding the door closed. It's a miracle she wasn't thrown from the car. If she survives this, I'm going to tan her ass so hard it will mark it permanently. When I get it open, I carefully pull her head back, not wanting to do more damage than might already be there. She falls gently against the car seat. The fucking car is an older model, from the seventies, and there's not an airbag in view.

"How is she?" Ghost yells, almost right beside me.

"Get the fuck away," I growl, not wanting him near her—not wanting *anyone* near her.

"Boss, don't move her. Let's make sure she's not got anything broken," Ride says, like I don't have a brain in my head. Asshole.

I reach over and turn off the car. Gently bracing her neck, while doing my best to get her head off the horn.

"Dragonfly, I need you to open those pretty little eyes, darlin'," I urge her softly, touching the side of her neck to check her pulse. It seems strong and steady, which reassures me a little.

"Oh my God! Is she okay?" Cherry says, and who the fuck let her over here is in for a world of hurt.

"Get her the fuck away from here. Ride!"

"Getting it handled, Marcum," he says, and I hear Cherry complaining in the background, but I ignore it. All of my attention is centered on Toi.

"Toi, honey," I whisper again.

"Boss, we got bigger problems," I hear Topper say, but I ignore him, because Toi's eyes start to flutter open.

"Boss..." he says again.

"That's it, honey, open those beautiful blue eyes and look at me."

"Boss, damn it!" Topper yells.

"Topper, I don't—"

"The car is on fire man! You have to get her out of it!"

I jerk at his words and look at the back of the vehicle. Fuck! I didn't even smell the smoke. Under the vehicle there's smoke and sparks shooting. I can also smell gas.

Shit.

"Dragonfly, I don't want to hurt you, but I have to get you out of here. I'll try to be as gentle as I can," I tell her. "Topper, you and the boys deal with Weasel's body and call a fucking ambulance for Toi, and get the fire department out here."

"Boys are already working on it, Marcum," he answers, as I get Toi in my arms and pull her against my chest.

Her eyes open and she looks at me through shocked, dilated eyes. They slowly close again and I instantly miss them, but I concentrate on getting her far away from the car.

"I never seen anything like that, man. She ran over Weasel. Plowed the fucker down without hesitating and she did it...."

"She did it to save me," I finish for Topper. "I know. I saw it all, man. I saw it all," I add, finally getting Toi a comfortable distance from the car.

"Guess we were both wrong," he says, and I don't know what he's talking about, but I don't much care right now.

"Dragonfly, it's going to be okay. I promise you, it's all going to be okay," I tell her.

"Marcum," she says in a broken whisper that wraps itself all the way around my heart.

"I'm here, Toi. I'm right here, baby."

"You're okay," she whispers, her eyes opening again. I pull her deeply into me then, still gentle, but some of the fear has left me. I cup the side of her face with my hand and hold her gaze.

"You made sure of that," I tell her. She starts to close her eyes again, but I don't let her. "You're not getting away from me now, Dragonfly. There's no getting away now," I tell her.

"But—"

"I'm keeping you, Toi. You sealed our fate, honey," I tell her. Her eyes go wide, but she doesn't argue. Instead she stares at my lips and I find myself fighting the urge to smile.

❧ 32 ❧

TOI

"Toi! Toi! Are you okay? Daddy said you got hurt!"

I jerk up as Desi and Harley come running into my room. Marcum carried me to an SUV after a medic checked me out. Then he kept me in his arms the entire ride back to the clubhouse. Still carrying me, he brought me to my room and put me in the bed with a gentle kiss on my forehead. He disappeared after that and I wondered where he went. Part of me is scared he's with that woman, Cherry. But, there's no reason for me to be jealous. Despite what Marcum said, we've not truly kissed, not a normal kiss that a couple shares.

His words were said in the heat of the moment.

"I'm good," I whisper, catching her as she climbs on the bed and wraps her little body around me. I look over at Harley, who is standing by the bed. He's watching me closely.

"I heard Babs and Topper talking," he says ominously. "You saved Daddy."

I lick my lips to moisten them, feeling nervous. I need to talk to him. Instinctively I know if I wrote down what I needed to say he would pull further away from me. It's not fair, but then life for a child is different than life for an adult.

I motion my hand, indicating I want him to come closer. I almost hold my breath, afraid he will reject me right out. I'm surprised when he reluctantly walks toward me. I brush the side of his face. I don't know a lot about kids, but I want to give them the love I always craved—and never received.

"Your dad is strong. He would have saved himself," I tell Harley. Kids need to think their parents are invincible and can protect them from anything—at least the good ones.

"He is," Harley responds, and he holds his body solid, but there's a war going on in his eyes and it just seems wrong for such a small child. "I'm sorry you were hurt. When I'm sick, Dad brings me chocolate milk."

"I'll have to ask him for some," I answer, trying to make Harley smile. He's such a little man, afraid to let go, and trying to be just like his father. The pain in his eyes hurts my heart.

"I'll tell them!" Desi speaks up.

"We'll see to Toi," Ghost interrupts. "You two better get back to your room. Your dad wants Toi to get some rest."

"But Toi needs us!" Desi cries.

"You can see her again before you go to bed," Ghost argues.

It takes some work, but after a few hugs and promises that I would feel well enough tomorrow to watch the Troll movie, Desi finally agrees. Her and Harley walk out of my room side by side. But, when Harley gets to the door, he looks back at me. I've seen that look before—that very same look. He's studying me, just like his Dad does from time to time. He finally turns around and leaves.

I sigh when they're gone.

"He'll come around. Harley was really close to Cherry. He thought of her as his mother. Closest thing the poor kid ever had."

"Oh," I answer. Partly because I'm tired and my throat hurts, I don't bother to respond with more. Inside my heart hurts. I had hoped I'd be able to reach Harley, but with Cherry back... Plus, I was leaving. Marcum will probably let me go now without issue—especially since he won't need my help with his kids.

The thought leaves me so sad, I close my eyes and decide to wallow in my misery.

❧ 33 ❧

MARCUM

I CLOSE THE DOOR TO CHERRY'S ROOM—HER NEW ONE. TOI IS IN her old one. I haven't talked a lot to her yet. I had to make sure she was locked down before I could stay with Toi. I told Cherry I'd talk with her in the morning and that she couldn't leave the room, and I have two men there to make sure that happens.

She swears she's innocent, but there's just something about all of this that tells me in my gut, there's something more. Cherry— the Cherry I once knew—wouldn't betray the club, or me. That much is true. But she wasn't fond of Weasel either. I just don't get it. I need to get to the bottom of it, but it's late and I need to be with Toi more.

I stopped by to check on the kids and tuck them in bed. I haven't told them anything about Cherry. I'm not sure I should. They both loved her; it's the main reason I made her my old lady. She fit into my life. Hell, at one time she even added to it. She made sense, which has always been a deciding factor in any choice I've made. *Until Toi.*

My older kids all know Cherry is here. Some are surprised. The oldest are more... wary. I raise smart kids. I've yet to tell Maxwell;

that conversation is coming tomorrow. I'm too fucking worn out to put up with his shit tonight.

"How's she doing?" I ask when I go inside Toi's room. I left instructions for String to stay with her. It doesn't make me happy that I find Ghost with his ass parked beside her bed. For that reason, there's a bite to my voice. He and I are definitely going to have words before this is over.

"She's resting. Ride had Kasha give her something to help her rest."

"Toi and Kasha don't exactly get along."

"Yeah, that might be understating it. But Kasha respects her. She told Ride she was out of line earlier, though she didn't bother to elaborate."

"Interesting," I murmur, even though I don't give a damn. I'm looking at Toi. She's lying in the bed with her hair fanned out over the pillow case, and she just looks so freaking young.

Too innocent for me.

And now...she has blood on her hands because of me. Her own father. I don't know what to do with that, or how to process it. I do know that if I go back to my unwritten rule, the one I uphold to all others, I have to admit that Toi is strong. She's more than strong enough to survive in my club. Fuck, I could see her thriving in it.

Here.

As my old lady.

"You hear me, Marcum?" Ghost asks, bringing my attention back to him.

"What?"

"I said Cherry being here is going to mean trouble, especially for Toi."

"It won't," I argue, but hell—he may be right.

"It will. Women get strange when there's competition and that's exactly how Cherry will view Toi. If she's back, it's because she wants to be where she was before. The very spot you're looking to slide Toi into as a replacement."

"Listen motherfucker, Toi isn't a replacement for anyone. What does or doesn't happen in my personal life isn't your business. So do us both a favor, and get over it before it causes some permanent damage between the two of us."

"I'm letting it drop."

"Good. Then if you don't mind, I've had a fucked up day and I want to be alone with Toi. We have things to talk about."

"I'll leave," he says unnecessarily, since his ass is getting up and walking to the door. "But I'll leave with a straight-up warning, Marcum. You hurt Toi, or she decides you ain't worth the trouble, I'm moving in and I'll do it in such a way she will *know* she comes first with me."

With that, he leaves. I let out a deep sigh. There's going to be trouble, I can feel it in my fucking bones.

❧ 34 ❧

TOI

I COME AWAKE SLOWLY, AS IF I'M DIGGING MYSELF OUT OF A thick fog. I half expect to see Ghost, but the room is completely dark, indicating I've been asleep for a while. I stretch, but I'm sore and stiff everywhere and I can't stop the whimper that comes out.

"You okay, Dragonfly?"

I freeze, every muscle in my body locking tight. Marcum is in bed with me, lying on my left side. We're not touching... unless you count the fact that my head is using his arm as a pillow. I start to sit up, but Marcum stops me by pulling me deeper into his body and turning on his side. He shifts so he can rise, resting his upper body on his elbow and looking down at me.

He reaches across me and turns on the lamp and I mourn the darkness for a minute. There I could hide, but with the pale light now I can see his face. I can see his beard mere centimeters from my face and I see his dark eyes full of concern... *for me.*

"You're here."

He smiles as if I surprised him. He brushes his fingers across my cheek gently, but that small touch manages to reignite my body. A body that seems to come alive when Marcum is near.

"Where else would I be?" he asks with a soft laugh.

There are a lot of answers to that and some might make me appear a jealous fool. These new feelings for Marcum are confusing. So, instead, I try to concentrate on the here and now.

"Why are you here?"

"I explained that earlier today," he says, and if anything his grin widens. It's the kind of grin I've seen him get around his kids. The kind that makes the laugh lines around his mouth and eyes deepen. The kind that makes his dark eyes warm and look like liquid.

"Maybe you could explain it again."

If I could freeze a moment in time, it might be this one. I have the attention of a sexy, virile male. I have all of his attention at the moment, and I'm talking. Not loudly, but then with our lips this close, it's not necessary. I almost feel... *normal.*

"Remember what I told you when I said I couldn't kiss you, Toi?"

I think back. I wish I could say I remembered it all, but at the time I was mostly mourning the fact he wouldn't kiss me. I suck my lips in, nibbling on them as I think over that non-kiss-semi-kiss we shared.

"I can see you're thinking hard about it," he laughs. His thumb moves over my forehead as if to erase the lines I'm sure have formed. "I told you I couldn't kiss you, because you weren't mine to claim."

"I remember." I take a deep, shuddering breath. I'm not sure I can forget the fact that he didn't kiss me. Maybe if he had, I wouldn't crave his kiss quite so much now. The mystery would be kind of gone, and I could put it behind me.

"I also warned you that if you ever decided I was yours, nothing would keep me from you."

"But..."

"No buts."

"I mean, I didn't. *Did I?*"

"You definitely did," he argues.

"I don't remember that."

"Doesn't matter. What does matter is what comes next."

At that declaration my eyes widen and I'm pretty sure I stop breathing.

"Next?" I ask, and my voice comes out a squeak—and I don't think it has a thing to do with the fact it hurts to talk.

"I finally get my kiss, Dragonfly. Any arguments?"

If I wanted to be logical, I'd say I had plenty—like how fast this is going, how he's all wrong for me, how I need to get away from Florida... The list is never ending. Yet, at the thought of Marcum finishing what he teased me with the other day, I can't force any of the reasons out of my mouth.

"I can't think of any," I whisper instead, and his smile deepens and blurs in my vision as he brings his lips to mine.

❧ 35 ❧

MARCUM

OVER THE YEARS ALL THE WOMEN I'VE BEEN WITH HAVE KIND OF faded into a haze. The old saying, *"You've been with one, you've been with them all,"* is exactly how I felt. There's not a thing a woman could do that would surprise me. There's nothing about being with one that is different. Maybe that's why I've gone so long without a woman. Those around me think it was because of Cherry and the way she left.

It would have been simpler if that was the reason.

Fuck, seeing her today... I felt nothing. There's a chance she is betraying the club, and that should have me upset, but hell... I can't even feel much about that. I resented having to see to her when I could have been with Toi. I don't know what the fuck that says about me, but it is true—just the same.

But Toi... Toi is special. I shouldn't have anything to do with her. I should stay the fuck away. I've been fighting it, trying with everything in me. Every turn I make has been spent with the intention of staying away from her. Tonight she made that impossible.

I tried to convince myself she wasn't strong enough to survive in my world. I used that as another reason I shouldn't touch her.

Then... tonight, with one single, selfless act—an act that put blood on her hands—she crumbled every fucking defense I had to use against her.

I told her, but I don't think she understood. It's time I show her.

"I can't think of any," her soft whisper breathes out and that's all the permission I need—the final wall between us comes crashing down.

I hold her face gently, keeping her still for me. I have done a lot of things with women in my life, but gentle has never been a part of it. Something about Toi makes me want to be gentle. I press my lips to hers lightly, letting my tongue seep between hers slowly, running it along them, just to tease. She doesn't open for me, but I don't sense rejection from her. I've surprised her. I suck on her bottom lip, being as tender as I know how—which is nowhere near what she deserves.

She tastes sweet like candy and I know it's a taste I'll quickly become addicted to.

"Open your mouth for me, Dragonfly," I groan, wanting more of her, but trying to let her be the one to give it to me. Soon, there will be a time when I'll demand what I want and she'll give it to me, but for now it's important she gives herself to me at her pace. ·

She lets me in slowly, and I try not to rush her—but the moment I can I slide my tongue inside her mouth and explore, I'm lost. I drink from her, learning her, and claiming her. She's shy. Maybe she's not sure yet of the two of us. I can understand that. As hard as I fought giving in to my desires, I doubt she ever saw me as her man... *but I am.*

I let my fingers move to her neck, needing to feel her warmth. I stroke the soft skin as I plunder her mouth. I allow my hand to move farther and palm one of her breasts. I do nothing but massage it, knead it in my hands but I'm rewarded when her body pushes up from the bed toward me.

She wants me, and for now, that will have to be enough.

I break away slowly from her lips, opening my eyes to gaze into hers.

Beauty.

That's what Toi is. Something beautiful in my world that's seen very little of it. When a man finds beauty, he'd be a fool to let it go.

I stand up and remove my shirt. Toi watches, her eyes never leaving me.

"What are you doing?" she whispers.

"Getting ready for bed, Dragonfly." I grin when her eyes dilate and her mouth opens in surprise.

She shakes her head no, and shakes it harder when I undo my belt.

"You're cute, Toi, but I'm getting in this bed with you."

"You were already in bed," she says so softly I have to strain to hear her.

"But I didn't get undressed. I thought I might have to get up for club business."

"You still might," she says, rather desperately.

"I've decided I don't care if there's a fucking fire and we're attacked on all sides. I want to sleep with you skin against skin." I wait for her to process my words, then continue—needing to make her understand. "I told you, Toi, you sealed your fate."

"What does that mean?'

"Just what I said. I'm keeping you."

She starts to talk, but instead reaches for the notebook, wincing when it hurts. I frown. I don't like that and if what Kasha said is true, using her voice won't cause more damage. If anything, it might preserve what she still has. She starts to write furiously on her paper, when I reach down and pull it away.

"When you want to talk to me, Dragonfly, you use your damn voice."

"It hurts," she squeaks, but you can hear the anger in it.

"Because you don't fucking do it enough," I grumble, raking my hair back away from my face. This wasn't how I envisioned my evening and it's not how I want to finish it.

"You're a jerk," she huffs.

"I know and you should get used to it. Now quit distracting me. I told you I was keeping you, and I am."

"Shouldn't you..." She stops to catch her breath and then continues, "ask me about this?"

"It's too late for that," I answer her, unbuttoning my pants and pushing them down. Her face colors and she almost jumps back in bed. I'd almost think she'd never seen a dick before. I reach down with my hand and stretch my cock, showing her just how fucking much I want her. I nearly groan when she licks her bottom lip hungrily. "Not yet, Dragonfly."

She looks up, shocked.

"I wasn't—"

"Your eyes were. You need to heal up. You checked out okay, but you're black and blue every fucking where I look."

"I don't think we should—"

"Oh, we will."

"Marcum..."

"Yeah, I like that."

"What?"

"You saying my name."

"Can you put on pajamas?" she whispers as I put a knee on the bed.

"Don't have any."

"Underwear?" she squeaks, trying to scoot away.

"Don't wear that shit."

"You can't get in bed with me naked."

I reach down and kiss her forehead.

"Get some rest, Dragonfly," I say with a smile, as I slide under the covers.

"Oh my God!" she says clearly.

"It's big, honey, but it's not that impressive. It will fit inside of you just fine."

"I... You... We..."

"That's it pretty much. *We*. Go to sleep, Dragonfly."

"I'm going to pretend you aren't here," she murmurs, turning around and giving me her back. She's wearing a long, white gown and while it's sexy, I want to take it off of her. That's for another night, though.

"Let's see how that works for you."

There's silence for a few minutes and as I pull her body into mine, I close my eyes at how fucking perfect it feels.

"Your... I can feel you poking my ass..."

"Not yet. Soon, though." She tries to wiggle away from me, but I don't let her go. "Toi, honey, I know I said I was going to wait to claim you, but if you don't stop wiggling your ass against my cock like that, I'm not going to be responsible." She goes deathly still and I grin.

"Sweet dreams, Dragonfly," I whisper, kissing the back of her head and holding her close. This may be the first time in a month that I get a good night of sleep.

Even with a hard-on that could drive a nail in cement.

❧ 36 ❧

TOI

I WAKE UP ALONE. THAT SEEMS KIND OF ANTI-CLIMATIC, AND even though I should be grateful, I find I'm disappointed. Which is crazy.... *really it is.*

I sit up and I moan. Everything hurts. I'm sore from the top of my head to the bottom of my feet. Then there's the guilt. I was too out of it to process it last night, but this morning it's front and center.

I killed my father.

I killed my father for a man I'm not sure I even like most of the time.

I killed my father.

What kind of person does that make me? My father was slime, there's not any love inside of me for him, that's true. But isn't this proof that his blood flows through my veins? I have to be just as horrible as he was to kill him like I did. In my head, I can still hear the sickening sound of hitting him. A dull thud that could be heard even over the revving of the engine. I did it on impulse, without thinking. I just wanted to save... Marcum.

I didn't want Desi or Harley to hurt. I didn't want his other kids, who I am just starting to get to know, to hurt. And... if I'm honest with myself... I didn't want Marcum hurt. He's an ass. We fight more than I've ever fought with anyone. But I'm not scared of him. In fact, when he's near... I feel more alive. I like him... I might even care for him. I have to wonder if he care for me. The change seems so sudden. And, do I have any right to be thinking about being with him, when whatever I do will be built over the blood on my hands?

I slowly get out of bed. I need a shower. Maybe that will make me feel better. It has to help the soreness. I go to the attached bathroom. It's tiny, a small shower and toilet with the sink out in the bedroom, but it's more than I ever had. That's when I admit that I'm comfortable here. Most of the time I'm even happy.

All the reasons why I was running away are still there. They're just smaller than the need I have to get to know Marcum better... to maybe do more than just kiss him.

Getting undressed is a slow, painful adventure and by the time I get under the spray of the hot water—I'm more than thankful. Marcum wasn't kidding. I look like one giant black and blue bruise. In hindsight, I probably could have slowed down as I approached the tree. I'm pretty sure I was in pure panic mode.

I close my eyes and get lost in the water. The heat feels amazing. I move my hands over my body, carefully, letting the soap wash away some of my worries. I need to go see Desi and Harley. I miss them and I'm hoping I can get through to Harley a little more. I want to see more of Marcum too. I wonder if he will be around, or if he'll be gone. He seems to disappear often. Then there's the fact his ex is back. I don't know what that means. He didn't seem concerned with her last night, but there has to be feelings there and she was really pretty...

"Look what I have here."

"Marcum!" I gasp when he pulls the shower curtain back and is looking at me. I do my best to cover my most female areas with my hands—caught completely off guard.

"I missed you, Toi," he growls. His voice is so dark and graveled that it instantly sends chills through me.

JORDAN MARIE

"Close the curtain," I try to order, reaching to turn the water off and twisting to the side so he doesn't see so much of my body.

"Not on your fucking life, Dragonfly. Now turn around here, I want to see you," he demands, and to make sure I do exactly that, he gets ahold of my arm and pulls me around to face him. I don't even get the water turned off, he moves that quick. I try to bring my arm back to shield my body, but wrestling with Marcum is useless. "You're beautiful, Toi."

"I don't think ... You shouldn't be here," I tell him, having to take a break, for both my voice to work and my thoughts to settle.

"I shouldn't have left this morning. The shower in this damn room is too small. I'll fix that soon."

I have no idea what that means, but I don't bother asking him. I have bigger concerns. The hot water already has my body flushed a pale pink, but the way he looks at me only makes the color increase. Shock rolls through me as Marcum drops to his knees, his hands on my hips.

"Put your hands against the shower wall, Toi."

"Marcum..."

"Do it," he commands in such a way I find myself obeying at once, leaving my body open to him. I'm thankful I'm in the shower because my knees went weak at the way he ordered me and I'm so wet, I have to fight not to touch myself in front of him.

"Good girl." His hand moves over my breasts, his fingers teasing them. I lose my breath as I look down and see his face. His eyes are centered on my body—on the way his hands move across my body. I've never felt beautiful before, but in that moment I definitely do. "You've got a beautiful pussy, Dragonfly," he praises, as his fingers run against the trimmed hair that I keep there. I feel goosebumps move over my body and I don't speak—I'm having enough trouble breathing. You can hear my deep breaths in the room overtop of the sound of the shower. "I'll have to shave you here, so you'll always be bare to me."

Those words change those goosebumps into full-on body shivers as I imagine him doing such an intimate thing to me... *to*

124

my body. He sounds like he owns my body now and I find I don't want to argue. If he has me under some kind of spell, I hope I don't wake up from it.

"You'll get wet," I tell him, as the spray of the shower runs down on his long hair and beard. He looks up and I know he probably couldn't have heard my words.

He surprises me though. His face softens in its desire, and with the water glistening on it like that—it takes my breath away. I've always been attracted to older men. There's something about the way they carry themselves, and the miles they've traveled that shows up on their bodies and in the fine lines of their face. It's attractive. I've never let myself step over the line with one—my father would have made my life hell. I can't stop myself from reaching down and touching Marcum's face now. He's really beautiful, right down to his untamed beard and the wild look in his deep brown eyes. I clench my fingers carefully into his beard, liking the way the coarse hair feels between them.

"Like the way you're wet?" he grins, and his grin is positively sinful. It takes me a moment to understand what he's saying. I'm thankful my body is already flushed, or he would see embarrassment on my face. I've never been around anyone who just speaks so... directly. "Spread your legs out for me a little more, baby," he tells me, and he applies pressure to the inside of my thighs to ensure I do. He didn't need to worry. I want to know what it feels like to have his mouth on me. I've never had a man go down on me before. I carefully slide my legs farther apart, bracing my ass against the shower wall. "I like the way you mind me, Toi. It makes me want to reward you," he tells me, and I gasp my reply, my body thrusting toward him as he slides his fingers between the lips of my pussy. "You like that, don't you, Dragonfly—so hungry for more."

"Yes," I murmur as his fingers graze against my clit.

"Do you want more?"

"Please," I ask, as I feel one of his fingers push inside of me. "More..."

"You might be in trouble, Toi," he growls, pushing two fingers deep inside of me now and stretching me.

"Why?" I gasp, trying to hold him inside of me.

"Because I like it when you say please," he responds, and I'm really too far gone to know what that means—to understand what he's saying. I don't care as long as he doesn't stop. I'm desperate enough that I give him what he wants.

"Please, Marcum. Give me more, please."

❧ 37 ❧

MARCUM

"PLEASE, MARCUM. GIVE ME MORE, PLEASE."

The words are spoken so delicately I can't be sure she said them, or if I'm dreaming she did. Either way, I can't stop myself from tasting her. I pull the lips of her pussy back, opening her to me. I can see her wet, swollen clit throbbing, and it calls to me. I flatten my tongue and tease the little button before sucking it into my mouth and pushing my fingers back in her tight little hole. She's so fucking tight; I've never felt anything like it.

Which is fitting, because in this moment, with Toi, I forget the past. She makes me feel clean, she makes me forget the filth and the shit I've done and still do on a daily basis. She makes me...

Fuck—she makes me feel.

Besides my kids, no one has truly done that in a very long time —maybe forever.

That realization rocks me to the core. I grab her leg and pull her into my face, burying myself in her. I wanted to take my time and fuck her with my tongue, bringing her to an orgasm by teasing her. I didn't plan on being the one to lose control first.

"That's it, baby, ride my face. Ride it fucking hard," I growl against her pussy before pushing my face back in and drinking her down. Fuck, she even tastes sweet and clean.

Melt-in-your-mouth-perfect.

Jesus.

I pull her even harder down on me. Using my tongue to fuck that sweet little cunt, hell even using my lips, nose, beard, fingers, anything to make her go wild. And she is... She's going completely wild. She's riding my damn face like a jockey riding a thoroughbred for the win in the Kentucky Derby. Her moves are wild, and unpracticed, but that makes me fucking glad. She's the purest thing I've ever laid my hands on. Too damn pure for me to touch her—but that ship has sailed.

I bite the inside of her thigh, making her cry out. With her voice, it's quiet, but still louder than anything she's given me before. I smooth my lips across the bite, before going back to lick up more cream from her juicy little pussy. I'm smothered in her cum. It's on my face, my tongue, I'm drinking it down my throat and it's coating my beard.

And still, it's not enough. I want it all.

Every. Fucking. Drop.

I run my fingers through her juices, then thrust two deep in her cunt, sinking in as far as I can. When I slide them out, I replace them with my mouth, pressing my chin against her cunt, sucking on her clit and running my tongue over it in different directions, my approach fast and hard. Then I take my fingers which are covered in her cum, and thrust them deep in her ass.

I don't go slow. If I were a softer man, I would have. I'm not. I'm hungry for her orgasm, I'm starving for her. She cries, her body tightening as my fingers breach past that tight ring of muscles. She tries to lift off of me, but I don't let her. I hold her down on my face with bruising force. A few minutes of tongue fucking her juicy little cunt and she softens, my fingers stretching her ass. I'll be fucking her here. Jesus. With just this taste, I know I'll be fucking her anywhere and in every hole I can get.

She's on the edge, I can feel it by the way she's thrusting down on me. I continue fucking her ass, but I pull away from her sweet little cunt, licking her honey from my lips. I push my other hand under her and slide my fingers in her pussy. I fuck her ass and pussy in tandem with my fingers. Toi slaps the side of the shower wall hard with her hands. She's whimpering, her breaths dragging through her body harshly. She's so close to the fucking edge that when she finally blows I know it's going to be beautiful.

Her head thrashes back and forth as I twirl my fingers in that tight little ass and fuck her pussy hard. I watch until the very moment her eyes open. They're wide, dilated and full of hunger.

"Marcum," she cries, the sound frenzied and broken.

I lick her cunt then, continuing to fuck her ass as she comes on my face and rides me all the way to the end.

38

TOI

I JUST CAME.

I just came...on Marcum. I should be dying of embarrassment, but I'm having enough trouble trying to catch my breath. I might be in some kind of trance, because I don't even notice that Marcum is washing me until I feel his hands wrap around me and squeeze my breasts. I look down and watch as the water washes the soap down my body.

"I..."

"I fucking love your body," he growls.

"Oh God," I gasp as he bites on my neck, still kneading my breasts.

"Hold your head back for me and let me wash your hair."

It's crazy. Marcum is still fully dressed. The only thing I don't notice on him is his club cut. He's wearing jeans and a red, long-sleeved, thermal shirt. The shower is so small that we are pressed against each other and there's not a lot of room to move.

"I can... I can bathe myself," I whisper, my voice much hoarser than normal. I'd never admit it to Marcum, but he is right. The more I use it, the easier it seems to be—even if the sound doesn't get much louder.

"I want to bathe you, Toi. You're mine and I need to be able to touch you anytime I want, and I want to fucking take care of you any way I want. So hold your head back and let me wash your hair," he orders against my ear. His breath teases my skin, even with the shower water—which somehow, is still warm.

"Okay, Marcum," I answer. I don't have it in me to argue. I doubt it would do much good in the first place, but I like his hands on me. I let my head go back and Marcum shifts so he's standing at my side and begins the process of washing my hair.

"Damn shower is too small. Tomorrow we use my shower, Toi."

I don't know how to respond to that, so I don't. Secretly, I'm just glad that he's planning on touching me again. I don't know much about being claimed by Marcum. What we just shared could have been the end of it, for all I knew. I'm glad it's not.

Marcum is surprisingly gentle with me as he washes and conditions my hair. I close my eyes, loving the feel of his fingers brushing through my hair. I moan as he finishes, and he rewards me by kissing the side of my neck. He shuts the water off and all too soon he pulls me outside and wraps me in a towel. He's still soaking wet, and his clothes are sticking to him, but it looks good on him.

"Get dressed, Dragonfly, and come down for breakfast."

"But..." I start, surprised. He always has Ghost or someone bring me a plate from the kitchen. As long as I've been here, I've never mingled with the club—not really.

"I want you to eat with me before I have to get some work done." I color at his words and he actually laughs. "I mean to eat food this time, Toi." I gasp in shock and that just makes him laugh harder.

Before I can reply he gives me a kiss. It's quick, but intense, and his tongue invades my mouth like a solider on a quest. When we break apart, he stays close for a minute, kissing my forehead.

"Marcum..."

"Don't keep me waiting, Toi. I want you downstairs."

"But—"

"And wear this when you do," he orders gruffly and walks out the door.

I'm left holding his cut, the heavy leather warm to my touch, and staring after him, wondering exactly what I'm going to do with this changing Marcum.... A Marcum I like—even if I shouldn't.

❧ 39 ❧

MARCUM

"WE NEED TO TALK, MARCUM, HONEY," CHERRY SAYS THE minute I sit down.

"Don't see why," I grumble, annoyed that she's here. I should have her locked up and monitored. After interrogating her some last night and talking with the men, I decided against it. I looked to Topper and Ride for guidance on this one, because I'm not sure I can be impartial. Our final decision was to let her believe we somewhat trust her, just to see what her next move is. My only request is we keep her from the kids, so I'm not sure how the fuck this is going to work full time. Hopefully Cherry will be gone soon.

I'm probably a stupid fuck, but she was a decent woman before. I don't think she's lying about the reasons she was helping Weasel, but something does feel different about Cherry.

Fuck. Maybe it's because I'm not thinking with my dick.

"You're angry with me," she sighs. I look at her then, appraising her. Honestly, I haven't paid her much attention. She hasn't changed a lot. Her hair is shorter these days, her makeup a little heavier, but mostly the same Cherry she was before. The same one who told me she couldn't live with me knowing I killed another woman so easily. The same woman who apparently never understood me from day one.

How could she, if she thought that I would let Jenna continue to draw air after knifing Max and the club in the back? She fucked with my son and got Tess shot. I almost lost them both because of her. Jenna knew what would happen; she wasn't a fucking stranger to this club, to the rules we lived by. If I hadn't retaliated, I wouldn't be sitting here. Fuck, I wouldn't be breathing. My world sniffs out weakness and if they find it, you're fucked.

"You came back to help out an enemy of my club," I start.

"I didn't know he was an enemy, honey. When I was here, he was one of the crew."

"Weasel was never one of the crew."

"He helped you sometimes. You used his skills and he had club privileges," she argues.

"I'd buy that from anyone else, but not you, Cherry. You lived behind my walls. Fuck woman, you slept in my bed. You knew how shit was done, and you still did it."

"I thought I was helping out the club."

"You want to help the club, you come to me," I shrug, as one of the club girls puts a plate of food in front of me.

"We didn't exactly leave things on good terms, Marcum, honey."

"That's a good reason for you to walk away and not get involved."

"Marcum, I still feel loyalty to the club and to you. I can't just turn that off. I don't want you angry with me."

I lean up on my elbows and look at her, really look at her. I didn't love her, but I should feel something... and yet, I don't.

That probably makes me a bastard, but it doesn't change the truth.

"I'm not angry with you, Cherry. If I were, you wouldn't be inside the walls of my club, sitting at my table."

She smiles at my answer and something flashes in her eyes that

I do not like. I don't know what it is, but it's different than any other emotion I remember from her and it sets off warning bells.

"I'm so glad, Marcum. I think we have a lot to talk about."

"If I was angry, you wouldn't be breathing right now. Then again, you know that. That's why you left," I remind her, driving my point home hard, because I've always been a firm believer in going with my gut. And, right now, my gut is telling me to keep an eye on Cherry.

Her face pales and it damn well should. My mood is soured, but luckily that's the moment Toi comes down the stairs.

She's walking a little tenderly and I can't help the cocky grin that spreads on my face. I wasn't easy with her, and I'll probably continue to be that way. Toi's like a drug that goes straight to my head.

She's wearing worn jeans that I've seen several times before, and a black long sleeved shirt that is just as familiar... Yet it's all different this time.

Because today she's wearing my cut.

I've got one of her own being fixed. I've never claimed a woman in this way. Even when Cherry was my old lady, officially, I never gave her a cut. This is a big step for me and you can tell that by the silence filling the room. I fight the urge to look at Ghost. He's the motherfucker I want to deliver my message to the most, but for the life of me I can't pull my eyes away from Toi.

Her hair is down and she takes my fucking breath and locks it in my chest. She's beautiful. I make a note to take her shopping for more clothes, and to fuck her soon. I don't think I can wait much longer. She stands back from the table, blushing and looking very unsure.

I walk over to her, drawn to her like a fucking moth to a flame.

"You look good, Dragonfly," I whisper in her ear, pulling her into my body. "I like your hair down."

"I had a bruise on my neck," she whispers back and I move my hand along the inside of her neck, lifting her hair. It's the hickey I gave her earlier. I haven't done that shit since I was a wet-behind-the-ears kid, trying to prove himself to the world. Toi makes me want to mark her entire fucking body, though. I grin down at her.

"I like it," I tell her pulling her hair over her shoulder, revealing it a little better.

"You're an ass," she whispers, but she says it with an almost-smile on her lips. I pick her up, cradling her against my body. "Marcum!" she gasps. "I can walk!"

"You've been in a bad wreck. I want to carry you."

"I'm fine," she says.

"I should probably tell you now, I like carrying you. I'm liable to do it often," I tell her, ignoring her protest. I walk her over to the table and sit down in the chair with her. The minute we sit down, the men start talking again. Toi tries to move off of my lap, but the chair beside me is where Cherry is sitting and Toi isn't getting out of arm's length from me. I keep her in my lap, not letting her go.

"I..."

"I want you here, Dragonfly."

"But—"

"Hearing your voice makes me happy. If you're not in my lap, I may not hear it, and I need to hear it, Toi. You stay in my lap."

She sighs, but she doesn't argue. I reach down and get a piece of bacon from my plate and hold it to her lips. She opens slowly and takes a bite, her eyes glued to mine. She chews slowly and I stab a piece of scrambled egg on my fork and hold it up next.

"Let me guess. You like feeding me too?"

"Got it in one, baby. Got it in one," I answer with a grin, and that grin only gets bigger when she takes the egg between her lips and I hear a chair scrape against the floor. I look away to see Cherry giving Toi a look I do not like. I make a mental note about that, but then I see Ghost walking out of the room. I lean down and kiss Toi's forehead. She has no idea what's going on, I see it on her face, but that's okay. Ghost and I do. It's too late for him and he knows it.

Toi's mine.

❧ 40 ❧
TOI

I'm PRETTY SURE I'm IN A COMA SOMEWHERE, COMPLETELY
unconscious and dreaming. That's the only explanation for how my
world has turned around since the accident. It's been three days
since Marcum brought me back to the club. Three days of him
sleeping with me every night and playing my body like an instru-
ment he created. Three days of him carrying me the minute he
sees me walking and three days of eating dinner in the large
kitchen at the club, while in Marcum's lap.

It also has two dark spots.

It has been three days that I have seen very little of Desi and
Harley. The older kids have stopped by to check on me, and Desi
always comes in every evening to hug me and tell me about school.
But I haven't seen Harley.

Not once.

The other dark spot is Cherry is still here. I haven't questioned
Marcum about it. As new as this is, I'm not sure *what it is.* I'm
pretty sure it's not my place to question him about his exes—at
least not yet. Still, I'm not blind to the way she looks at me. And
I've blocked out most of that day, but she didn't seem as sweet that
day in the car as she tries to be here. At least I don't think so.

Maybe I'm projecting because I don't like her being here. I'm not jealous... At least I'm not going to admit that I am. That would be silly, right? To be jealous over a man that....

Shit. I don't know what Marcum is. I don't know what we are.

Maybe there's more than just two dark spots, after all.

I shake it off and take a quick shower. Marcum hasn't showered with me again since that first time. Truly there isn't room in here, but I always miss him now—which is annoying. When I get out of the shower I go to my bed and find a box laying on it. I had the door locked, so that in and of itself is worrisome. I tug my towel a little closer and look around the room, wondering if I should hurry and get dressed. I still seem to be alone so I open the plain white box. Inside there's white tissue paper and a pink envelope. I take out the envelope and push the paper aside, finding a vest—or cut as Bab's explained they're called—that mirrors the one that Marcum had me wearing. It was his and it dwarfed me. It was heavy but it was warm and somehow comforting, because it smelled like him. I can tell right away that this one is my size. I pick it up, instantly missing Marcum's scent on it. This one still smells like leather, though, and that's close. It's black, the front has my name embossed in white lettering and the club's insignia beneath it. When I turn it around is when I lose my breath.

Property of Marcum.

Property... I don't know how I feel about that. Everything in me should rebel, but I think I like it. My brain is such a mess, and I'm trying really hard not to think about my father. I just don't think I can handle it all right now. So, I'm living in a world of denial.

I go to my dresser to find some clothes to wear. It won't be hard. I only have a few outfits and I've interchanged the tops and bottoms a million different ways since being here. I hadn't worried about it when I was planning on leaving. I don't know what I'm doing in this new reality, so pretty soon I'm going to have to find a job—a paying one.

There's a banging on the door that startles me. I turn around still clutching the towel.

"Toi! Harley and I need to talk to you!" I look at the clock and frown as I hear Desi. They should be in school right now. I grab an old robe that was here when I moved here, off of a hook on the wall and put it on. I barely have the waist cinched when the clamoring on the door happens again. I unlock it and it opens so swiftly that it almost hits me. Desi throws herself in my arms with such force that I stumble. I sit on the bed before we fall. Harley comes in behind her and Desi might be crying, but Harley looks mad. He's got so much anger that I can almost feel it and it's directed solely at me. Behind him comes Cherry and I immediately get a sick feeling in my stomach.

Whatever this is, it can't be good.

✦ 41 ✦

MARCUM

"Delivered the package, Marcum," Ghost says coming back in and looking like he could kill someone—most likely me.

I'm a twisted motherfucker, but I had him deliver Toi's cut to her. I thought he would call me on my shit, but he didn't. Which is good, but frustrating. I find the more I think of the way he looks at Toi, I want to punch his damn face in.

He sits down and stares at me, his eyes locked on me and there's anger rolling off of him in waves. I look around the group of men that have assembled around the room. All of my officers are here, along with the ones that once held an office and have stepped down for younger blood. I've not. Being the President of this crew is what I was born to do. Stepping down isn't in me, even if some of these young fucks think it'd be for the best. I've been challenged a couple of times and I handed them their ass on a platter. I might have some miles on me, but I got a fuck of a lot more to go.

My mind instantly goes to Toi. She definitely deserves better, but I'm not giving her up.

"Have we checked into seeing exactly what Weasel was up to his last days?" I ask Ride. He's my second in command, and the fucker that I trust the most, with maybe the exception of Topper. It just happens that Ride has the muscle to back up what needs to be done. Topper is deadly in a fight, but mostly because of his weapons. Fuck, I'd say Ride could rip a man's head off of his shoulders with one hand. The fucker is that big.

"I still have some checking to do. Whatever the fuck it was, he was keeping it quiet and being pretty fucking stealthy about it."

"Shit," I mutter. There's a course of grunts around me, because we all know that's trouble. Weasel didn't get his nickname without reason. "I'm going to call an old friend. He's had some dealings with Kuzma. Word is that fucker works closely with the Garcias."

"That's an ugly can of worms you're opening boss," String warns.

"That's why I'm opening it slowly. I'll talk with Anthes about it and see what he can find out. Now, everyone go and do the shit that needs to be done," I growl, tired already of meeting with them. They all stand up, but my eyes land on Ghost. "All but, Ghost," I order. Everyone stops. There's an undercurrent going on, and though they may not understand all of it—they understand enough.

"Brother—" Ride starts.

"Stay out of it, Ride," I warn, my gaze not leaving Ghost's. His stare is just as fixed. The room clears out rather quickly, and the door closes, but Ride is the one who closes it. "I told you to leave," I yell at him again, still not taking my eyes off of Ghost.

Ghost takes his cut off and I do the same. We know what's about to go down. This isn't about the club. *This is man to man.*

"Way I figure it, one of us around here needs to keep our head on straight so you two fuckers don't kill yourselves."

"It's none of your business," Ghost growls at Ride.

"There's something we can agree on," I answer and I take my rings off one at a time, seeing how he is too. I don't want it said I loaded the fight when I have his ass packed out of here.

"Whatever happened to the old saying, *bros before hos?*" Ride asks sarcastically.

"She's not a ho," I growl, and I can respect that Ghost answers the same, right along with me.

"She's not yours either," I taunt Ghost when we start circling each other.

He makes an angry jab at me, that comes nowhere close. It was done out of anger, but he hasn't lost control; he's merely feeling me out and wondering exactly when I'll attack.

"You shouldn't touch her," Ghost yells, taking yet another jab into empty air.

"You're pissed 'cause you didn't get in there first," I mock, defending his blow easily. He's going easy on me. Does he think I'm so damn old that I can't hand him his ass? He's about to learn that's a mistake.

"She's been through a lot. She needed time to heal."

"She needed a man. Trust me brother, I give Toi exactly what she needs," I smirk and he swings at me again. He almost gets me this time, but I still manage to side-step the blow.

"Are you going to hit back or dance around like a fucking girl?" he complains, irritated when he can't connect to flesh.

"I'm just telling you that I have Toi taken care of. She even begs me for it and takes it so fucking sweet your teeth would hurt," I taunt.

"Fuck, that's low, Marcum," Ride laughs, shaking his head. It is. I'm a fucking asshole, but it's also exactly what makes Ghost let go of what control he had. He charges at me head on, crying out like a fucking wild boar attacking prey. He hurls his body at me and sends us both careening through the damn air a good foot before we crash into the table. The hard pine of the table slaps against my back and fuck, that's going to hurt in the morning. Ghost clamps his arms around me, but he can't dodge my knee that comes up to sucker-punch the fucker in the nuts. When he curls into his own body from the blow, I raise both arms up and chop down on the asshole, connecting at the side of his neck. He goes down like fucking lead.

"Get up, motherfucker," I growl, kicking his sorry ass with my boot. He climbs up and he's not bleeding and that needs to be rectified. I want him bleeding.

"You're too fucking old for her and she sure as hell ain't your kind of woman," Ghost barks. I pop my hand out quick and hit him in the mouth. That's what he gets for saying that kind of shit to me. Especially when it's the same old shit I've been using to stay away from her.

His lip starts bleeding—not a lot, but enough that the deep red running from the corner makes me way too fucking happy.

"You don't know shit!" I growl, even though he does. He's not wrong. I am too fucking old for Toi and shit, she's not like any of the other women I've messed with. She's better than me, she's better than any fucking other person in my life that I've had. She's the kind of girl that can stand toe to toe with Tess and not be less. She fits. She's the kind of mother I wish my kids always had.

"I know she's younger than Dawg. I know that you have her tending to all those fucking kids like a damn slave. Fuck, half of those kids aren't even yours," he growls wiping the blood from his lip and succeeding for a minute, but only a minute because more keeps coming.

"They are mine."

"Fuck. You took most of them in, knowing it wasn't you who made them. Treated those whores like you thought they were worth something. Which is fine. You want to claim a hundred kids that you didn't father, then whatever, but you don't need to pass them off to Toi to take care of. She deserves better!" he growls and then he throws a punch.

I don't dodge this one. I'm frozen, because his words surprise me. I didn't realize my brothers knew that most of my children weren't mine. Hell, even the twins aren't mine biologically. At least that's what the mother said. But they needed me and the mother was a fucking dime-bag whore. So I took them. Same with the others. Shit. If I want to be technical, the only child I'm sure I fathered was Maxwell. It doesn't matter. I love them all and I claimed them the moment I knew they were growing. The kids don't know, and I'll never tell them. I'm their father and I dare anyone to tell them differently.

I fall back a few steps with the savagery of Ghost's hit. Now he's drawn blood too, but he drew more than me. The blood he drew isn't visible, but it's there. There's only three people—besides the women involved—who know I didn't father most, if any, of the children. They are people who I trust—or trusted—with the secret. At this point, I doubt it would hurt the older kids, but it might destroy Harley and Desi. I don't like that my secret is out and eventually I will find out how the motherfucker knows. Right now, I just want him to hurt.

I push myself up and I throw a punch connecting with his stomach, and then another, another, and yet another. I let my rage fuel me. I try to concentrate in the area of Ghost's ribs and I attack him as if my life depended on it. He gets in a few good punches of his own—enough that I know I'll be wearing bruises tomorrow.

"Shut your fucking mouth," I warn him, though the words come out ragged and winded as we continue our fight. "Those are —" I take a deep breath and deliver one more shot, this one harder, meaner, and aimed for the fuckers face. I uppercut him and it's so hard he instantly drops, his face going to the side at an odd angle. "—my children!" I growl with the hit, anger vibrating through me. I stand over Ghost and he's out. He's moving his head but he's definitely down. I spit at the ground as blood begins to pool into my mouth. "You don't talk about my kids. You don't know jack shit, and you don't go spouting off about them. Fuck, you know nothing about when it comes to my life," I warn him and he better fucking listen. The next time I'll end the motherfucker. No one brings my kids up in this shit. *No one.*

I rub the back of my hand against my busted lip, looking down at Ghost. He stares at me, but he doesn't say anything. Maybe he's taking my warning in. He fucking better.

"Marcum, man," Topper says. He's standing at the door.

"Motherfucker, doesn't anyone know what stay the fuck out of this means?" I growl, turning to look at him.

"I hear you, dude, but we have a situation."

"What in the hell is it now?"

"Harley and Desi are upstairs in Toi's room and Harley, man, he's freaking out."

"Fuck..."

"It gets worse, man. Cherry is with them."

"I told you sorry fuckers she wasn't to get around my kids," I growl, grabbing my cut and throwing it on, leaving my rings where they are. Even now, my knuckles are swelling.

"That's just it, man. We were keeping Cherry under control. Harley followed String down the hall and we didn't know it until it was too late."

"Fuck. I should fucking beat every one of you dumbasses," I growl, perhaps unfairly. Right now, however, I don't give a rat's ass about being fair. I take off toward Toi's room, hoping I can stop it before whatever is going on becomes a shit storm.

❧ 42 ❧

TOI

"WHAT'S GOING ON?" I ASK, BUT WITH MY VOICE YOU CAN barely hear it over Desi's crying.

"Can't hear you, honey. Oh, that's right, your voice is broken," Cherry says and she smiles like she's being friendly, but I see the spitefulness in her eyes.

"Toi's not broken!" Desi argues, holding me closer, her little hands wrapped around me and linked at my neck. I pat her on the back and try to soothe her as best I can.

I ignore Cherry. There's not much I can do about her, and she's not my main concern anyhow. I focus on Harley—*a very angry Harley*. I hold out my hand to him, trying to get him to come to me. I can't explain why, but I don't like that Cherry is so close to him. Something about her just seems off and if it's because I'm jealous? So be it. I still want Harley away from her.

Harley stubbornly remains where he is. He takes a stilted step toward me. Cherry slyly puts her hand on his shoulder and he instantly stills. I clear my throat.

"Come here, Harley," I urge him. I see the indecision war inside of him and my heart breaks for the little boy. Whatever is going on is truly hurting him. I have a bad feeling that Cherry is at the root of it all. I have the strongest urge to scratch her eyeballs out. I hold out hope he'll come to me, but when he doesn't, I have to close my eyes at the pain it brings me. I may not know exactly what I feel for Marcum, but I love Desi and Harley. I love them like they're my own kids and having him turn me away while he's hurting drives a knife through my heart.

"Were you leaving?" Harley asks and at first, I don't understand, then I feel a sick flush move over my body as his words hit home.

"Harley," I start, but he doesn't let me finish.

"Were you running away from here? Are you the reason my dad almost got hurt?" he asks, and the anger and pain on his face makes him appear so much older than his years. He looks like a mini-adult standing there and that makes me sadder. Kids Harley's age should be innocent of the world and the tricks adults play. Tricks I'm sure Cherry is using—even if I can't prove it.

"I told him you wouldn't, Toi! I told him you wouldn't just leave us like that! I told him Cherry was lying!" Desi cries.

My gaze snaps to Cherry, who is frowning at Desi. It's quickly replaced with a look that I suppose is meant to resemble regret—It doesn't quite make it.

"He overheard me talking to my father. I didn't know he was around," she says, and I want to throttle her. Instead, I try and focus on Harley and Desi.

"It's not that simple, Harley," I begin.

"You were going to leave us?" Desi says with tears in her eyes and her lip quivering.

"I didn't want to," I start, hating everything about this.

"I told you, Desi. They all leave. No one wants to stay with us," Harley argues. He pulls away from Cherry then and goes toward me, but it's not to hold my hand or let me get near me. He wants his sister. "Let's go."

Desi looks up at me and my heart is breaking.

"Why did you want to leave us, Toi? Don't you love us?" she asks. She slides off my lap and I want to hold onto her. I think about forcing her to stay, but I don't. Something instinctively tells me that would be the wrong move.

"I didn't want to leave, not really, babies," I try to explain, but I start coughing because I've never been this emotional while trying to talk. The weakness shames me. Especially when Cherry is standing over there, looking close to gloating.

Can't she see how this is tearing up the children? Couldn't she try to help—for their sake?

"But you were," Desi says, her little voice trembling as her body shakes with sobs she's trying to hold back. "You told me you loved me..."

"I do love you, Desi! I love both of you." I'm really stretching my voice now, but I need to try and reach them.

"We don't love you," Harley says, his voice stoic. "You're nobody! We don't want you here anymore!"

"That's enough, Harley!" Marcum's stern voice comes from the hall. He looks like he's been in a physical fight and...he's mad. *Furiously mad.* I can see it, but I wouldn't have to. His anger is so powerful you can feel it in the room.

All of us jump, probably even Cherry, though I'm trying to pretend she's not here, so I don't look.

"I was just telling the truth!"

"You will treat Toi with respect and that's final, son," he says harshly.

"I won't and you can't make me. I hate her! Desi and I both hate her and we don't want her here anymore!" he answers remaining stubborn. My heart feels like it's breaking. He runs from the room and Marcum gives me a look I don't quite know how to read, and then follows his son. Desi looks at me; she looks more than a little lost.

"I love you, Desi," I whisper, and I feel my own tears now, but I try to hold them back.

She doesn't say it back, but at least she doesn't say she hates me. She leaves the room, though and that is painful enough.

"I'll just go see if I can help Marcum calm them down, honey. These kids trust *me*."

Cherry puts an emphasis on the word 'me' and if I had anything left in me I would go after her, but I don't. I'm coughing from talking for so long at the highest volume I can manage. I feel raw both physically and emotionally.

"It'll be okay, Toi." This comes from Ride, who is somehow standing by the bed handing me a bottle of water that I keep on my nightstand. I wish I could believe him, but I don't. I just keep seeing Harley's and Desi's faces and hating myself for hurting them.

I take a drink of the water and then one more. When my coughing eases, I lie down on the bed and close my eyes, feeling completely lost.

It's then the tears begin.

❧ 43 ❧

MARCUM

"I DON'T CARE WHAT YOU SAY, DAD. I'M NOT SORRY!" HARLEY says stubbornly when I walk into his room.

The kid might not be mine biologically, but damn if he isn't so much like me it hurts to see sometimes—even as it makes me proud. The truth is, I've not done a lot in this life I'm proud of, but these kids... They make me proud. It doesn't matter to me if it was my seed that fathered them, I've been their dad and I'd kill another man for trying to take that away from me. They're mine. I let Maxwell down so much in life. Hell, I didn't even know he was alive for the first years of his life. Maybe there's a part of me trying to make sure these kids—kids I love—never know the emptiness Maxwell had, at not having a father.

Fuck, I was just a kid when I gave Max's mother my dick. Too fucking young to know better and too full of cum to care.

"Son, you don't have a right to be upset at Toi."

"She was going to leave us," he says stubbornly. Desi is a little more forgiving. When I squat down on my legs so that my son and I will be more eye to eye, Desi comes over and climbs up on my lap. I balance the both of us while I stroke her hair gently, holding her to me. I keep my gaze on Harley. I know he's hurting; I see it in his eyes. My son may act like a badass, but inside he's just a little boy looking for something he's always missed having—his mother.

The one thing I've done a piss-poor job of giving him.

As if on cue to my thoughts the door opens.

"I was just checking on—"

"I have my children, Cherry. You need to leave."

"But, Marcum. Honey, I just wanted to see if there was anything I could do."

"You can leave and let me talk to my children alone. You and I will talk when I'm done," I order her. I want to say a fuck of a lot more than that—but I can't—not in front of my kids.

She must see my anger. I'm doing my best to hide in front of Harley and Desi, but Cherry has to see it, because she backs out of the room.

"You shouldn't talk to Cherry like that. She cares about us."

I try to let that remark slide. I can't find it in me to let all of it go however. I can't prove it, but I'd lay odds Cherry has fed Harley's need to dislike Toi. I don't know why the fuck she would. She left the club, she left me, but my gut tells me that's what is at play here. Plus, if there's one thing I've learned over the years, it's that a woman is not fucking logical.

"Son, let me ask you a question. How can you take up for Cherry, and yet be mad at Toi for the same damn thing?"

"I—"

"The only difference is that Cherry left. She did that on her own, no one made her. Toi is still here."

"But she was leaving," he says stubbornly, but I see something on his face and I hope my words are getting through to him—at least a little.

"Have you given her a reason to stay, Harley?"

"I—"

"I'm going to tell you something I learned a long time ago, son. A woman needs to feel wanted."

"You saying Toi didn't feel wanted?"

"She had reason to believe she wasn't and that's adult stuff you won't understand right now, but Toi cares about you and Desi and she doesn't deserve your anger."

"Whatever," he huffs, turning away from me and going to sit on his bed—effectively dismissing me.

I sigh and kiss my little girl on the top of her head, before helping her stand and then straightening up.

"You're a lot like me son, maybe too much. Someday that pride is going to get you in trouble."

He doesn't respond and after winking at Desi and getting her settled, I leave them alone. I have several stops to make before I can get back to Toi and I have a feeling that Toi needs me.

I sure as fuck know I need her right now. Christ. *When did life become so fucking complicated?*

✿ 44 ✿
TOI

"ARE YOU CRYING, DRAGONFLY?" MARCUM ASKS, ONCE HE SLIDES in bed beside me. Instantly the warm heat of his skin envelopes me, giving me what I've missed even if I didn't put it into words.

"I'm trying not to," I tell him quietly.

"They're just kids, sweetheart. They'll get used to the way things are and come around, eventually," he says.

I frown. This conversation is a little surreal with Marcum, considering how quick the relationship he and I have has changed in such a short space of time. Does he truly believe the children will come around? Did they come around for Cherry when he was sleeping with her? How many times have the kids had to get "used" to a woman in their lives?

I don't ask him any of this, however. Marcum is like a freight train and honestly I can't handle that right now. He just barrels in and things have to be his way; he won't accept anything less. Right now, I don't want to ride that train. I don't think I can. So I remain quiet—at least about that.

"What time is it?"

"It's late, honey. Go to sleep," he mumbles, and his beard tickles against the back of my neck. He tightens his hold on me and I know that's my cue to rest. I feel so unsettled though. What am I doing with Marcum? What are we? Why is Cherry here? Why was Marcum gone for so long? All I have are questions and no answers. The worst part is, I'm not sure I have a right to ask the questions... Because I don't know who I am to Marcum...

And maybe that's the whole problem.

"Marcum?" I begin nervously.

"Go to sleep, honey."

"Marcum, who... *what* am I to you?"

I know the exact moment he processes my question, because his body almost goes rigid behind me.

"Come again?" he responds.

"What am I to you...?" I ask uncertainly.

"What are you to me?" he parrots, pulling away from me. I roll to my back, so I can see him. He stays on the bed, but he's sitting up now. The room is mostly dark; there's a stream of light shining through the window from the moon, but that's it. "Are we really doing this shit now, Toi?" he asks and I can't help but flinch when I hear the anger in his voice.

"I... I just..."

"You what? You want to dissect shit at two in the morning?" he mutters, scratching his fingers through his beard. I watch the moonlight catch the silver of his skull ring and look at the ink covering his fingers.

I didn't realize it was so late and I try to tamp down the jealousy that bubbles up that Marcum has been gone that long. Was he with Cherry? Did they work together on how best to deal with the kids? Because he didn't ask me; he just told me they'd come around.

"Maybe you should leave."

"Maybe I should..."

"Leave," I finish, really wanting him gone, unable to deal with an angry Marcum when I have so many emotions rushing through my head right now.

"What in the fuck, Dragonfly? What in the hell is wrong with you?"

"Nothing."

"You're wanting me out of your bed. That sure as hell don't sound like nothing."

"I asked you a simple question. It's not my fault you got... *pissy.*"

"Pissy!?!?" He roars the word. I wouldn't be surprised if the walls didn't shake. I sit back against the headboard, pulling my knees up to my chest, and the blanket up to my neck. I wouldn't be surprised if his screaming didn't cause people to come running into the room.

"Pissy," I answer, and I really wish I could scream it back at him.

"I'm a grown ass man, Dragonfly. We don't get *pissy!*"

"Will you stop yelling at me? It's not fair that you're yelling at me when I can't yell back!"

"Dragonfly—"

"I just wanted to know how you felt about me. I mean, it was a simple question," I grumble, getting out of bed. I stomp to the small bath and find my robe, frustration, fear and anger all combining to take over my mouth. I don't watch my words, I don't even care if he can't hear me as I walk around. I hear me and that's all that counts.

He doesn't deserve to hear me!

"Toi—"

"It's an honest question. You barely spoke to me. You were *pissy* with me constantly, and mean and rude! You made me talk when I didn't want to. You made me talk—"

"Toi, honey—"

"...even when it hurt me! You didn't care, you just kept pushing it and pushing it. Then all at once, you decide to *claim* me—whatever that means."

"It means you're mine. Now, Toi—"

"People aren't property, Marcum! You can't just claim them. And why did you claim me? I'm not even convinced you like me."

"I think I proved that already, but if you want me to remind you..." He ends his statement with a shrug and a really sexy grin that I have the strongest urge to punch.

"That didn't prove anything. You've done that with a million women. Your five hundred children are proof of that! For all I know, you've done that with a bunch of women before you came up here to my bed tonight!"

"And that's it," Marcum growls and then he moves. *And I mean he moves.* He moves so fast that if I had blinked I would have missed it. All at once he's standing up in front of me, he has his body close to mine, his hands wrapped around my wrists and holding me tightly—so tight it's bruising in nature.

"What are—"

I don't get to finish the question because Marcum picks me up one minute and the next I'm sailing through the air, covering the small distance to the bed. My body lands on the mattress and I bounce, as my hands come out to catch myself.

"I claimed you, Toi. I don't do that. I've never fucking done that," he growls. "I've only ever claimed you."

"Liar!"

"I hope you're ready, honey, because I'm going to set your ass on fire for that. It will be so red you won't sit for a damn week."

"Quit being an asshole. Marcum! What are you doing?" I ask, almost swallowing my tongue when I finally notice that his dick is swaying back and forth, completely hard. In fact, it practically dances as he prowls the few steps to the bed.

"I'm going to spank you for being *pissy*. And then I'm going to fuck you raw until you can't throw attitude at me."

Oh shit...

❧ 45 ❧

MARCUM

"I CAN TELL FROM THE LOOK ON YOUR FACE YOU'RE STARTING TO rethink shit, darlin', but it's too late now," I tell her with a grin.

I don't know how the fuck to explain it. Never in my life have I enjoyed arguing with a woman before, but damn if it's not fun as hell with Toi.

"Marcum, maybe we should talk about this," she says, backing up on the bed, which makes me grin even more.

"I don't want to talk."

"You don't?"

"Hell no. I've got other things I'd like to do with you."

"But we're fighting!"

"We aren't fighting. You're being pissy and I'm about to set you right."

"Set me right?" she says, obviously getting her fucking panties in a knot again. Why I think that shit is cute, I don't know—but I do.

"I've never claimed another woman like I've claimed you, Toi."

"What about…"

"Spit it out, Dragonfly. Time's a wasting and I got some handprints to put on your ass."

"You're not."

"Toi, now," I warn.

"Cherry! Okay. You claimed her. You can't deny that."

"Are you jealous, honey?"

"Stop that! You don't get to do that!"

"What's that?" I ask. I'm on the bed, stretching so my head is next to her hip. I can't resist letting my hand travel up her thigh, through the gap of her robe. She slaps my hand and fuck, here I am laughing.

"Make me seem like the jealous girlfriend. Cherry was your woman, everyone knows that," she huffs.

"She *was* my old lady, honey."

"See, you admit it," she growls—and she literally growls.

I lean down and place a kiss against her warm hip, tasting her. I let my tongue dip to her skin, teasing the flesh right before I take it between my teeth and tease it gently. At the same time, I let my hand travel slowly along the inside of her leg. I can feel the heat from her pussy before I get close.

Fuck, she really is perfect.

"I wasn't a fucking choir boy, Toi. You know that. But what I gave Cherry isn't what I'm giving you," I confess, straightening my fingers out to push against the inside of her thigh. The tips of my fingers are brushing the lips of her pussy. I'm so close to the promised land, I could weep. It's that fucking good. She's wet too, and getting wetter. She can try to growl at me all she wants, but it's not anger I'm making her feel—*at least not all.*

"You mean your dick," she mutters. She tightens her thighs, and maybe she thinks that's to keep me away from her sweet honey, but if anything, her hips push toward me.

"I mean, Toi, you get a part of me I've never given another woman."

"What's that?" she whispers, trying to pout. I hear the excitement she's trying to keep at bay, however.

"My heart, honey," I tell her, my fingers pushing between the lips of her pussy and zeroing in on her clit.

"You... you love me?" she asks, her eyes wide.

In that moment I hate myself, because I see the hope she's harboring and too innocent to hide from me.

"I don't really do love, Dragonfly," I admit, almost wishing I'd just gone ahead and lied to her when I see her disappointment.

"Then what are you talking about?" she asks, moaning because I'm massaging her clit over and over. She's losing herself to the sensation as her legs open, giving my hand more room.

I shift my position so I'm stretched above her. My fingers find her entrance and I slide them inside, while keeping my thumb pressed against her clit.

"I gave you my cut. I fought my own man over you and soon, Dragonfly, you're going to have my name."

"Your name?" she whimpers when I begin fucking her more purposely with my fingers. She's going to come soon—but then, that's what I want. I watch as desire and pleasure clash on her expression and her head rocks back and forth.

"You're going to marry me, Toi. You're going to be my wife."

"I am?" she cries loudly, at the same exact moment I push her robe up her body and run the tip of my tongue over her clit.

"You're the first for me, Toi."

"What?" she asks.

"You're the only woman that I've looked at and seen forever in her eyes. I'm keeping you Toi. You're never getting away from me, Dragonfly."

"Oh God, Marcum. I'm going to come."

"You're going to marry me too, aren't you, Toi?"

"But—"

"Aren't you, honey?"

"Yes! Anything! Just please, Marcum, finish me... Oh God, please make me come."

"That's my girl." I smile. Hell, I'm close to fucking laughing again, but this time with complete happiness. My club is in fucking chaos, my kids are upset and Toi somehow has worked a miracle. I suck on her clit and twist my fingers inside of her, raking them against her walls. She disintegrates in my arms, jerking and quivering under my mouth. I use my body to keep her pinned to the bed, refusing to let her move. I eat her pussy and slowly bring her back down. Her fingers are twisted in my hair and she tries to hold my face exactly where she wants me.

Eventually I look up at her. Her breathing is so ragged her body is shaking with it. Her eyes are closed and she's so beautiful like this.

Beautiful and mine.

"Toi, honey. I'm going to need you to see the doctor tomorrow," I tell her.

As predicted, her eyes open and for a moment I find myself drowning in a sea of blue. Jesus, she is breathtaking.

"What?" she asks. "Why?"

"Your voice, honey."

"Marcum, I told you there's nothing they can do. I've been like this for a long time."

"Then why have you been yelling at me, Toi?"

"Because... Wait... I..."

"Have been yelling at me, honey. Practically this whole time."

Her mouth opens. It closes and then opens again and then tears begin falling from those beautiful blue depths. I don't mind these tears though, because my Toi is happy and I can't help but feel like I had a part in that.

Yeah. I'm keeping her.

❧ 46 ❧

TOI

"Toi stop being sad," Marcum grumbles, helping me off his bike.

"Can't help it," I whisper—and it is a whisper. Last night I was talking normal. Heck, I was yelling and then I woke up this morning... and it's back to the way it was before. Marcum won't admit it, but I saw the disappointment in his face too.

"We'll go see this guy and see what he says, honey."

"I hate doctors." I mumble the words, not that Marcum would know that because you can barely hear me. In truth, he probably doesn't. The parking garage is loud with cars starting and moving around us.

"I've picked that up about you, Dragonfly," he answers, shaking his head.

We're silent on the elevator ride and during the wait in the doctor's office. I'm silent because I'm nervous. Maybe Marcum is regretting his promises to me and that's why he's quiet—I'm afraid to ask. I don't know why I'm having such a hard time taking him on his word, but I am.

"Mr. and Mrs. Kincaid, the doctor will see you now," the nurse announces and my heart beats erratically in my chest.

"Mr. and Mrs.?"

Marcum doesn't answer my question; he just squeezes my hand. I start to question him further, but before I can we're ushered into a small office. There's a man in a white doctor's coat sitting behind the desk and when we walk in, he looks up with a smile.

"Mr. Kincaid. It's good to meet you, and I take it you are Toi?" he asks, extending his hand. Marcum nods, but he doesn't reach out and shake the doctor's hand.

"Hi," I whisper and I shake his hand. Marcum grunts beside me and I get the distinct impression he doesn't like that I shook hands. Which is crazy, but I don't think I'll ever understand Marcum.

"I had your old doctor email me your records. It's been a long time since you've had a thorough examination, Ms. Kincaid."

"I... Uh... That's not my..."

"We already know what she's had done, Doc. I want to know what you can do to help her."

"Yes, well. I've been going through the notes. You say Toi was talking normal last night?"

"She always talks normal," Marcum growls and I don't know why that makes me feel good, but it does. "She just can't talk very loud. Last night she did."

"What was she doing last night when she was talking normal— uh... louder?"

"Fighting with Marcum," I confess.

"Having sex," Marcum says over top of me and I feel my face flame in embarrassment.

"You did not just say that," I hiss.

"It's the truth, Dragonfly. Nothing to be ashamed of."

"Well, okay then—and you were able to maintain a regular speaking voice?" the doctor asks, interrupting us.

"Yes, although I didn't realize it at the time."

"She did. Hell, she let out a few good screams," Marcum says with a grin, relaxing back in his chair and propping his foot up on the doctor's desk.

I'm starting to get the impression that he doesn't like this doctor that much. When we get alone I'm going to ask him why he brought me to someone, if all he was going to do was antagonize the man. That's if I don't kill him for embarrassing me first.

"I see. And according to the information my nurse has here. You were involved in a recent car accident, Ms. Kincaid?"

His question shocks me. I look over at Marcum. I've not really allowed myself to even think about that day. I feel my body shake as pictures come to mind. I don't think I can deal with it. Then I feel Marcum squeeze my hand.

"Yes, my wife was traveling with her father. He lost control of the vehicle and hit a tree. Toi was thrown free, but I'm afraid her father was in the vehicle when it caught fire."

He delivers that statement so calmly. My hand jerks in his, and he squeezes tighter. I hadn't even asked how the situation was being handled. I was just glad cops weren't knocking at my door with arrest warrants. That doesn't say the best things about me, either. I know my father was slime... He was...

But I killed him.

"From studying your old records and from the history I have. I think the wreck might have caused a shift in the damaged vocal cord."

"What does that mean?" Marcum asks.

"In cases like Toi's, there's a surgery that can be done—I see that it was recommended for you several years ago, Ms. Kincaid."

"Yes..." I admit. There's no way I could afford it—though I tried for a while. I don't tell him that.

"Right. Well, ideally, they want to do the surgery soon after the first injury. Time usually lessens the effectiveness. But the fact that you regained your voice—even briefly—is a good sign, Ms. Kincaid, a very good sign."

"So she needs this surgery?" Marcum asks. "How soon can we get it scheduled?"

I jerk in my seat.

"No," I whisper. Both men train their gazes on me.

"Toi—"

"The surgery is expensive," I whisper to Marcum and I hate him for making me admit it. "And there's no guarantee it will work." I add that last part and my voice squeaks. I barely get the last word out.

"She's right. Especially considering the amount of time between the first injury and this one. Still, I think it would be worth a shot. In essence, we'd be rearranging her damaged vocal cord to place it in a position that would increase its reverberation. It is a relatively simple surgery, but as Ms. Kincaid said, there's no guarantee, and as with any surgery there could be some high risks."

"Like what?" Marcum asks.

"She could lose her voice completely."

"I see," Marcum says and I feel him staring at me. The weight of his stare is almost physical. I don't look at him though. I just want to leave.

"I really suggest the two of you talk it over and if you want to proceed then I'll make sure to work Toi in quickly. In the meantime, I would like some updated scans and films done, so I can better prepare if surgery is the choice."

"Set it up, Doc," Marcum says and I turn to look at him, not sure if I'm upset with him. I don't know what I feel. I just know it revolves around Marcum.

He stares at me, as if daring me to tell the doctor differently. I don't.

I'm too confused.

❦ 47 ❦

MARCUM

"You have to talk to me sometime, Dragonfly."

I breathe loudly. I'm annoyed; she's not spoken a word to me since we left the doctor's office. She didn't even order food. I ordered for her. We're sitting at a mom-and-pop restaurant and have been here long enough to get our burgers and fries and Toi still hasn't spoken to me. I can't tell what's going on in that pretty little head of hers and it's starting to worry me.

"Here's your refill. Can I get you anything else?"

"We're fine," I tell the waitress, my eyes still on Toi. She's staring out the window, effectively ignoring me.

"Here's your ticket then, sugar. You pay up front," she says, putting the slip on the table.

"Toi—"

"Is this what being with you is going to be like?" she asks, her voice soft and tender.

She looks so genuinely upset that I can't stand it. Without thinking about it I get up and walk to her chair and then pull her up. I sit down in her seat and fix her on my lap. Because her seat is fixed so my back would be to the entrance, I scoot it, angling it to the side, and pushing the empty chair that was there a few feet over.

"Talk to me, Dragonfly."

"Marcum, people are staring," she complains, her body tense in my arms.

"I'm not fucking you, Toi. I'm holding you. Let them stare. I don't give a fuck about any of them, only you. Now talk to me."

"I'd say no, but it wouldn't matter," she responds.

"What are you talking about?"

"You. You just bulldoze in where you're not wanted and takeover." She starts coughing from straining her voice. I grab her soda off of the table and hand it to her.

She grudgingly takes a drink. When her coughing subsides, she lays her head against my chest, almost as if she's too tired to argue further.

"Toi, I'm just trying to take care of you."

"I can take care of myself."

"You were doing such a good job of it before."

"I don't like doctors, Marcum, and it may surprise you, but I don't really want this surgery."

"It could help heal you, Toi," I answer with a sigh. I don't understand why she's being so stubborn about this.

"I don't think I'm broken."

"That's not what I meant and you know it. I would want you if you could never speak."

"It doesn't sound like it. If me not being able to speak normally bothers you..."

She stops, breathing deep and taking another drink and I know it's because it pains her. Which should be a reason she jumps at this damn surgery. If I live for a hundred more years, I doubt I will ever understand a woman.

"Toi—"

"If it bothers you, then you should just leave me here and let me live my life—*alone*."

I have a lot to say about that and none of it is good. I'm about to get into it with her—yet again—over the same damn shit, when the bell to the front of the diner makes a noise. It's habit, but I look up on instinct. What I see sends warning bells churning through me.

"Well, look what we have here. If it's not Marcum. Funny seeing you on this side of the county. You slumming it today, old man?"

"Toi, honey. You sit in the chair beside me. You don't look at these motherfuckers, just look at me. You understand?"

"Marcum—"

"Just do it, honey. I'll explain later."

I sit Toi in her own chair right beside me. I don't know what's going on, but I do know it's no coincidence that three of the main members of Retribution just walked into a diner where I'm eating.

I lean back in my chair like I'm the most relaxed motherfucker on the planet.

It's show time.

✣ 48 ✣

TOI

"HOUND, FANCY SEEING YOU HERE," MARCUM SAYS.

Until this moment, I haven't been paying attention. I was too pissed that Marcum was wanting to stare at him and not talk. It has been a while, so I didn't recognize the voice of the man that yelled at Marcum either. But I know the name and when he responds I definitely know that voice.

"There's not a damn thing fancy about this place. Mind if Graves and I join you?"

"Would it matter if I did?" Marcum asks.

"Not a fucking bit," Hound answers.

"I thought so."

I know Marcum asked me not to look at Hound, but that order pissed me off. Honestly everything he's done today has pissed me off. Marcum has a way of taking over my life and telling me how things are going to be. His testosterone levels have to be sky high, but I'm kind of sick of his caveman ways. Plus, I know Hound. He's one of the few friends my father had I liked. Liked in a distant kind of way, because that look in his eyes was a little too intense and Hound is not my type, and he may not know it—but I'm definitely not his.

"Toi, baby girl, is that you?"

I feel Marcum go stiff beside me and I feel the air thicken. I clear my throat and look at Hound—which is a completely stupid name, but short for Hell Hound, which from everything I heard fits him. He's sexy in a deadly kind of way. His head is shaved, but he has this beard that covers the lower part of his face. He has the deepest blue eyes that I've ever seen; and when he looks at me, he scares me at times. There's this huge tattoo on his neck of a black skull. It's surrounded by ornate black plumes that remind me of smoke, but it's the eerie red-orange eyes, nose and mouth of the skull that make it look... kind of creepy.

I smile at him. As far as Hound knows, I can't talk and for some reason I don't want that impression to change.

He picks up my hand and pulls it toward his lips. Just like that Marcum's hand snaps out and grabs mine. I let out a startled gasp of surprise, and look at him. His face is hard and he's staring straight at Hound.

"If you want to stop breathing, keep trying to touch my woman," he says quietly. He may be quiet, but his words sound like steel.

"Your woman?" Hound asks, surprised.

"You've got about two seconds to let go of her hand," Marcum adds. His voice is that same quiet voice that sends chills down my spine—and definitely not the good kind.

Hound drops my hand, but now he's looking at me. Graves is silent beside him, but his gaze is trained on me too and just as intense.

"Mind telling me what in the fuck brought this on?"

"I do. It's not your fucking business," Marcum says and he pulls my hand back to his lap, blatantly putting it near his cock. I might have pulled it away, but I'm thinking it's best if Hound thinks I am agreeing with Marcum. Which, most days I am, but today... he's being an asshole.

"Rachelle!" Hound calls out and within a moment the waitress comes back.

"What's up?"

"Give me your pen and ordering pad," Hound says and that easygoing personality he usually uses with women is gone. The waitress does as she was ordered and Hound pushes it toward me. "Are you okay with being claimed by Marcum, baby girl?" he asks me, his voice dropping down and almost tender—but then, Hound has always been that way with me. I know he feels sorry for me, but that's not all of it and he treats me like a small, frightened child... or maybe a China doll he is afraid might crack.

"You doubting my fucking word?" Marcum growls and his voice might have been steel before, but right now he sounds like he could slice through steel... shit, maybe melt it down.

"Toi and I go way back. I want to know she's happy. If she is, then you and I have no beef. If she's not... then we have problems," Hound says easily.

They stare at each other for a few minutes. Marcum surprises me first.

"Tell him, Dragonfly."

I frown. There he goes issuing more orders, like I don't have a mind of my own.

"Here's your pen, baby girl," Hound says, pushing the pen and pad again. I start to reach for it and Marcum shows he's an ass again.

"Use your damn voice, Toi," he sighs.

"You're an ass," I hiss at Marcum. My voice isn't like it was the other night but it is a little louder than earlier—probably because I've been resting it.

"Fuck. You can talk?"

"Guess you don't go back as far as you thought," Marcum smirks.

"Guess not. I have to wonder what other secrets you kept from me, baby girl," Hound says and I don't think it's a good thing that Hound has me on his mind about anything.

"Keep calling her baby girl and I'm going to enjoying cutting out your tongue and serving it to my men for dinner," Marcum tells him.

Hound almost smiles.

"You claiming this ass... *Toi?*"

"Most days," I sigh.

"I didn't know you wanted to be an old lady. Graves and I would have stepped up long ago."

"It's good you didn't because I would have gutted you to get to her," Marcum says and I get the distinct feeling he's not joking.

"I'm not your kind of girl," I tell them, elbowing, Marcum.

"All girls are our kind of girls. Some just take a little more work. You would have been work we enjoyed."

"Would you like to tell me why you're here, Hound, before my patience snaps and I kill you? Because I got to tell you, I'm not liking the way you're talking or looking at my woman and the longer I sit here, the more I want to end you."

"We saw your bike outside. Thought we'd pay a friendly visit," Hound shrugs.

"I'm sure," Marcum says. His fingers move back and forth on my arm, the rough callused pads of his fingers teasing my skin. I'm annoyed with him, but I can't deny that I love his touch.

"Aren't you a little old for Toi?"

Marcum growls, his body tensing up again. I close my eyes, because I'm probably the single most confused woman on the planet. Then, I take my hand away from his lap and link my fingers into his hair.

It startles Marcum, I know it does, because he turns to look at me.

"Apparently I like old cavemen who constantly order me around."

"Like, Dragonfly?" he smirks.

"Most days," I whisper, and then to prove I'm stupid as well as confused, I kiss him lightly on his lips.

I don't know what I expected. Maybe I thought he would kiss me back, or demand a deeper kiss. Instead, he turns away from me and focuses on the men again. In fact, I get the distinct impression he's blocking me out. The reality of that kind of hurts.

"Let's get on with this. I need to take Toi back home and fuck her. Why in the hell are you here taking up my air?"

"And there's the asshole again," I mutter, mostly to myself, but Graves laughs. Hound just looks at me and there's something different in his look this time.

"I misjudged you, little one. You're much stronger than I gave you credit for. It's good you found a man who recognizes this."

I don't know how to answer that, so I don't say anything.

"Cut the shit, Hound. What the fuck do you want?"

"I don't think I can answer that. Or we will be fighting and I don't think Toi would appreciate me killing you."

"You could try." Marcum shrugs.

"Word on the street is you've attracted the attention of the Garcia bastards, Marcum. That's dangerous eyes to attract—even for you."

"Ask me if I give a fuck," Marcum responds with a shrug. On the surface he looks very relaxed, but my hand is back on his leg and I can feel the tension he's hiding. I press my hand in tighter. I don't know why, really. I just want to remind him I'm here.

"Still. You have something valuable now. I'll admit I didn't know how valuable until today, but you should watch out."

"I didn't get where I am by being stupid. I don't need you to warn me, Hound. You know who I am. Anyone wants to fuck with me, you tell them to bring it on. I'll dance on their fucking bones. Let's go, Dragonfly," he growls, standing up.

"Dangerous words for a man who holds gold in his hands," Hound says. Marcum's body goes still.

"Gold?"

"Five million."

"You're fucking kidding me."

"You didn't know."

"I do now. You get word back. Spread it wide. Anyone fucks

with what's mine and they won't need to worry about money. They won't need it where I'll send them."

"I'll spread it," Hound says, and I'm confused as to what they're talking about, but I know it's not good.

"Good, and tell them where I send them, they'll go in fucking pieces," Marcum growls.

"It will be done," Hound agrees.

Marcum wraps his arms around me and pulls me deep into his side—so deep I almost can't walk. Rachelle the waitress is still there and Marcum looks at her. "They're paying for our damn bill." Then he almost pulls me toward the door.

"If you need backup, my crew and I are available."

"Why? We have no alliance," Marcum says.

"No. Bu, Toi deserves happiness." Hound shrugs.

"I'll be the motherfucker to make sure she gets it. You and your crew can stay out of it," Marcum answers and with that, we're gone.

I have no idea what just happened, but I'm not stupid. There's big shit going down and I got a bad feeling I'm smack dab in the middle of it.

49

MARCUM

When we got back, I took Toi straight to her room and ordered her to stay there. I put Topper at her door and gave him a brief report of my run-in with Hound and Graves. Then I ordered a meeting.

When I woke up this morning, I had no fucking idea how the day was going to go. I sure didn't expect it to go to fucking hell the way it has. Now I'm sitting here looking at my men about to declare a fucking war that will put all of their lives in danger.

I don't take that shit lightly. These men put their lives in my hands and in our life you know the risks, but that doesn't mean you don't take every fucking precaution you can to stop it.

"What the fuck is going on, Marcum? You look like you're about ready to shoot someone's balls off," Ride mutters after the silence gets to be too much for him.

"Better watch your berries, Ghost," String laughs. The other men join in a bit, but the mood is fucking somber and they feel it. For his part, Ghost doesn't respond. He's watching me, but it's not with the anger he has been showing me.

"Got word today there's a contract out on one of our own."

"Motherfucker," someone growls. I don't know who, but there's a chorus of similar words spread around the room.

"Who the fuck would do something like that? We've beat down most of the fuckers around here to cement our hold," Moth demands.

"I don't know the specifics. Ghost, that's your job. By the end of the day I want to know every fucking detail you can get on the contract, the terms and exactly when and who ordered it."

"Do I have an idea of where to start looking?" he asks.

I take a breath and then let him have it—let them all have it.

"Garcias."

Silence fills the room. Each one needs time to digest it. This is not good news, nor is it simple. My men aren't afraid of shit, but a smart man would be wary about this entire thing—and my men are smart.

"They put a fucking contract out on you?" Ride yells, slamming his fist down on the solid oak table. It shakes under the impact, but doesn't give way.

"No," I answer, rubbing the side of my neck.

"On Dawg? Fuck, that man deserves some peace," String complains.

"It's not on Dawg," Ghost answers and his eyes are trained on me. He reads me better than any man in here, but then he would—at least about this.

"Yeah. It doesn't involve Dawg, though I'll be talking to him about bringing in the family for lockdown."

"Then who the fuck is it on? Has one of us pissed in their food bowl?" Ride questions.

"It's on Toi," Ghost answers before me.

Hearing it said out loud, even though I've been going over and over it in my mind makes my gut feel raw. I've got to end this before anyone gets their hands on Toi. I can't lose her. I can't let them get their hands on her either. I don't think they'd kill her, but they'd destroy her in so many other ways that she would wish she was dead. I've had visions of that in my head since this morning. I just can't figure out what the fuck they want her for. *How in the hell did she even get on their radar this heavy?* There has to be an answer, I'm just not finding it.

"We go on lockdown tonight. Topper and Moth are in charge of bringing in supplies. Bring in your family and get shit done quickly. You know the drill, it's not our first rodeo. Just get it done."

"Does Toi know?" Ghost asks.

"No, she heard bits and pieces. I don't think she understood. If she puts it together she'll think it's on me."

"Is that wise?"

"No fucking idea. I just know I don't want my woman scared —or worse..."

"You think she'll turn herself in to protect you," Ride answers.

"I don't know," I answer, but in my gut I know the truth.

"She killed her own damn father for Marcum. She wouldn't even blink to save any of us, if she knew we were at risk because of her. That's the kind of woman she is," Ghost answers.

He sees Toi too. I really want to fucking hate that man, but I can't. I'm even starting to like him more than I did before.

I'm still not giving Toi up to him though.

50

TOI

"Can you explain why I'm being moved into the basement?" I ask Marcum. Topper has been at my door all day. Babs finally agreed to distract him long enough for me to slip out, and I've been waiting in Marcum's room ever since. Which means I've been sitting in his room for over two hours. I thought about looking for him anywhere else. I knew that if I did that, I'd be sent back to my room and guarded even heavier.

"How'd you get out of your room? I had Topper guarding you," Marcum growls, slamming his door.

"That's another thing I'm not happy about. Why am I being guarded all of a sudden?"

"When you find your voice, you don't hesitate to use it, do you, Dragonfly?" he asks, rubbing the side of his neck.

"I've been saving it up. So? Are you going to tell me?"

"We're all being moved into the basement, not just you," he says finally, taking his club cut off and putting it on a table.

"Oh. Is this about the conversation with Hound this morning?"

"You're going to explain how you know them," he says, not confirming my suspicions, but not denying them either.

"You're going to eventually answer me too," I respond, and he smiles a little. I don't know why him smiling should make me happy, but it does.

He pulls his shirt off, and it must be said that Marcum is completely sexy. He is covered in ink, most of it dark and black, but it looks good on him. There's this tree on his chest. It's inked over his heart and that one tattoo always grabs my attention. The roots are dipped in red ink and it looks like it is growing out of his heart. On the tree are branches everywhere and each one has leaves. Harley and Desi's names are on one branch and the names of all of his children are there, right down to Max. There's a new tree intertwining with it and the leaves are green and Tess's name is there, along with his grandkids. It's beautiful and it says so much about the man. And what it says is in direct contrast to everything I've ever heard or known about him. Hell, it's in contrast to everything I know about *any* man.

Marcum is a protector, a soldier who takes it on himself to protect his family. I've never known anyone like that. That could be why I'm attracted to him, I don't know. I know that after seeing him with his kids, I found him much more attractive. He's like this gigantic puzzle and every time I manage to work another piece in... I fall a little more under his spell.

"What are you thinking when you look at me like that, Dragonfly?" he asks, his voice hoarse as he stands at the foot of the bed where I am.

"That you are beautiful," I tell him honestly. And I begin falling back on the bed as he stretches his body over me.

"You might need your eyes checked, honey," he whispers just as my head lands against the soft mattress of his bed. His hands come to hold each side of my face, gently. His fingers brush against the skin as his dark eyes look down at me. He's rough... all over and there's nothing soft about him. But he can be soft with his children and that's beautiful. He can really be soft with me at times and when he is... *I get lost in him.*

"You're beautiful to me," I tell him, quietly.

"My Toi, always so sweet. Open your mouth for me, honey," he whispers, as his lips touch mine. I give him my mouth, my tongue wrapping around his as he kisses me. It's a different kiss from any we've shared. It's slower, just as intense, and it's sweet.

I wrap my arms around him, loving the feel of his warm skin. Never have I been attracted to a man like I am with Marcum. It's physical, but it feels like more than that too—which should scare me, but I can't stop it. When it's over he kisses my eyelids, and then my forehead, before sliding off the bed. I came here to talk to him, but disappointment fills me as he gets up. I definitely wanted to continue that kiss. He's been making me come continuously and it's always good... Yet it never goes further than that.

When I found out from Topper that the men were moving me into the basement, I thought Marcum was done with me. After all, he moved me to be close to his children. I'm in his private wing of the club. Moving me would mean he wants me away from his family—away from him. That's the real reason I'm in his room now. I felt panicked at the thought that Marcum was done with me.

With a sigh, I sit up and look at him. Surprise fills me when he starts undoing his pants. I bite my lip, waiting for the moment he frees his cock. He's obviously hard—I think Marcum stays hard.

"Undress for me, Toi," he orders, his voice laced with so much need my body shivers in response.

I swallow down my nerves and stand on legs that feel like rubber. I don't remember doing it, though I know I did—but in moments I'm standing in front of Marcum completely naked, with my breath coming so harshly that my heart is slamming against my chest.

"You're overdressed," I tell him, my hands twisting nervously at my stomach as I fight the urge to cover myself up.

"Lay on the bed, Dragonfly." I swallow but I sit down on the bed, and then slide up it, lying down, but keeping Marcum in my sight at all times. "I've been trying to hold myself back with you, Toi. I didn't want to scare you off and I wanted to give you time to heal up, but honey... I need you," he says with a frank type of honesty that I've been craving from him. I was starting to worry he didn't want me, so it's good to hear that he's been purposely trying to hold back.

"I want you too, Marcum. I need you," I tell him. A million things are running through my brain and I want to tell him each of them, but it all boils down to the same thing. I really do need him.

He kicks off his shoes and pushes his pants down. Through it all, I don't think he takes his eyes off of me. Then, he literally crawls over top of me, the look in his eyes so intense I lose my breath.

"You need me, Toi?" His deep voice rumbles as he drags his hands up my sides.

"I do... I was... afraid," I confess.

"Why were you afraid?" he asks as one of his hands goes immediately between my legs. "Fuck... you're always so wet for me, Dragonfly. So fucking hot, wet and ready for me."

He's right. I am wet for him, I should be ashamed, but I'm not. No one has had this effect on me, absolutely no one but Marcum.

"I was afraid you were... done with me," I whisper, just as he gently moves his fingers over my aching clit.

"Christ, woman, you really don't listen. I told you last time what I wanted with you. I've tried to show you that you're special to me," he mumbles against my skin as he kisses along the side of my neck and then moves down, leaving a trail of kisses all the way to my breast. Then, he sucks my nipple, pressing it hard into his mouth—to the point that it's almost painful. He somehow twists the nipple in his mouth, his teeth raking against the sensitive nub, at the same moment his fingers pinch my clit. My body thrusts up against him, a soft cry leaving me. "What more can I do to show you what you mean to me, Toi? What can I say that will finally get through to you?" he growls as his mouth bites softly into my skin, making a path down my stomach.

I grab him by his hair. I know where this is going and, as much as I love it when he uses his mouth on me, that's not what I want this time. I want to confess to him that I'm afraid his interest in me is solely based on the fact that I saved his life. I don't want him out of a sense of duty, but I don't know how to tell him that. Plus, telling him that right now will only make him stop. That's something I absolutely don't want.

I pull on his hair to stop him from moving down.

"No," I tell him when he raises his head and his gaze locks with mine.

"Toi?"

"I don't want your mouth this time, Marcum. I want you."

"Dragonfly—"

"I want to feel you inside of me. If you really mean it, Marcum. If you're going to keep me, then really make me yours," I tell him, using what courage I have to get that plea out.

51

MARCUM

I WAS PLANNING ON CLAIMING HER COMPLETELY ALL ALONG, BUT I wanted to make it slow. I wanted to give her my mouth first. I didn't plan on Toi begging me to take her. Her sweet words slide down inside of me like the most expensive whiskey.

Women in my life have been hardened by life; they're cold in certain ways. It's always been that way from the first to the last. Toi is completely different. I thought she was too weak for my life, but she proved me wrong. I'm starting to realize that she's the complete opposite of weak. She is the strongest woman I've met. Life may have had her bending backwards to survive, but it didn't harden her, it didn't make her jaded. Through everything she's experienced, it's made her stronger, but appreciative... loving.

I knew what Max found with Tess was rare; that's why I encouraged him to face hell so he could keep her. I was even envious to a point. But, not once did I think what he found would ever happen to me.

I was wrong.

Toi is sunshine in my world—a world that has been cold and empty for as long as I can remember.

I don't know why I keep hesitating, except for the fact that Toi is special. But, fuck... she's right. I'm too old to keep waiting and if she's worrying that I'm not claiming her because I don't want her —I need to stop it.

I go back on my knees, straddling her body as I pull the lips of her pussy apart. Her juices have coated the outside of her lips until they shimmer. She's so wet it makes my balls ache.

"Is this what you want, honey?" I groan as I hold my cock in my hand and run the head of my shaft against her wet pussy.

"Yes," she hisses, and it's like music to my ears.

I should use my fingers to ready her for me. I don't know how experienced Toi is, but I doubt she's had much. She's tight, I haven't fucked her deep with my fingers, because I wanted my cock to be the first part of my body to stretch her. I want her pussy shaped to fit my dick like a glove. I don't want to hurt her, but she's so wet I should slide inside of her pretty easy. I just have to keep my head about me, remember to go slow. That won't be easy. That's for damn sure. Toi is a drug to my system.

"Put your feet flat on the bed, Toi, and open up for me honey. I want to watch as I sink inside of you," I murmur, my gaze glued to the pre-cum on the head of my dick, the way it clings to her clit, and the strand stretching as she rocks against me.

She whimpers as she does exactly as I tell her, and I reward her by leaning down and flicking her clit a few times with my tongue before sucking it in my mouth. Her back bows off the bed, her head pushing against the mattress. She's a fucking work of art like this. I pull back up, and run my shaft down her wet little slit, poising my cock at her entrance. I push just slightly, waiting until I have her attention.

"Marcum," she cries. Her soft voice wraps around me and claims me just as surely as the woman herself has. "I need you."

"Fuck baby, I need to hear that from you always," I growl and I'm not fucking lying. When they lay me in the ground I want the last words I hear to be Toi, moaning she needs me.

"I need you," she gasps again, her hands coming up to grab each of my sides. Her fingernails bite into me with the fierceness of her demand. The sting of pain makes my dick throb impossibly harder.

There's no way to hold back after that, I push inside of her.

The muscles of her tight little cunt squeeze my cock so hard it's almost painful and that's when I feel my cock pushing through her body, destroying her innocence.

Toi...

"You're a virgin," I groan as I claim her and take what no other man has ever had.

❈ 52 ❈

MARCUM

I PULL OUT QUICKLY, FROM SHOCK AND FEAR. I KNOW TOI IS young, but she's not that young. How in the hell did she remain a virgin this long?

"Marcum, no!" she cries, her body shuddering underneath me. "Come back," she whispers. I place my hand on her stomach, palm flat. Her pure, white skin a stark contrast to my rough, ink-covered hand. Her light to my dark... and that's how it is with everything about us. She's the opposite of me in every single way possible, and yet she feeds this hunger inside of me that nothing and no one has ever touched before.

"You're a virgin," I repeat, trying to process it. I look down at my cock and see the telltale sign of blood on my shaft. *Toi's blood*. A potent mixture of hunger, of pride and fucking ownership surge through me. I grasp my cock tight and stroke it once, my hand sliding over a mixture of our desire and her innocence.

"Marcum," she whispers and I look into her eyes, needing this contact with her. I push just the head of my cock inside of her, my hand still flat against her stomach.

"You gave me your innocence, Toi," I growl, sinking another inch inside. "I'm the only one you've let between your legs."

"Marcum, I—"

"I'm going to be your last, Toi. From this moment on, I'm all your firsts, and I'm the only one that ever touches you," I growl. I sound like a fucking moron, but I've never had this gift from a woman. Fuck, I've never wanted that from a woman.

I want everything from Toi.

I push all the way inside of her, not stopping until I'm sunk up to my balls.

"You feel so good," she whispers.

"You're mine, Toi. Admit it."

"Marcum—"

"Say it," I growl.

"I'm yours, Marcum," she whispers, giving me the words. I reach down between us and massage her swollen clit as I begin to ride her. I move inside her in slow, measured thrusts that curve my cock deep inside her, so fucking deep and still it's not enough. I'm starting to think it will never be enough. I grab a pillow, use my hand under her ass to lever her up higher. She cries out because fuck, that takes me so deep I'm pushing against her cervix. I shove the pillow under her and then fuck her hard. She wraps her legs around me, pulling me in deeper and I keep manipulating her clit, desperate to make her come.

"That's it, baby, come for me. Come for me," I growl when I feel her muscles clench down on my cock, milking it. I know the exact moment she goes over the edge. Her eyes open up and she locks her gaze on me. Her mouth opens and she gives a low, keening cry as her body shakes underneath me.

"Marc...um," she moans, my name a broken whisper full of wonder. In that moment, I feel reborn. In that moment, a decision is made. I will make sure Toi never regrets giving herself to me. I'll earn the gifts she has given me. I'll earn every damn one of them... And the one I want the most is the one I never believed in.

Not until this moment.

I feel my own climax roar through me and as I bathe her womb with my cum, I lean down and take her mouth, kissing her as I empty myself inside of her.

With our bodies shaking and our breath shuddering through us, I wrap my hand gently at her neck, feeling her pulse.

Fast. Hard. Strong.

Alive.

"I'm going to make you love me, Dragonfly. I'm going to make you love me," I vow to her, right before I kiss her again.

❦ 53 ❧

TOI

I'M GOING TO MAKE YOU LOVE ME.

Marcum's voice echoes through my thoughts.

I feel like I can't breathe. I touch my neck where moments before Marcum's hand was.

He wants me to love him.

I don't know what love is. I've never had it in my life and I've never wanted it.

I'm going to make you love me.

He once told me he didn't do love. Why did he say he wanted me to love him then? I know I'm starting to panic—what I don't know is why.

"What are you thinking, honey?" Marcum asks, coming back into the room. He gathers me up into his arms and I curl into him.

"About you," I whisper.

"I like that." He grins and kisses the top of my head.

"Where are we going?"

"I'm going to bathe my woman."

"Bathe me? First, you carry me everywhere, then feed me, and now you want to bathe me? Marcum, did you have an obsession with playing with Barbie dolls when you were a child?"

"Fuck, no. Barbie is fucking scary."

"What?"

"She had no pussy. That kind of shit can scar a man. Boobs without nipples and no pussy? Jesus. And don't get me started on Ken."

"You're insane," I laugh softly, kissing the side of his neck.

"If I am, you've driven me there, Dragonfly."

He lowers me down into an old claw-foot tub. The hot water wraps around my body, instantly relaxing me even further.

"This feels like heaven," I whisper, leaning back against the tub and closing my eyes.

"You feel like heaven," he counters and his hand goes between my legs and he holds me there. My eyes instantly open up and my gaze locks with his.

"Marcum—"

"I didn't use a condom with you, Dragonfly."

I go instantly tense. I didn't even think about birth control. My face drains of color despite the heat of the water. My stomach churns. Oh God. I just had sex with a biker, one of the most fucking virile bikers in history without protection. What if I'm pregnant?

"Oh God," I whisper, closing my eyes.

"Dragonfly, I'm clean I swear," he says and another thought enters my head.

Oh God... what if one of the millions of women he's been with had something...

"Oh God," I say again, but this one sounds much more painful —because it is.

"Dragonfly, I'm clean. I swear it to you. I'll even go with you and have tests done so you can see for yourself—and I haven't been with another woman in a fuck of a long time. You don't need to worry," he says and I bite my lip and look at him. He's being honest. It's written all over his face.

"You could have made me pregnant. God knows you seem to make a woman pregnant just by looking at her."

"Toi," he says, shaking his head as his lips spread into a smile.

"God, how could I be so stupid?"

"Stop that. What we shared was not stupid, Toi. It was beautiful."

"It was stupid."

"It was special," he argues and I have to admit I like that he thinks that. I take a deep breath, trying to calm myself.

"What if I'm pregnant, Marcum?"

"Then we have a beautiful baby and we love it."

"You don't do love," I remind him, closing my eyes.

"Maybe you're the one that can change my mind, Dragonfly."

"You have a hundred kids, Marcum. The last thing you need is another one."

"I would want a child with you, Toi. Fuck, I want that more than you will ever know."

"Marcum... We don't... I mean what we have... It's new and..."

"It's real and it will be forever, Dragonfly. I've told you before and you need to realize it. I'm not giving you up."

"But Cherry is back and..."

"She's here until we figure out what the fuck she is up to," he sighs, starting to wash me.

"What she's up to?"

"Maybe I'm wrong, but I can't believe that it's a coincidence she's the one Weasel had taking you away from me."

I frown... Something is nagging at me.

"She did yell at me when you first showed up. She said something about having to salvage everything. She was afraid I got her caught... I didn't pay much attention and then with the accident..."

"Fuck..."

"I'm sorry. Was that important, do you think?"

"It could be. Dragonfly, we need to talk," Marcum says with a sigh.

His face is completely serious and all at once I'm scared about what he's going to tell me.

"I—"

"Let me finish washing you, honey, and then we'll talk," he says and butterflies are fluttering nervously in my stomach.

54

MARCUM

"I thought we were going on lockdown?" Toi asks as I lay her down on the bed.

She's right; I really should take her down there for the night. But, I can't bring myself to do it. I want this night with her alone. We have a bedroom down there, but it's small and it will be loud because it's right off the common area. There's very little privacy with everyone down there and that's not what I want with Toi—not after what we just shared.

"I decided tonight we'd break the rules. I want you to myself."

"I'm not going to argue with that," she whispers, stretching. "You changed the sheets..."

"I'm a man of many talents," I tell her with a grin as I slide into bed with her.

"I already discovered that."

I look at her with that reply. She's grinning and she's happy. I see it all over her and I love that I get that from her. I'm a selfish bastard when it comes to Toi. I want to be the only one that gives her joy like I see on her face right now. I want her completely tied to me in every way possible. It seems only fair since that's where I'm at with her. Toi is all I think of and she's definitely all I want.

Which is why I'm about to give her a piece of me I've given very few people.

"I could become addicted to you," I tell her, pulling her into my body.

She rolls to her side and holds me, her arm coming across my stomach and her head resting on my chest.

"I'm hoping," she whispers, placing a kiss on my chest.

We lay like that for a little bit, the room quiet. I'm content in ways I've never been before. My fingers are sifting through her damp hair and it occurs to me I've never done this with a woman. In all of my years, not once have I held a woman through the night, breathed in her scent and felt like this... like my soul is at ease. My club is at war, my woman has a price on her head and the world is going to hell around me. That's still there, but right now with Toi I'm centered, I'm calm and I'm fucking happy.

"You're thinking way too hard," she whispers, her voice sleepy-soft.

"Some things aren't easy for a man to confess, Dragonfly."

"Then don't..."

"I want to. Fuck, as strange as it is for me, I don't want to hold anything back from you. I've been telling you for a while now, Toi, you're special to me. I don't think you fully believe me."

"Marcum—"

"Don't deny it, Dragonfly."

"I wasn't going to. I haven't had the experience to—"

"I noticed," I smile, still feeling like a fucking king because I'm Toi's only man—I don't care what kind of son of a bitch that makes me. It's the truth.

She slaps me playfully, and sighs.

"I just mean, you've had so many women, women who have—"

"Honest to God, Dragonfly, I remember none of them when I'm with you. Fuck, the longer I'm with you, I don't remember any of them in my life. But, even if I did, you can't judge what you and I have by the past, Toi. My past is just that. I'm giving you the future and everything I am—which, fuck, baby... It's not a lot, but it's yours."

"They matter, Marcum. They're the mother of your children and I've grown to care for them, even if you did kind of force me into that situation."

"This... what we're doing isn't what I had planned, Toi. You need to know that. Believe it or not, I wanted to protect you from your... from Weasel. I didn't see past that. I was a dick, I admit it—"

"You still are a dick," she sighs and I laugh.

"That's probably not going to change, honey. I'm too fucking old to change that much."

"I figured."

"Quit distracting me, woman. I'm trying to reassure my woman so I can sleep because she wore me out."

She shifts, rubbing her body against mine and draping her leg over my hip.

"You don't feel worn out," she says.

"You angling for my dick, woman?"

"Maybe, but condoms this time are a must."

"That ship has sailed."

"No, just because it happened once doesn't mean we can't be careful from here on. I love your kids, Marcum, I do. I'm not adding another one to your brood."

"My brood?"

"You could field your own football team."

"We have a problem, Dragonfly. Because I want a child with you. Fuck, I need one with you."

"You have kids and grandkids, Marcum."

"But they're not ours."

"I don't want to talk about this right now," she says pulling away from me. She sits up, pulling the sheet around her chest as she goes.

"Why not?"

"Because I just gave you my virginity! The last thing I want to discuss is your strange, twisted need to have a million kids! I don't really want to be one in a number of women who you breed and then forget, Marcum!"

"Did you ever notice that when you're alone with me, your voice comes back? Or the fact you can yell like fucking crazy?"

"Because you make me crazy," she huffs.

"Or maybe you feel safe with me, Dragonfly. Hell, maybe I even relax you, like you do me. You ever think of that?"

"I don't feel relaxed right now."

"Because you're getting your tits in an uproar over nothing."

"My tits... *over nothing?*"

"That's what I said."

"You populating enough children to fill a third world nation is not... *nothing.*"

"I haven't."

"Whatever. I'm going back to my room. I should have known asshole-Marcum would show up," she mutters, her voice breaking and going back to quiet, but I'm not sure it's because of her injury or the emotion I hear causing it.

"I only have one child, Toi."

"Marcum, I'm really not in the mood for this. I told you I love your kids. I just don't want to discuss—"

"The only child I have that I'm one hundred percent sure of is Maxwell."

"I really... Are you serious?"

"I was too young to be sticking my dick in any woman. Max's mother was a piece of work, but she can't really take the blame for that. She was in a state facility for a while. Crazy as fucking hell. I didn't know it at the time. All I saw was a chance to fuck a good looking woman and that was a lot more appealing than my hand."

"Jesus."

"I didn't even know about Max until later in life. I reached out to him, but by then he hated me. He had his reasons and really none of them were wrong." I still feel guilt that will never go away when it comes to Max.

"He cares for you now. I've seen it."

"We're finding our way. When he got in trouble, he came to me and I've done everything I can to make sure he never regretted that."

"What about the other kids? Marcum, they adore you."

"And I love them. They're my children. I may not have fathered them, but they're mine either way."

"You don't know if—"

"Some there's just no way. I wasn't with them physically, but they were in a bad way. Their mothers came to me, knowing I could give their child a decent life. That sounds fucked-up, considering who I am and the way I live my life, but it's true. It is what it is, Dragonfly. Others? I used protection, always, and I know that shit is not a hundred percent, but it's pretty fucking effective. The truth is none of it matters. They're mine. Kids should never feel like they don't have someone who gives a shit about them in this life, Dragonfly. *Never*."

"Like Max did?"

She sees me. Again the thought hits me, clear to the fucking bone. She sees parts of me no one ever has before and she does it effortlessly. There's so much guilt inside of me about Max, about the fucking way he grew up. If I had known... I could have made it different. I would have been there for him...

I clear my throat, trying to sort through my brain, but all I can think is...

Toi understands me... and she cares.

Those two facts might seem small, but they feel fucking huge.

55

TOI

THIS MAN... THERE'S SO MUCH MORE TO HIM THAN ANYONE realizes—more than I realized. I want to reach out to him right now, hold him close and comfort him, because I can see pain in him now where before I thought it was only hardness. It's pain he carries around and hides. I don't do that, however, because instead I think back over his beautiful children and how they love him, how he loves them. In his own way, Marcum saved them, he gave them a home.

He protected them.

Kids should never feel like they don't have someone who gives a shit about them in this life, Dragonfly.

Believe it or not, I wanted to protect you...

Oh God.

I look around the room for my clothes. I'm feeling way too exposed right now. I cling to the sheet I have wrapped around me like a lifeline. I find my pants and shirt, and that will have to work. Before I can make it to the bathroom to change, Marcum scoops me up in his arms. He carries me back to the bed, despite my protesting and kicking at him. He holds me tighter, stilling my movements and sits on the bed with me. He pulls me so my legs drape over the side of his lap and then he turns my face to his.

"What's going on in that head of yours now, Toi?"

"I'm another one of your projects," I whisper. I can feel tears stinging the back of my eyes and I hate them. I feel raw inside, because...

Because Marcum matters. He matters so much...

I love him.

I'm such a stupid fool! I love a man and to him I'm just a little lost lamb he needs to protect!

"*Motherfucker,*" Marcum growls and then he leans back so he's lying on the bed, taking me with him. He pulls me so I'm facing him, and he holds his hand at my neck, his fingers pressing into my jawline so I can't look away. "You are not a fucking project, woman."

"You admitted it. You wanted to protect me!"

"Christ, you women get everything so twisted. Why is that a bad thing?"

"Because I don't want to be a charity case to you, Marcum. Another lost soul you try and protect."

"Fuck, baby, have you seen me? I'm not a damned guardian angel. Most of my fucking life I've sent people to their death. Don't try to romanticize me."

"You see me just like one of the kids. You want to protect me from life!"

"So? Jesus. I want to protect you, but I don't see you as my kid. You're young, Toi, but you're a woman—a damn beautiful woman and I'm not a fucking monk."

"What does that mean?"

"That I want you. I fought it like hell, but it was always there. You deserved better, and I'm way too fucking dirty and old to touch you, but I couldn't walk away. It was always you for me, Toi."

"It was?" I ask, confused. I feel hope warring inside of me, though and as much as I try and beat it down, I can't.

He pushes the sheet from my body, and I let it go. I'm riveted into place by the heated look on his face. It's a mixture of anger and need, and it makes me feel alive.

"Of course it was. I'm feeding you my dick. I beat the fuck out of my own man over you. Jesus, woman, I'm sharing shit with you I don't share with anyone. How can you think you're not special to me?" He growls out the question as his hand connects between my legs. He might be angry, but the soft glide of his fingers over my clit doesn't feel angry.

"Marcum—"

"My whole life, Toi, there's never been another woman... fuck... another person who gets inside of me like you do. I want you. You're like a fire inside of me and I need you as much as I need food or air. But that's not all of it. I trust you, Toi. I trust you in ways I don't even trust most of my men, and they've pledged their lives to me. I told you about my children when only Max, Tess and Topper ever got that information from me. You *are* different, honey. You're not like any of the others, you aren't a damn project... *Fuck*," he hisses, stopping his tirade as I wrap my hand around his cock. "Toi..."

I stroke his cock once. He's so wide my hand doesn't go around him completely, and I love it. I love everything about him. I guide him to my entrance, pushing my foot into the mattress to get a better angle.

"I love you, Marcum," I confess quietly as I thrust upwards, taking him into my body. "I love you," I tell him again, my pussy bearing down on his cock and groaning as he pushes deep inside of me.

"Christ, Dragonfly."

"I love you," I whisper again, as he takes over.

He doesn't give me the words back, but that's okay. He says I'm special and I believe him. He trusts me and for Marcum that feels like a huge gift. He also needs me; that's enough. It's more than enough and when his orgasm takes over, I follow him. I do it with one thought on my mind too...

I hope he does give me his child.

56

CHERRY

I LISTEN TO THEM GRUNTING LIKE PIGS IN THERE. SHE'S worming her way inside of him, in ways I never could. I tried with him too. I gave him a fucking year of my life as his old lady and he never appreciated it. Not once.

He told her about his fucking kids. I cared for the damn brats for a year before he finally claimed me as his old lady, then I devoted another year to them and he never told me that shit. I had to hear it from Babs.

I did everything for him and then he wanted to kick me out of his fucking bed? Telling me he just wasn't happy anymore. He kept looking at Max and Tess and I didn't measure up. The fucking prick. He didn't exactly measure up either, but that didn't seem to bother him. There were days I couldn't stand him, but being the old lady of the club president had some damn nice perks. I liked them and I wasn't about to give it up.

Then came the news about Jenna. Jenna was a bitch, that's true. I didn't care much for her. Still, Marcum alone knew that Jenna was my sister's kid. He didn't care. Fuck, he didn't hesitate to end her. He didn't even tell me about it. I had to find out months later. Then he tries to spout out all these rules about family loyalty.

I couldn't stay, not with the things I had done. If Marcum had found that out, then he would have killed me, just like Jenna. He wouldn't have even hesitated. I didn't get this far in life not to know the golden rule. You have to take care of yourself. Which is why I'm here. Toi has a five million price tag on her head and I want my money.

Thanks to Marcum trusting the little bitch, I know the exact way to do it now. I smile as the plan begins to form in my mind. I regret the path I have to take. I don't like kids much, but the twins are good kids. It's best they learn that life is fucking hard now. I'm doing them a favor really.

I walk quietly back the way I came. If all goes well, I'll have that five million in my hands and be somewhere sunny and warm within a week.

And Marcum? He and his bitch can rot in hell together.

It's no less than the bastard deserves.

✥ 57 ✥

MARCUM

"You sure look fucking happy to be a man on lockdown," Ride complains.

"Fuck off," I laugh, knowing he's right. It's been three nights since I claimed Toi and every fucking day just gets better. Jesus, I'm craving her even now and I just left her bed a couple of hours ago. I made her come with my mouth and left with her whispered I love you in my ear.

"Marcum man, are you listening?"

I look up at him and push thoughts of Toi to the back of my mind. That's not as easy as it probably should have been, but Ride is right. We're in lockdown and I need to concentrate on getting Toi free and clear of all this shit.

"Sorry man. What were you saying?"

"I don't think I've ever seen you like this," he says and I shrug.

"You haven't. It may have taken me a lot of fucking years, but I found it."

"It?"

"She's it, brother. The kind of woman that feeds the soul and cuts out the bullshit. Building a man up, not tearing him down. Toi's it for me."

"Christ. I'm happy for you man. Truly. I don't want to catch that shit, but I'm happy for you just the same."

"Finding a good woman, Ride, would be the best thing that could happen to you."

"Fuck no. A woman makes a man weak. I'm fine the way I am."

I shrug. It's his loss, and before I found Toi, I was pretty convinced I'd never find the woman who could reach me like Toi does.

"Suit yourself," I tell him, right before there's a knock at the door. Ghost comes in and behind him Topper. If he brought Top in, then I know it's not going to be good news.

"Marcum, we need to talk," Ghost says and I sigh. Yeah. You can see the worry all over his face. Whatever this is, it's not going to be good. Him and Topper come in and that's when I see it. Topper is carrying a bottle of Jack and three glasses.

Fuck.

"I'm going to need another glass," Topper says, putting them down on the desk. I grab the Jack and start pouring, giving each man a glass.

"Fuck it, I got a feeling I'm going to need to drink straight from the bottle. Hit me," I tell Ghost.

"The owner of the contract... It's not good, man," Ghost starts.

"The Garcias own it," I tell him, waiting for the hammer to drop.

"Alvaro himself owns it."

"Jesus fuck. Why would he issue a contract on Toi?"

"Alvaro bought her."

"What the fuck are you talking about? I know Toi, she hasn't got near that fucker. Someone like that would scare the shit out of her."

"He met her once. I doubt Toi remembers," Ghost says.

"If she met him, she'd remember. Alvaro isn't that fucking easy to forget."

"She was ten."

"What the fuck?"

"Weasel sold her to Alvaro."

"The fuck you say," I growl, my entire body vibrating with anger.

"Alvaro's been out of commission. Remember the fire? It nearly took him out. Left him completely screwed up, scars everywhere, bastard was lucky to survive. Brother, he'd give Toi nightmares now and he was pretty fucking scary before," Ghost answers, and fuck, I do remember. I was actually contacted about taking that job, but I had a fucking brain and wanted to steer clear of the Garcias. One of Alvaro's own brothers wanted him dead and tried to hire it done. When I turned the job down, they hired some wet behind the ears mess-up from out of Texas. He got Alvaro, but he didn't finish the job. Alvaro had the would-be assassin hunted down and tortured to death, but his brother is still breathing air, so I doubt he knows the whole story.

"So he hadn't claimed Toi earlier because of his injuries?" I ask, still not clear on what Alvaro's game plan is here.

"Exactly, but he's back now and he wants her."

"With his position and power, not to mention his money he could hire a woman to warm his bed, doesn't matter what he looks like," I growl.

"He wants Toi."

"That's what Weasel was doing? Luring his daughter away from here so he could pay his debt to Alvaro? Jesus Christ." I take a swig of the Jack. The whiskey burn in my gut is nothing to the burn I'm feeling at the idea of Alvaro with his hands on Toi.

"If he gets a hold of her, he'll break her," Ghost says and because he cares for Toi, I see the same worry in his eyes that's mirrored in mine.

"He won't get her. I'll fucking burn the Garcia empire down and set fire to Alvaro myself and this time nothing will save him," I vow.

"Boss, their reach is pretty fucking long. Not saying we don't have markers we can call in and some pretty damn strong alliances, but there won't be a lot of them willing to tangle with the

Garcias." That comes from Topper. And he's not wrong, but I need to bring in some muscle just as strong.

"Then it's time I call in my biggest marker."

"Anthes?"

"He has a direct line to Kuzma. Kuzma has wanted me on his payroll for years. He's about to get his fucking wish."

"Christ, brother," Ride says, rubbing the side of his face.

"Get out," I tell them, picking up my phone. I see it in their eyes.

Acceptance.

They know they can't stop this—and they can't. If the only way I can save Toi is to sell my soul to the devil—*then so, fucking, be it.*

58

MARCUM

"HAVEN'T HEARD FROM YOU IN A WHILE, KINCAID."

"That's the truth. How's Ana?"

"Pregnant, just like I like her," Roman laughs.

"She's too good for you," I say, taking another drink and embracing the burn.

"Don't I know it," he agrees and then gets silent. "Not that I mind you calling, but considering we never talk, I'm going to say this isn't a social call."

"I need a meeting with Kuzma."

"Fuck, Marcum. That's not the kind of son of a bitch you look to do business with. He finds you, and if you're smart you try never to get on his radar in the first fucking place."

"We both know I'm already on his radar," I answer.

"Fuck, man. Why? You don't need the money. Why would you let yourself get under Kuzma's thumb?"

"Why do all good men fall?" I ask philosophically.

"A woman," Roman says after a moment. "You let a woman in."

He doesn't ask. It's a statement, short and concise... *and completely fucking true.*

"A good one. Took me a lifetime to find her and I'm not letting her go," I tell him easily.

"Fuck."

"Pretty much."

"I'll set it up. Hope you know what you're signing up for man."

"Appreciate it, and I don't have a choice."

"I hear you. I'll be in touch," he says, hanging up. I stare at the phone and taking another drink before laying it down.

And so it begins.

❧ 59 ❧

TOI

"Hey Toi, you doing okay?" Tess asks, coming to sit beside me. We've been in lockdown for a week and Tess has to be going crazy. It's not easy for me, but I was used to living here. Tess had a great home on the beach and she has to miss it. Today is a little better; Marcum has fixed it so we can all be outside enjoying the warm air. The fresh air is good for the children. Marcum didn't want to chance it before, but he said he was making headway on the threat to the club. He's got some kind of big meeting set up today. I don't know the particulars and I haven't asked. If Marcum wants me know—he'll tell me.

"I'm good. You look tired," I tell her, offering her the empty chair beside me.

"Hard to sleep when you're as big as the side of a house," she laughs, rubbing her stomach.

"You're not that big," I smile.

"Close enough. You're talking better these days."

"I am. There's moments my voice is almost normal. The new medications the doctor prescribed are helping. It's a short term fix, but it's been nice. Marcum still wants me to have the surgery."

"You don't want it?"

"I do... but..."

"You're afraid?"

"A little. What happens if it doesn't work? Or I lose my voice altogether?"

"Then you'll adapt. Sounds simple for me to say, but I'm still not wrong. People adapt when they don't have a choice. It's all we can do."

"Speaking from experience?"

"In a way. Max and I went through hell and there was a time in my life I thought I would never have him with me again. I held on for Maddie, because I had to. It was a dark time, but I survived and if Max hadn't come back, I would have continued to survive—because I had to..."

"For Maddie," I whisper.

"Exactly," she answers. I sigh, more than a little lost as I look over at Harley and Desi playing. Cherry is there. Marcum was doing his best to keep them separated, but with lockdown that's been impossible. Mostly because Harley kept seeking Cherry out. It shouldn't, but it hurts me to see them with her. It hurts me that Harley hardly talks to me right now.

"That was a very sad sound, Toi."

"Yeah."

"The kids will come around, you know. They care about you."

"Desi maybe, but I think Harley might actually hate me."

"He's just confused. And Cherry was nice to me at a time when I desperately needed a friendly face, but she's not the same person now. I don't know what's going on, but I truly believe she's playing on Harley's love for her. I see it, Max sees it and Marcum sees it. Once things get back to normal around here, it will get better."

"I care about them... I love them," I whisper.

"Just like you love Marcum?"

I think about denying it, but there's no reason. It's completely true.

"I do love him."

"It shows. He loves you too, you know. I can tell."

"Marcum doesn't *do* love. Whatever that means," I laugh.

"No man does, honey." She giggles and I smile at the sound. I look back over at Cherry and the way she brushes Harley's hair as he talks to her. My heart squeezes.

"I shouldn't be jealous, but..."

"But you are. It's understandable, though. I would be too. You've found your home and Harley, as stubborn as he is, is your family too."

"God, he is stubborn."

"Just like his dad," Tess agrees. I look at her with a frown. "Marcum told you," she says reading me like a book. "He really does care for you, Toi. I hope you appreciate that."

"I... uh... I don't know what you mean," I stammer, clearly lying, but what Marcum told me, he told me in confidence and even if he admitted that Tess and Max knew, I don't feel comfortable discussing it. Tess puts her hand on mine and smiles gently.

"It's okay. Besides, I think in this instance Marcum is completely wrong. Harley couldn't be more like him and Desi clearly has her daddy's eyes."

I look at the children and I find myself smiling.

"I really hope you're right, Tess."

"I am," she says and as I watch the children, I believe she is too.

❧ 60 ❧

MARCUM

"Jesus, baby," I groan. "You got to stop."

"Mm..." she moans around my cock.

"Baby, I can't hold back much longer."

She slides her mouth off me with a grin. "I don't want you to."

"When I give you my cum, I want inside of you," I growl, and I lift her, pulling her up my body until she straddles my cock. "Take me in, Toi. Please, honey," I growl, knowing I'm about to blow and needing in her when I do. I don't care if I am begging. Her body is the sweetest heaven I've ever known.

She reaches down between us and guides me inside. She's wet and ready, just like I knew she would be. That's a gift I never fail to give thanks for.

"It just gets better and better," she moans, her voice soft and loving.

I reach up and grab her breasts, squeezing each in my hands, her hardened nipple pushing against my palm. She's right. It does get better and better.

"I'm not going to be able to hold back long, Dragonfly."

"I'm almost there," she gasps and I can feel it. It doesn't matter that I've only been inside of her mere minutes. She gets that worked up sucking on my cock. She likes going down on me almost as much as I like it—and that's a fucking lot.

"Then ride your man, honey. Ride me hard and take me with you," I order her, but I didn't need to worry.

Her head goes back, her long blond hair cascades down her back, her eyes are closed in passion and she's magnificent. Her body tightens on me, she slides up and down on me, rolling her hips, and I can feel my cock scrape against her inside walls. My balls begin to tighten. I'm coming, but I don't want to go without her. I reach down and pinch her clit, grabbing her hip and grinding her down against me.

"Marcum," she cries right before shattering. I follow her, when she's like that I can't help it. I close my eyes and groan as I empty myself deep inside of her.

She falls down against me and I cradle her to me, our bodies still joined. We stay like that while our breathing calms and this might be my favorite time with Toi. I wrap my hand in her hair, thinking about how my life has changed since meeting Toi.

"What was that?" she asks.

"What, honey?"

Her head raises slowly and she looks toward the door, the frowns.

"I thought I heard a noise."

"It was probably my damn heart. I'm too old for the workouts you've been giving me," I joke.

"Yeah, right," she laughs. "Can we just stay in bed today?"

"I wish we could sweetheart, but I'm meeting with some men today. I got to try and clear this shit up."

"You haven't told me what you're clearing up."

"I don't want you worrying. Just know I'm handling it."

"You have to stop trying to protect me, Marcum."

"Not possible, sweetheart."

"Can you at least tell me why this is happening?"

"Let's just say your father left a mess and I'm trying to clean it up," I tell her reluctantly. I didn't want to tell her, but I know she won't just let this drop. I feel her body tense and if it were possible I'd kill her father all over again.

"What did he do?"

"You don't need to worry about that, Toi. I'm dealing with it."

"It's my father, don't you think I have the right to know?"

"No."

"No?!"

"That's what I said, Toi."

"How can you say no?" she huffs. She pushes against my chest to get up, but I hold her tighter, not letting her. I flip us, so that now she's lying on the bed and I'm over her, I've pulled out of her, and I should be limp as a fucking ragdoll, but I don't think that's possible when I'm near Toi.

"I can say no because it's my job to protect you," I tell her, capturing her wrists with my hands and pinning them to the mattress.

"I don't need protecting!"

"Dragonfly, you have nightmares almost every night."

"You know about that?" she asks. She goes completely still with shock. I could almost smile.

"Honey, I sleep beside you every night. Of course I know."

"I could be having a nightmare about anything," she hedges.

"You also talk in your sleep."

"That doesn't mean I can't know what's going on. Your need to constantly protect me is unnerving me."

"Then think of it as me protecting my family."

"What?"

I pull myself off the bed, sitting beside her and putting my hand on her, gently. I splay my fingers out and hold her stomach.

"You could be carrying my child, Toi," I tell her, holding her gaze with mine.

"But...we don't know that, Marcum."

"Sweetheart, you're going to have my son or daughter. You need to get that in your head. And it's my job to protect you both."

"Marcum..."

"I promise to tell you about it all—"

"Finally."

"After I make sure you and our child are protected."

"Will you please—"

"Toi," I respond with a sigh. I hook my hand along the side of her neck and pull her close to me. "You've changed my life sweetheart. I need you and our child to be safe. Without you, I couldn't make it."

"Marcum..."

"I'm serious, Dragonfly. If something happened to you, I'd lose it."

"You can be really romantic sometimes, Marcum Kincaid."

"Don't spread that shit around, it will ruin my cred," I smirk.

"Kiss me before I find another reason to get pissed at you," she whispers, and I kiss her.

And I do it smiling...

❧ 61 ❧

HARLEY

I MISS TOI. DAD SAYS SHE CARES ABOUT ME, EVEN THOUGH I'VE been mean. She's been nice. She fixed homemade chocolate chip cookies the other day and brought them to us. I told her I wasn't hungry, but I did eat one after she left. No one ever made me cookies before. Maybe Dad's right and if I was nice to her... she wouldn't leave.

She seems happy here. She likes Desi and she likes Daddy. Maybe if I tried, she will like me again.

Desi was still asleep when I snuck out of my room.

I'm nervous. My tummy feels like it has butterflies. Daddy always says a man has to own up to his *ree-spons-bill-tees*. I do want him to be proud of me again.

I get to the door and I start to knock, but I hear Daddy.

"What honey?"

I start to walk away. Daddy is always calling her honey. He really, really likes her. Cherry said if she doesn't like me, she'll convince Daddy to send me and Desi away. What if she's telling Daddy to send us away now?

I walk back to the door and put my ear against it. Toi speaks really quiet sometimes. Her voice is broken, but if I try really hard maybe I can hear.

"Let's just say your father left a mess and I'm trying to clean it up."

That's not good. Cherry said the reason we have to stay in the basement was 'cause someone wanted to kill Daddy. Is that Toi's fault? I'm almost afraid to listen more. If Toi is the reason Daddy is in trouble, I don't want her to stay.

I finally decide to listen, maybe it's not Toi's fault.

"Then think of it as me protecting my family," Daddy says. I think Toi says something, but I can't hear it, but I do hear Daddy's next words. *"You could be carrying my child, Toi."*

Daddy's going to have another baby? He's going to have a baby with Toi? Will he still want me and Desi if there's another baby? Cherry said Daddy will want a new family with Toi and won't need us anymore. Is she right? I press my head to the door, hoping I heard wrong.

"After I make sure you and our child are protected."

I hear Daddy and I take off running. He didn't say Desi and I needed protecting. Just Toi and his new baby.

Cherry was right. Daddy has Toi now. He doesn't need me and Desi. He doesn't even worry about us anymore.

❦ 62 ❦

CHERRY

I WATCH AS HARLEY RUNS TO HIS ROOM AND SLAMS THE DOOR. He's coming from where Toi and Marcum are staying. It doesn't take a rocket scientist to figure out who has upset him. That kid is starting to get annoying. I don't remember him being so needy when I was here last time. Desi is easy. She's a tad too needy, but usually I can put her in front of the television and ignore her. No such luck with Harley. I've been working extra hard with him though. I need a way to make Toi feel insecure and I'm pretty sure the key to that is Harley. Plus, I know it's making that bitch miserable to see me and Harley together. That's been enjoyable.

I sigh as the boy goes in and closes his door. I guess that's my cue to be the thoughtful, loving mom he's made me into. I can't wait until I get Toi delivered to Alvaro. I'm taking my money and finding a sandy beach, clear blue ocean and a tall drink... and best of all—no kids. I'm too damn old to play nursemaid. Before, I had no choice. Marcum didn't know how good he had it when I was here. He didn't have to worry about a damn thing. Now he's getting what he deserves.

I paste a concerned look on my face and open the door. It's

time to go add fuel to the fire. Toi doesn't know it yet, but her days here with Marcum are definitely numbered.

❦ 63 ❦

TOI

I LOOK AT THE PLATE OF BLUEBERRY MUFFINS I HAVE IN MY HAND in disgust. This is my second baking-bribery-attempt in a matter of days. This is what I've been reduced to. Buying Harley and Desi's affections. Which would be okay at this point—if it was working, but it's not. Harley wouldn't even eat the cookies I made last time.

I stand at their door. I can hear Cherry's voice from where I'm standing and I want to turn around. I don't trust her. Marcum says he needs her here to keep an eye on her while we're on lockdown. The problem is she keeps staying close to Harley and Desi. I want to demand that Marcum stop it, but I know that will come off as petty jealousy and really—I am jealous. Still, I can't help but feel she's using the kids. I'm going to have to approach Marcum about it. He actually thought it was a good thing she's keeping to herself except for the kids. He sees it as proof she's not behind whatever mess is going on. Men can be so damned blind.

Cherry is trouble. I feel it.

I take a breath, praying my voice holds up. I hate when it doesn't and Cherry is around. She never misses an opportunity to make me feel less. It's so weird. Ever since the accident my voice

JORDAN MARIE

has been doing much better. Part of that is the medicine regimen the doctor put me on, but a bigger part of it I think, is that I'm relaxed and even... *happy*. I'm trying to strike up the nerve to finish the scans and get the surgery Marcum wants me to have, but he's agreed to table the discussion while everything is going on with the club.

"Hey. I was wondering if you guys would like some muffins," I say and my voice sounds way too overly cheerful to my own ears. I look around the room, immediately disappointed because Desi is not here. It would have been good if she was. She's the one person who likes me and it sure would be good to see a friendly face right now.

Instead, Cherry and Harley turn to look at me. One face is full of hate and one is full of victory.

Both make me very nervous.

"Hello, Toi. I'm afraid this is not a good time."

"Is something wrong? Harley, honey? Are you okay?"

Harley blinks. His little face is pale and I can tell he's been crying.

"You're having a baby!" he accuses and my face goes white.

"What? Who told you that?"

"I heard you. I heard you and Daddy! You're having a baby!"

"Well... I mean, I don't know, Harley. We've talked about it..." I stutter, not knowing how to handle this.

"You want to replace me and Desi! You want to take my Daddy away!"

"What? Of course I don't. Harley no one will ever take your Daddy away. He loves you," I tell him, trying to reassure him.

"I hate you! I don't want you here! Everything was good until you came!"

He grabs the plate of muffins I have and throws them to the floor. The plate shatters. I immediately get down and start picking up the pieces, not wanting Harley to get hurt.

"Harley, it's not okay for you to act like this. I know you're hurt, but you don't understand," I tell him, and I curse myself silently because my voice is breaking. Every muscle in my body is tight right now, so it makes sense, but this is the worst time possible for it to happen.

"I understand! I heard Daddy! He's got to protect his family, his *new* family!"

"Sweetheart, what's going on right now, your Dad is trying to protect all of us."

"He wouldn't need to if it wasn't for you!" Harley accuses me and I feel my stomach squeeze when I see Cherry smiling.

"What do you mean?"

"I'm afraid Harley overheard me talking to Babs about the lockdown," Cherry says.

"What did he overhear?" I ask, knowing it's bad from the self-satisfied smile on her face.

"She said your dad sent you away to some men for money because he didn't want you anymore!"

"I... Harley..." I start coughing, my voice trying to seize.

"Your daddy didn't want you, so you're trying to steal mine!"

"Har... ley," I cough out.

"You're going to get my daddy killed! I hate you! I wish you had never come here! We don't need you! We have Cherry and Daddy was happier when she was here!"

"Harley..."

"I hate you! I wish you'd die!" Harley screams and he takes off running from the room. I turn to go to him and Cherry grabs hold of my arm.

"I think you've done enough here. I'll see to Harley; he trusts me."

"He doesn't know," I get out before I start coughing, "what a fucking liar you are," I finally finish.

"Really, you should watch your language around Desi and Harley. They're good kids."

"What was Harley talking about?"

"Oh... you don't know. Isn't it just like Marcum to try and keep the truth from you?" she responds, as another cough breaks free.

"What truth?"

"Your father sold you to the Garcias."

"The Garcias?" I question. I've heard of them—vaguely, but I don't completely understand.

"Exactly. And if Marcum doesn't hand you over, he might as well sign his own death warrant. No one goes against the Garcias around here and lives."

"I…"

"If you don't mind, I really need to see to Harley. He's more important than a woman who is putting the entire club at risk and all because she spread her legs for the right man."

I want to respond, but I feel like I've been sucker punched and I'm hurting so deeply I can't seem to catch my breath.

All I can do is watch her leave while I'm coughing and feeling completely alone.

Is Cherry right? Am I going to get Marcum and his men killed? Is that why he's keeping all this from me?

❧ 64 ☙

MARCUM

I STARE AT THE PHONE AND I CAN'T DENY THERE'S A SOUR feeling in the pit of my stomach. I'm now on Kuzma's payroll—provided he gets the Garcias off my back—which is a formality at this point. He gave me his assurance that Alvaro would back down relatively easy. Apparently Toi killing someone and being mine will have tainted her. Bastard paid for an innocent and that's what he wants. Fuckers like that need to stop breathing.

"How long you going to be beholden to the man?" Ride asks, bringing it down to what's important.

"You know how this shit works, Ride."

"Jesus. Marcum, man..."

"I'm good with it."

"Bullshit."

"For Toi, I'm good with it," I tell him and I'm not lying one fucking bit. If I have to be Kuzma's hitman for the next five years, and probably stay under his thumb for the rest of my life, big fucking deal. I've made worse bargains and gained a lot less. If this keeps Toi safe, then I do not give a damn.

"So, lockdown is over?"

"Kuzma got word this morning. Start moving people up top today around noon."

"Noon?"

"Better safe than sorry. Can't hurt to give it a few hours and be cautious."

"You worried, man?"

I look at Ride. I have this unsettled feeling in my gut, though I can't put name to it.

"Let's just say that it seems too easy."

Ride agrees right away, nodding his head.

"Does seem mighty anti-climactic."

"If it's indeed over, I'll take that any day," I laugh as Ride gets up and walks to the door.

"That's because you're getting old," he says with a laugh and I give him the one-finger salute. Bastard's not that much younger than me. "Whoa!" he says once the door opens and Toi is there. He catches her before she falls, because she was trying to wrench the door open.

She's crying and I get up immediately and go to her, lifting her in my arms and carrying her over to the couch. Ride quietly shuts the door as I settle Toi in my lap.

"What's going on, Dragonfly?" I ask as her almost silent sobs shake her body. I can't stand to see her like this. She was fine this morning and my woman should never know the kind of sadness which is bothering her right now.

"Harley," she cries, the word becoming muffled until it's so quiet I have to strain to hear it, but once I do, I breathe a little easier. Harley is having growing pains where Toi is involved and it hurts her, but it will get better. It's just going to take time.

"I told you, honey. This will get better. Bub just has to get used to us being together. Once he sees that you being here is permanent, it will be fine. You just keep loving him, it will get through to him," I try reassuring her, combing through her hair with my fingers.

"You don't understand."

"Tell me." I kiss the side of her head, unable to stop my smile. She cares about my kids so deeply. Toi has so many things about her that I love, but her heart might be my favorite.

"He said he hated me, Marcum. He was so hurt."

"Hurt? Honey, what's going on?"

"He heard us talking this morning. He thinks I'm pregnant."

"Fuck..." I groan. This wasn't how I wanted my son to find out.

"Or maybe that bitch told him. She's using him, Marcum. I know you said you'd deal with it after the lockdown, but..."

She stops talking as she starts crying again. I know Cherry is a sore spot for her and I don't trust Cherry, but I haven't stopped the kids from seeing her while on lockdown... because I didn't want them to fucking hate me and have Harley resent Toi even more. I don't know what Cherry's game is, but I honestly thought she cared for Desi and Harley. Fuck, I'd rather deal with a man any day of the week. Women are too damn conniving.

"I'll deal with it, honey," I reassure her.

"I want her gone, Marcum. She's toxic."

"I will deal with her, I promise," I assure her again.

Toi cries a little longer, but eventually the sobs subside. She lifts her head and looks at me. I was feeling better, thinking Toi was through this crisis. She knows I'll take care of everything. She has a right to be mad, hell I'm mad at myself. I should have taken Cherry out of the picture much sooner. But, when Toi looks at me, it's not anger I see at all. It's something else entirely.

"Are we on lockdown because of me?"

Fuck.

"Dragonfly, I told you that your father left a mess... I'm just cleaning it up." I try to skirt the truth as much as I can.

"My father sold me," she whispers and anger wars with concern.

"Who told you that, Toi?" I growl.

"Is it true?"

"Who the fuck told you?"

"Are you going to war because of me?"

"Toi, who the hell told you this shit?" I demand again.

"Is it true?" she repeats.

"I'm handling it."

"So, it *is* true."

"You don't need to worry, honey. I've got this handled."

"We're on lockdown. Your men are in danger, your kids are in danger because of me," she whispers, shaking her head no.

"I just got off the phone ending the war. We're all fine. Everyone will start moving back upstairs in a few hours."

"How did you take care of it?" she asks, still not trusting me.

I hold the side of her neck, enjoying the feel of her pulse against my palm.

"You've never had one before, Toi, but you need to realize that you have a man in your life now that will take care of you. A man who will protect you, always."

"I couldn't live with it if your family got hurt because of me," she says, her head going down. I pull it back up and bring her closer to me.

"You're forgetting one thing, Dragonfly."

"What's that?" she asks, her big eyes—so beautiful—staring at my mouth.

"You are part of our family now. You're a part of me now," I tell her and I'm rewarded with the sweetest words I've ever heard. I'll never get tired of them either.

"I love you, Marcum," she says and I take her lips.

Our kiss starts soft. She fills me with so much emotion that I don't know how to begin sifting through it. When we finally break apart, both of us are breathing harder.

"Damn it, Toi, I want you, but I have work to do."

"I want Cherry gone. I know you think it's jealousy, Marcum but..."

"Is she the one who told you about your father?"

"Yes... and Harley."

"She fucking told Harley about that shit?"

"She said he overheard her talking to Babs, but..."

226

"That fucking bitch," I growl. "I'll deal with her. Fuck. I'll do it right now."

We get up and the only thing on my mind is getting to Cherry and shutting her down. I'll have her out of this damn club by nightfall. We've barely made it out of the door of my office before sirens start to go off.

"What's that?" Toi asks. I can't hear her over the siren, but I can tell what she's asking by her lip movements. Plus, fuck that's the question on my mind. The siren going off means there's an attack topside. Topper and Babs come running around the corner.

"What the fuck is going on?" I ask Topper.

"Ride sent me down. Fucking blast at the garage, man. The men are up there, returning fire.

"You see to the women and get them and the children in the shelter. Then meet me up top."

"You think it's the Garcias?"

"If it is they lied to Kuzma," I growl.

"Marcum," Toi cries and I look down at her.

"I need you to keep the kids safe, Dragonfly. Stay here and do that for me."

"But—"

"I got this, Toi. Remember?"

"I don't want you to get hurt," she whispers.

"I won't. Trust me, the club and I have been through worse shit. I just need you to make sure the kids are safe. Can you do that for me?"

"Yeah..." she whispers.

"That's my girl," I tell her and I give her a quick kiss. I am running toward the stairwell that leads topside when something occurs to me. I turn back around. "Hey Top!"

"Yeah, man?"

"Lock Cherry down. I want her away from my kids. She doesn't breathe the same air as them and Toi. You hear me?"

"Got it," he says, but he says it to my back because I'm already heading upstairs.

🜲 65 🜲

HARLEY

I MADE TOI CRY. I WAS SCARED. CHERRY SAID SHE WAS GOING TO take Daddy away from me. She said they won't need me no more because they'll have new babies. She's right too. My real mom didn't want me or Desi. She gave us away. At least Toi likes Desi. I look over to where they're curled up in the corner playing cards. Toi keeps hugging her and now they're laughing. Desi will be fine, but not me.

Toi won't want to keep me at all now, especially after I made her cry. She ran straight to Daddy and he'll take her side, especially since they're going to have a new family. Cherry's not here. Topper said Dad wanted Cherry to stay in her room away from everyone. She got mad. I heard her yelling to Topper and blaming Toi. Topper didn't deny it. Toi hates Cherry too. Cherry warned me that they'd get rid of her too and they are. She said all we had to count on was each other because once they got rid of her... I'd be next.

I thought maybe she was wrong. But I heard Topper and Babs talking and Topper said Daddy was going to send Cherry away after the lockdown. If Cherry goes, I have to go with her. She's the only family I have left and she loves me. She told me she does.

Everyone is busy playing and talking. They don't even know I'm around. I saw Toi look over at me a few times, but that's it. I don't want to stay here and watch her be nice to Desi. Desi's mad at me now too, and all because I yelled at Toi. I don't belong here anymore. Cherry's right.

Unless we're on lockdown, we're not allowed down here. But, Desi and I sneak down here and play all the time. I walk over to Babs and I don't really want to, but I don't think I have a choice. It's now or never.

"I gotta go to the bathroom."

"I'll get one of the prospects to go with you," she says. I knew I'd have to have someone take me there. If I tried to go by myself, they'd never let me.

"Spence, can you take Harley to the bathroom?" Babs asks.

"I could take you," Toi says coming to where we're standing and surprising me. She reaches out like she's going to touch me, but she takes her hand back before she does. I look down at the ground. For a minute, I wanted her to touch me. She used to hug me all the time. I kind of liked it—even if I said I didn't.

"Whatever."

Toi looks back at Desi and hugs her. "We'll finish our game when I get back, okay, sweetheart?"

"Okay, Toi," she says. Desi doesn't look at me. She's still mad at me. She won't miss me when I'm gone either.

"Maybe your brother will join us when we get back," Toi says.

My heart speeds up at first, but then I remember what Cherry said. Toi's just trying to look nice in front of everyone else and make me and her the bad guys.

I start walking away and Toi follows me. We go down the hall from the big room everyone is staying in and there's a restroom at the end of it. Toi opens the door and I stand there.

"You can't go in with me."

"I just want to make sure it's safe," she says and she walks in looking around. "Okay, sweetheart. I'll just be right outside."

"I can go to the bathroom by myself," I mumble, annoyed she's here. I won't have as much time this way.

"I promised your dad that I'd keep you safe," she says her voice strained. I was thinking she was worried about me, but she's just making sure Daddy won't be mad at her.

Figures.

I stomp into the bathroom and lock the door. Then I go straight to the back stall. There's two stalls in here and one is really small. But, the other one is big. It also has a secret panel! Desi discovered it when we were playing hide and seek. For a girl, Desi is really good at that game. I go to the long mirror hanging on the wall beside the toilet, and reach under the frame at the bottom. There's a button I push and it pops, causing the mirror to swing out and revealing a tunnel. It just goes back into Daddy's bedroom down here, but that's all I need. From there, I can get to Cherry's room. She can get us out of here. She said she could. It's really dark and I'm kind of scared, but I hurry. I don't want Toi to discover I'm gone until me and Cherry get away. Cherry's going to take me to live with her forever.

She'll be my mommy again.

🎕 66 🎕

TOI

OKAY, I KNOW KIDS CAN BE SLOW, BUT HARLEY HAS BEEN IN there for thirty minutes. I realize he's probably making me wait on purpose, but this is getting ridiculous so I knock on the door.

"Harley? Are you okay, honey?"

He doesn't answer. Not that I really expected him to. I really don't know how to reach him. I'm hoping once Cherry is gone, I can find a way to get through to him. My heart is still hurting from hearing him tell me he hated me. If we get through today I'm going to throat punch Cherry. I'd like to do more, but I figure that's as much as I can get in before Marcum intervenes.

Marcum.

I'm worried about him... about everyone really. I know he said he could handle this, but if anyone gets hurt because of me...

"Harley, honey I know you're not happy with me, but could you at least tell me you're okay?" I ask the door.

I'm not really surprised when all I get in return is silence. I hate to break into the bathroom; if I do that Harley will hate me. I war with myself for a few minutes and then sigh heavily. "Harley if you don't answer me, I'm going to have to come in there," I threaten.

I hear footsteps down the hall and look up to see Babs and Desi heading our way.

"We got worried about you and Desi said she needed to use the bathroom too," Babs explains.

I rub the back of my neck, feeling tension gathering there. I try to breathe deep and relax, because I know that my voice goes crazy if I'm stressed.

"Harley's locked himself in the restroom," I tell her with a sigh. I try the doorknob, while pushing my body against the door, but it doesn't budge.

"That little hellion. I swear he was such a great kid too. Cherry is doing a number on him," Babs mutters.

"What does she mean?" Desi asks, her eyes big and round.

"Nothing, honey," I tell her. I don't want to badmouth Cherry; kids don't need to be brought into the screwed-up world of adults.

"Here, let me try this," Babs says, holding out a bobby-pin she took from her hair.

"You know how to pick a lock?" I ask, wondering if I could get her to teach me.

"When you're the old lady of one of our boys?" she laughs. "Girl, trust me, it comes in handy."

She works with it for a few minutes and I'm looking over her shoulder trying to will it to open.

"Is Harley in trouble?" Desi asks carefully.

"No honey, of course not. I'm just worried about him."

"He's probably just pouting in there. Marcum is going to have his hands full with that one," Babs says. Eureka!" she cries as the door opens. I push in first, anxious to get my hands on Harley and hug him—and then maybe shake him.

"Harley!" I open the small door to the first stall and it's empty. "Harley, answer me," I grumble. I open the next door and it's empty.

"Did you walk away or something? Maybe he came out when you weren't looking," Babs says from behind me.

"No. I've been standing out there this entire time. There's no way he came out there. Maybe he left through a window?"

"Honey, we're underground here. That's why the boys had us moved to this part. On this side of the basement we're deeper down. There are no windows."

"Is Harley in trouble?" Desi asks again, her voice wobbling.

I crouch down so I'm at eye level with her. I know she has to be worried about her brother. Heck, I'm terrified. My heart is beating so hard that it is slamming against my chest.

"No, honey. He's not in trouble, it's just there are some dangerous things going on right now and we need to make sure he's safe," I tell her, gently holding her little face and trying to reassure her.

"He's with Cherry," she whispers. "She told him to come get her."

"Why would she say that, honey?"

"She thought I was napping, but I wasn't."

"When was this, honey?"

"Before Harley made you cry. She told him that you would send him away now, because you are going to have your own baby. Are you going to have your own baby, Toi?"

"Not right now and even if I did, I would never send you or your brother away."

"You wouldn't?"

"Of course not. I love you guys. You, Harley and your daddy are my family now," I tell her, my heart breaking at the fear I see in her little eyes.

"Cherry needs her damn ass kicked," Babs growls. I definitely agree with her, and once I get Harley back safe, I'll be doing the kicking.

"I love you, Toi," Desi cries, throwing her arms around me.

"I love you too, baby." I pick her up, her legs wrap around me too and I hold her close. "Now if we just knew where Harley disappeared to," I sigh.

"And how he managed it," Babs agrees.

"I told you, he's with Cherry," Desi insists.

"There's no way he could have gone down the hall to her room, honey. I never moved from the bathroom door."

"I know how..." Desi says cautiously.

"You know what, honey?"

"I know how Harley dis'peered," she says.

"How?" Babs and I both ask.

"Through the mirror."

"I think you watched that Narnia movie too much, baby cakes," Babs says.

"No! Really. I'll show you," Desi says, already wiggling to get down. She practically jumps down and then goes in the largest stall. She fumbles around with the mirror and it pops open.

"Fuck me," Babs whispers and I think the very same thing, but resist saying it because of Desi. "I better go get one of the boys," she says, turning away.

"Take Desi with you," I order her.

"Where are you going?"

"To Cherry's room to find my son," I growl, taking off running down the hall.

🎋 67 🎋

MARCUM

"WHAT THE FUCK IS GOING ON?" I GROWL, LOOKING AT WHAT'S left of the third dirty bomb we've found. It was a coordinated strike and damn sophisticated. I've got some heavy duty security around the club, but we are not fucking prepared to have bombs dropped in by a fucking drone.

"Welcome to the age of robotics," Max growls, grinding a piece of the burned drone into the charred ground. It was a rude bomb to have such a sophisticated drop. There were three bombs. One was explosive and centered on taking out our garage and all of our fucking bikes and cars. The other had fucking nails exploding and was centered on the club itself. If we had our family in there...

Fuck, just the thought of what would have happened if Toi and the kids had been in there scares me to death.

The third bomb was another one filled with nails and it dropped on our guardhouse. It took out three of our best prospects. They dropped one right after the other and then...

Nothing.

"I'd say we should do some scouting and try to track the fuckers down, but..." Ride shrugs

"Our garage is fucking toast?" Ghost growls.

"We've got two SUVS in the garage by the swamp. Use those, but I doubt you will find shit," I answer, raking my hand along the side of my face.

"You think it was the Alvaro and his men?" Max asks.

"Probably. I need to get Kuzma on the phone."

"Jesus we're in the middle of a fucking mob war," Topper mutters.

"Weren't you the son of a bitch who was complaining shit was getting too calm?"

"Don't remind me, Dawg. Damn, I'm going to need a drink."

"You and me both," I agree. I take out my cell and hit the button for the programmed number I put in earlier. I take a few steps away from the others and after the third ring Kuzma picks up. Max falls into step behind me. I hate that I'm putting his family in danger, but it's damn good to have him by my side.

"Kincaid, my employees don't normally call. They wait for my call," Kuzma answers

"I'm not your damned employee," I growl.

"You can't back out now. I handled your—"

"You didn't handle shit. My club just got hammered, the garage is a complete loss and I've got casualties."

"Garcias? They gave me their word the contract would be canceled."

"Well, maybe they're getting even at having their plans derailed. Fuck if I know, but you promised to get the assholes off my back and keep my woman safe. Got to tell you man, I'm not feeling fucking safe."

"I'll deal with it," he snaps.

"Not if I deal with it first," I tell him, hanging up the phone before he can respond. This is why I don't like dealing with fucking suits.

"Marcum, we got problems," Moth yells from within the club.

I crash through the doors, looking at the carnage and debris everywhere. I get ahold of Alvaro and I'm going to slice his balls off with a dull knife and feed them to him.

"Tell me something I don't already fucking know, Moth."

"Harley's missing."

Fuck. Fear slams through me and crashes hard against my chest, my heart stopping.

"What the fuck do you mean?" Max asks.

"Toi took him to the restroom during the lockdown. She let him go in alone, and when he wouldn't answer she broke in and he was gone."

"Someone took him?" I ask, still barely able to catch my breath.

"No man. He found the passage to your room."

"Motherfucker, that boy is too damn smart for his own good."

"Have you searched the place? I want it turned upside down. You hear me?" I yell, breathing a little easier. So he's hiding out somewhere in the club. I'll make his fucking ass bright red for worrying me... after I hug him. "Where's Toi? She'll be upset. We find him, I'll want her to—"

"Marcum, buddy..."

Something in Moth's tone scares me.

And I mean it fucking scares me.

"Spill it."

"Toi followed him. Babs said she was going to Cherry's room. Desi told them that Cherry had a plan to take Harley and leave."

"Son of a bitch!" Max roars from somewhere behind me.

I'm heading straight to the passageway that Toi used to leave the last time. Cherry helped Weasel, trying to take Toi from me before. I have no doubt she's trying to do the same shit now. She better hope when I find her, Alvaro has already ended her. Because if she's breathing when I find her I'm going to choke the life right out of her.

❧ 68 ❧

TOI

I'M KICKING MY OWN ASS. I SHOULDN'T HAVE WAITED SO LONG before I checked on Harley. I gave him entirely too long—which gave that fucking bitch Cherry way too big of a head start. I get Harley back and I take out my frustrations on that fake redhead, I'm going to set Marcum's ears on fire. He locked Cherry up, but there wasn't a guard around! Harley got her free easily. I mean, I know we were under attack and he had his men involved in that, and then watching us... but still. He hasn't seen her as a real threat this entire time.

"Big, strong, he-man, macho ass. You can't underestimate a woman. We might have tits, but we can also be more dangerous than a man, and mostly because men never worry about us."

I'm muttering to myself and I need to stop it, because talking is getting harder. I've used my voice too much today and I missed my last dose of steroids and medications. Marcum's right. I need to stop worrying and have that surgery. I'll cave in if we all survive this. Being afraid seems ridiculous, considering everything that we are going through now.

I swore the last time I was in this damn tunnel I wouldn't come back. In fact, when this is over and I kill Cherry, and Harley and I are back with everyone else, I'm going to demand that Marcum destroy these damn things. Who has secret passages and tunnels in their home? I ignore the fact it probably comes in handy when you're an outlaw motorcycle club with a leader who can piss off the Pope without barely trying. Hell, he could have tested the patience of Mother Teresa. Yet I love him and when he's not making you want to pull out your hair he can be unbelievably sweet and caring.

A man who is everything I always wanted and never thought I'd find. I need to tell him that if I survive this. I know there are moments he still beats himself up about so many things when it comes to us. He doesn't realize I don't care about his past, or what he does. He doesn't know that to me he is the most amazing man I've ever met. I don't care about his age or that I'm closer to Max's age than his. I love him. I've told him I love him, but I've never told him the rest. I need to.

I will.

I stop walking and strain to hear. It's light, but I can hear someone up in front of me. I take a shuddering breath and pick up my speed, trying to remain quiet. I make my way through the tunnel by feeling the walls. If I had been smart, when I discovered Harley and Cherry already gone, I would have grabbed a damn light.

As I turn a curve, I can see light ahead. It's coming from outside and it's entirely too *déjà vu,* for comfort.

"Cherry maybe if we told Daddy we wanted to stay, he would let us. He wouldn't have to love us, but we could still stay," I hear Harley say and tears sting my eyes. I'm going to enjoy sending Cherry to hell.

"You know better, Harley. I told you what he said to me. He doesn't have any place in his life for either one of us now. That bitch wants us gone," she mutters just as they push on the old door, opening it.

I blink from the glare of light, trying to adjust my eyesight and then I stop thinking. Her words and the pain she's causing an innocent, confused boy are nearly destroying me. I run as hard as I can.

When I get to them, I see shock on her face and I can hear Harley yell, but I'm focused on Cherry. I jump the last little distance, hurling my body into her and tackling her to the ground. I pull at her hair, I claw at her face and I'm pretty sure I'm more than ready to rip her throat out with just my hands. The only thing that stops me is Harley's cry and the sound of guns cocking and preparing to shoot. I freeze. Cherry must have heard it too, because she goes still underneath me.

I look up and see three guns pointed down at us. The men are all impeccably dressed in suits. Who wears suits and packs rifles like they're sporting? It's like something out of a damn Al Paccino movie. That's not what chills me though. It's the man standing directly across from me. His face is scarred, obviously from a fire. He's wearing a patch over one of his eyes and the scars are so thick there are ridges on his skin. He's wearing a suit too, but his hands are as pink as his face, telling me the scars are just as deep on at least some of the rest of his body.

How does a man survive a fire like that?

The thing that scares me the most, though, is that he's holding Harley by the neck, and there's a pistol pointed at his head.

"My bride, finally I have you." The man smiles and my heart flips in my chest.

Oh shit.

Cherry grabs my hair and yanks it, pulling me to the side as she gets up. She stands up and kicks the shit out of my stomach. I curl from the pain. Even though the chance is minuscule, I pray that I'm not pregnant.

"Bitch," she says and spits on me. I hear Harley cry and I try to open my eyes, afraid they will hurt him.

"I told you I would get her, Alvaro. All it took was bringing the kid and she followed like a dog. She thought she was being so quiet. I had to stop several times just so she'd catch up with us."

Well, shit... so much for thinking I was being all stealthy.

"You done well," he says and his voice is so cold. He's not even talking to me this time, but it still chills me just the same.

"Good. Now did you bring the car and the money, like we agreed?" she asks.

"I have everything ready for you," he agrees and I see his face. I've seen evil before in my father, but this man makes my father look like a pussycat. I don't think Cherry realizes what's going on, but I see it from a mile off.

"Good. If it's all the same to you, I want out of here before Marcum and his men show up for her or the kid."

"Cherry, are you... you're taking me? We can't leave Toi..." Harley cries, his body shaking in the man's arms.

"Give me my son, please?" I ask the man reaching for the little boy. He looks down at Harley and then at me. His face tilts and I get the feeling he's testing me, measuring me. I don't care. I just need to get Harley. I need him in my arms, but more importantly —I need to try and shield him. "If you give him to me, I'll do anything you ask, please. Just let me hold him," I beg.

"Interesting. The child is not yours and yet you claim him?"

"I do. I love him."

My words seem to shock him. For whatever reason, he shoves Harley toward me. I catch him in my arms and he cries harder, but he hugs me tight.

"Sorry, kid. You'll learn, though. It's a tough world and people like you and me, all we have to depend on is ourselves," Cherry says, and for a minute I think I see regret in her eyes.

"You used me," Harley says. His little body is still shaking, but his tears slowing down, and he's still holding to me tightly. "You used me to get Toi," he says, shuddering, but proving he's as smart as Marcum when it counts. He's definitely Marcum's child. I need to make Marcum believe that if I get the chance. I look at the gun the scarred man is holding and I can't help but think that it's not going to happen.

Cherry looks at Harley and it's definitely regret I see on her face now, but she turns away, refusing to look at the little boy she's leaving behind—probably to die.

"I need my shit so I can go," she growls.

I see the man raise his pistol and I pull Harley deep into me, drawing his head to my chest to shield him.

"Don't look, Harley. Don't move," I urge him quietly in his ear. He knows, God bless him, he knows though because he's crying again and his body is shivering so hard, it's shaking me.

"I've got exactly what you deserve," the man says, and he shoots her.

"But..." Cherry cries and falls down on the ground. He shot her in the shoulder. I'd like to think it's because he's a bad shot, but I know better. He wants her to suffer. "Why?" she cries.

"Because you're a viper and you spit on my property," the man says as calmly as if he was talking about the weather. And then he unloads his gun—in her head.

Blood splatters and I scream as it hits my hand and the sleeve of my shirt. It even splatters on the back of Harley's shirt. I look at Cherry lying in front of me, her skin instantly pale, almost blue and her eyes open... and I want to vomit.

"Toi!" Harley cries, but I hold his head tighter, not wanting him to see what I'm looking at. He should never see it.

I don't want to see it.

❧ 69 ❧

MARCUM

THE BOMBS WERE A FUCKING DISTRACTION. I SHOULD HAVE SEEN through it. There's no way I could have been completely prepared. Alvaro's purse is to damn deep. Who uses fucking drones for bombs? Shit, I admit it, it takes balls of steel to even try that. What happens if a drone fails and you blow yourself sky-high? I miss the old days when a gun was the biggest firepower you had at your disposal. If I survive this shit, I'm going to have to find a man I trust to figure all this shit out. I won't be caught with my pants down again.

If I get the chance.

I know where Alvaro is. I radioed in my men. The problem is we're without our rides, We're basically all walking except for the two SUV's. The Garcias will have the majority of their men in the clearing and since the mess with Toi and her father last time, I will try to have some surprises there. It might be enough, but I doubt it. We're too scattered and licking our wounds from the blasts, and it doesn't help that Alvaro has been set up for a while. Toi left the door to the tunnels open and I found the clip she always wears in her hair at the entrance. I know she left it on purpose. It's burning a hole in my pocket now. I hope I get the chance to give it back to her.

There's so much I haven't done; things I want to do—if given the chance. I never spoiled Toi. I was planning on it, but I haven't gotten the chance. Now I might never get to.

"Wait up old man," Max growls from behind me.

"You need to go be with Tess, Maddie and..."

"They're safe. Somebody has to have your back."

"I got men. I don't want you hurt because of me."

"You were there for me when I was losing everything. You held it together for me, Marcum. It's my turn to help you."

"I've been a shit father and you know it. Because of me your life was hell and when I finally found you, it was too late. You hated me."

"I hated the world. Not really you. No one twisted my arm to stay here you know."

"I thought you did it just so you could tell me to fuck off daily," I joke.

"You always were smart for an old fuck," Max laughs.

"There's every chance I'm not going to survive this, boy."

"Bullshit. You're invincible."

"I'm being serious. I need you to listen to me. We're just a few minutes away from the clearing. When we get there, you hang back and hide with the gun. Maybe you can get some shots off—"

"You're speaking out of your ass and you know me better than that shit."

"Fuck, you're stubborn."

"Just like my old man," he agrees. "So, what's your real plan?"

"To save Toi and Harley."

"That seems simple," he says sarcastically.

"If I manage it, you have to promise me you'll take care of them and Desi. The other kids are older; they'll have the club, but Desi and Harley are young. They need protection and... Toi..."

"Old man, we're going to see the other side of this."

"Maybe, but probably not. I'm a realist," I tell him, stopping at the mouth of the tunnel and turning to look at him. The flashlight he's holding casts us in a dim light, but I see the worry on his face clearly. "Promise me you'll take care of them. I know I don't have the right to ask anything from you, but I need to know they'll be okay without me," I practically beg him, putting my hand on Max's shoulder.

"I'll take care of them," he reassures me. "You never have to worry about that."

"I've been a shit dad," I say again.

"You were there when it counted the most and I was an ungrateful punk-ass kid that didn't see you were always trying to be there," Max interrupts. He slaps his hand down on my shoulder and looks at me. His face is so much like mine. I doubt he'd appreciate me bringing that up—I'm not the best looking fucker.

"I suck at this emotional shit," I growl.

"Then save it and give it to me later."

We both know there probably won't be a later, but I let it slide.

It's go time. We turn the corner and the door's open. I hear gunshots and take off running. I break free outside to see Alvaro emptying his gun in Cherry's head. My eyes lock onto Toi and Harley and I make the one rookie mistake I'd kill one of my men for. I run headlong toward them.

🦋 70 🦋

TOI

"IT'S TIME WE LEAVE," THE MAN SAYS, STANDING OVER ME and Harley. He's reaching out one of his hands. My stomach turns and it has nothing to do with his scars, but the coldness I see in his eyes—and the fact he just shot Cherry without blinking an eye. I admit that I wanted to kill her, but still...

"Harley stays here," I tell him standing up and shuffling Harley behind me.

"The kid?"

"Yes. I want your word that you won't harm him, that he can stay and go back to his father."

"What is he to you?" Alvaro asks, tilting his head down as if to see me better. Perhaps his vision is damaged in the one eye he uses. I don't know, but having all of his attention is something to fear and I do—though I do my best to not show it.

"He's my son."

"Toi, this is my fault, I'm so sorry. I'm so sorry," Harley cries and I turn to face him, bending down so he can see my face.

"Sweetheart, I need for you to be brave. Your daddy and Desi are going to need you."

"I don't want you to go. I thought you hated me," he cries, his body shuddering again as he tries to control his sobs.

"Oh honey, I could never hate you."

"Let my family go," Marcum yells from the tunnel which is about twelve yards away from me now. God, he looks good, but I don't want him here. Alvaro will kill him just like he did Cherry and that thought scares the hell out of me and causes tears to sting my eyes. I can't watch Marcum get shot. Even if I can't keep him, I can't let anything happen to him.

"Get behind me now," Alvaro orders me and I want to tell him no, to fight—something. *I can't.* He has a gun pointed directly at Harley. *I'm trapped.* I put my body in front of Harley once more and walk to the side so we get behind Alvaro.

"I'm not telling you again, man. Let my family go."

I'm pretty sure Alvaro smiles. It's hard to tell from the scars and twisted skin on his face, but he makes a noise like a laugh. Where my voice is light, Alvaro's is hoarse and dark sounding. Maybe it was altered from the fire he was obviously caught in, or maybe he's just so evil it resonates in his voice. Whatever it is, I'll have nightmares about it for years—if I survive.

"Who are you, that you think you can order me?"

"Marcum Kincaid."

"Am I supposed to know you?"

"You're on my land. I'm pretty sure you are responsible for blowing up my garage. So yeah asshole, I think you know me."

"I was told grown men tremble around you and yet I could take you out with one shot. I don't understand."

"Try it. Before you can pull that trigger, with that fucked up hand of yours—you'll be dead," Max says from behind Marcum.

"Goddamn it, Max," Marcum growls rubbing the side of his face. "I told you to stay back."

"I'm like my old man. I don't listen," Max says with a wry smile, but you can tell he's not happy. There's not anything in this situation to find joy in.

"Dragonfly, you didn't stay where I put you," Marcum yells.

"I'm sorry, Daddy," Harley calls out.

"It's okay, son. This is my fault, not yours. You understand?"

"This is all rather touching, but if you don't mind, I'm taking my bride and leaving."

"Harley, go to your daddy."

"But, Toi..."

"Go now, don't argue," I order Harley. I look up at Alvaro, "I'll go, but I want to make sure my son is safe."

"Whatever," he says as if he could care less.

"Go, Harley," I order him again, pushing him gently toward his dad. Marcum holds out his arms and Harley runs to him.

I watch as Marcum lifts Harley up in his arms, holding his little body close, and Harley cries in his father's arms. I commit the image to my memory. This man and this boy are such a huge part of my heart. The thought of never seeing them again makes me ache.

"Toi, you're not going anywhere," Marcum calls out, stopping me from turning around to get into the man's limo. "Harley go stand behind Max and the men." I look over at Max and see that Ghost and some other men have fallen in line now, they all have their guns aimed this way. My heart leaps into my throat.

"I love you, Marcum," I tell him, because I know he's going to fight for me. I've waited my whole life to have someone do that, and now that he is... *I want him to stop.* "Let's go," I urge the man, needing to leave before Marcum or the others get hurt.

"That fire must have burned your pride away, Alvaro," Marcum yells.

Alvaro grabs my hand, stopping me from moving, and turns once again to face Marcum. Men on both sides have weapons drawn. Any way I imagine what happens next... is bad, and with each moment that passes my fear increases. I'm practically choking on it now. It literally hurts to breathe. I can hear my heart pounding, my pulse beating so hard that it roars in my ears.

"You're growing tedious, Marcum Kincaid. I paid for my bride twice and now, I'm keeping her."

"You didn't pay anything. They both ended up dead."

Alvaro smirks and he even manages a small laugh. It sounds so evil that I want to block it out. "Whatever," he answers. He sounds so pleased with himself.

"I have a proposition for you, Alvaro."

"What could you possibly have that I want? I have the woman," he says, and as if to prove his point, his hand moves to my breast and squeezes it hard, causing me to cry out in pain.

"You that anxious to try and claim what I already own?" Marcum asks. His words hit me wrong, but I'm too scared to be upset. I know he's just trying to get a rise out of Alvaro.

"Once she has a real man, she will forget you."

"What if I could give you something you want more?" Marcum asks, and his tone chills me down to my toes.

Please God... don't let him mean what I think he does.

"Nice try, Kincaid, but I don't think that's possible. I'll be going now. I'm sure you understand Toi and I have a lot of things to catch up on."

"How hot were those flames in that whorehouse in Dallas?" Marcum asks. "From the looks of you it had to be bad. You must have thought the devil himself was coming to claim your sorry ass."

"What do you know of my accident?"

"Quite a bit, since I'm the one who was contracted to do it, you sad fuck."

I hear Alvaro growl and then the sound of the gun discharging as he pulls the trigger. I see Marcum's body fall back with the force of the shot, and I scream. I try to run to him, but Alvaro grabs my arm and refuses to let me. My shirt rips as I try to get free, but I can't get away.

All I can do is watch helplessly as Marcum hits the ground and his blood blooms against his skin in a sick, overly-bright red.

❧ 71 ❧

MARCUM

I GRUNT AS THE BULLET RIPS THROUGH MY SHOULDER, TEARING through the skin, muscle and cartilage, and I'm pretty fucking sure it hit bone. I might have overplayed my hand a little. I needed to get his attention though. Now I need to rein him in enough to get Toi to Max. I need her safe. I don't give a fuck what happens after that.

"That's for trying to lie to me, Kincaid. I know who tried to kill me. I tortured him for over a year."

"What did you do, have him look at your face?"

That wasn't exactly reining it in. I'm angry because there's no scenario I come out of this and that's a sad realization for a man who suddenly has everything to live for. If I could I'd dice this motherfucker up. I've got a weapon—the asshole didn't ask for it yet—but I don't dare risk it with Toi where she's at right now. Alvaro doesn't like my taunting, though, and I know that by the way he shoots me again, this time just a hair lower than the prior shot.

"Motherfucker!" I growl out, even though I wish to fuck I could have kept silent. That one was more painful though. There's instantly more blood too, so I have to wonder if he hit

an artery. I need to be smarter and get Toi safe before I let him finish me.

"Marcum!" Toi screams and I hear Max cursing in the background. He's itching to kill the motherfucker, but he knows as well as I do, he tries anything and Toi will probably die. I can't let that happen. She needs to live on.

"I grow tired of you," Alvaro growls.

"The man you killed only took the job. It was offered to me first, and I turned it down. I can give you the man who ordered it all."

"Then tell me."

"I'll tell you what I know, for a price."

"Have you looked around you, Kincaid? I have the girl. My men have me protected and your men all have guns pointed at them. Why would I pay you *anything*? Besides, where you are going, you won't take anything with you."

"My men have your men surrounded. Maxwell over there was a sniper. They're not shooting for one simple reason—they know I don't want them to. You want out of this still breathing, Alvaro, you'll give me what I want."

"What is that?"

"An exchange."

"Of what?"

"You let Toi go to my boy and I'll tell you everything."

"Let my bounty go? Not hardly."

"Then you can have me instead," I tell him.

"Marcum! No!" Toi yells, her voice raw with tears.

"I already have you. Perhaps you've failed to notice."

"Agree to my deal and I'll make sure my men know to let you go—unharmed."

"Interesting. You sacrifice yourself for the woman?"

"In a heartbeat," I answer without pause.

"No...." Toi cries again, the sound tortured as if it's being ripped from her. I have to force myself not to look at her. I can't do this if I see her.

"Let me get this straight. I let Toi go, you tell me what I want and then I can do whatever I want with you? Then, I leave and there's not a damn thing your men will do to me."

"That easy."

"What's to stop them from attacking once I no longer have Toi? Perhaps you think I am stupid."

"I told you—"

"You should stop wasting your breath. From the looks of you, you don't have much left."

"Here's how this is going to go. I will let Drummond hold Toi, ten feet away as a show of good faith. You will kneel at my feet and tell me what I want. I'll let Toi go when I'm satisfied and there's a bullet in the back of your head."

"What's to keep you from keeping Toi?"

"Nothing, but then you'll be dead. It will no longer be your concern."

"One of my men stands with yours. I want someone close to Toi."

"Very well."

"Ride."

"Here, man."

"You're in charge of the club now. Pick a man to protect my woman."

"Marcum, please, don't do this. Oh God, please don't do this. I'll go with you, Alvaro. I'll go, just please stop this," Toi is crying, her voice so raw and thick with tears. I've still not looked at her.

I can't.

"Damn it, Marcum. This is suicide you're wanting me to help with," Ride growls.

"Pick someone. Don't have a lot of time," I tell him, and I mean that literally. I'm feeling dizzy as fuck. I'm bleeding out. It won't be long before all this is academic. I've been close to death before. A man pulled out in front of me in a truck and I piled up my bike on my way back from Miami. I felt death coming for me then, and I feel it now. I have to fight it back. I need Toi safe.

"Ghost," Ride says and his choice cuts me to the fucking bone. I hate it. It's who I would have picked. He'll protect Toi until he dies, I just couldn't bring myself to name him. It's one thing to die for Toi, I have no regrets doing that, but giving her to Ghost... That slices me raw.

Ghost walks down to me and takes the bandana from his head, wrapping it around my arm, pulling it so tight.

"This is not going to matter," I tell him, but I'm hoping it does buy me a little more time before Alvaro finishes the job.

"Miracles can happen. Once I have Toi, Max will shoot the son of a bitch," he says, but we both know by the time he can get Toi safe, it will be too late.

"Take care of her. I need her happy and living free. I need to know she gets that."

Ghost stares me down for a minute and nods his head.

"Enough with the talking," Alvaro interrupts. "I'm growing weary."

"I was wrong, Marcum. You are the best man for Toi," Ghost says as he walks away, but it doesn't matter now.

Nothing does except that Toi is safe.

72

MARCUM

I LOOK BEHIND ME AND SEE THE MAN PULLING TOI A FEW FEET away from Alvaro. There's another man patting Ghost down, taking his guns and tossing them back toward Alvaro's car. Ghost tries to take Toi in his arms, but she pushes him away and instead tries to run to me. I should have never looked at her. Ghost catches her at the waist, pulling her back.

Pulling her away from me.

"No! I don't want this! Marcum don't do this to me. I don't want to live without you," she cries. "I love you!"

My body jerks as I hear Alvaro's gun ring out again.

I'm going to die, there's no way around it. I feel it as another bullet tears through my shoulder. I can feel the hot lead carve through muscle and sink into the fucking bone. My body careens forward, my head slamming against the dusty ground. I look up to keep my eyes on Toi.

Death is coming for me now. There's no escaping it and I know Toi knows it too. I see it in her eyes—that realization that the future we had planned is being ripped away. Her hand goes to her stomach, and I want to scream out at the unfairness of it all. My head begins to swim and I blink to try and clear my vision, but all I can see is what we would have had.

Toi holding a child to her breast—our child—her head covered in light blond hair, like her mom's. Her perfect face a reflection of Toi's. So beautiful...

"I already killed my brother. Do you think I am stupid?" Alvaro asks, trying to pull me back, but I don't let him.

"Marcum!" Toi screams, falling to the ground and burying her head into her hands.

I see her standing in the kitchen, our child at her feet laughing with Tess as Desi and Harley play with Maddie. She's so happy she's glowing. Her long blond hair falling down her back. My ring shining on her hand. She looks over at me and mouths the words she knows I have to have from her. "I love you."

I feel Alvaro kick me and I blink to look at Toi again. Just one more look...

"Marcum, don't do this. God please, I can't be without you," she sobs, pain etched on her face, tears falling so hard there's no way she can see me, except in a blur.

I've failed her.

Just like my old man, I've lived my life by a set of rules, all of them unwritten—but they're inside of me as solid as concrete. The main one was to live without regrets. Failing Toi has regret barreling inside of me with the force of a freight train, and there's so much regret inside of me, I'm fucking choking on it.

I never wanted to fail her. I feel something kick me again, but I block it out... I want more of Toi. My eyes close as I feel myself slipping away.

"I love you," she whispers, touching my face. I lose myself in her eyes, as she moves her body, taking me in deeper, riding me into heaven. "I love you, Marcum," she cries again. I love her like this, wild in passion—free. "Marcum!" It's a broken cry that soothes the emptiness that was there before Toi became my life.

"Hush, Dragonfly. Hush for me, you'll wake our babies," I tell her, taking her mouth in a kiss.

"You stupid, stupid biker. Did you really think I wouldn't know everything? I only let you give yourself up so I could kill you. But I'll tell you a secret," Alvaro says, yanking my head from behind to pull me closer so he can yell in my ear. The pain increases, reality beginning to invade, leaving me desperate to return to my dreams... "I'm going to kill you and then I'm going to take the woman back and then I'll spend days upon days showing her what a real man is," Alvaro promises.

73

TOI

"HE'S DYING! DO SOMETHING!" I YELL, BEATING ON GHOST'S hand.

I yell as I watch Alvaro pull Marcum's head back. I pull, trying to break free, but Ghost doesn't let me. Alvaro points his gun at the back of Marcum's head.

"Now!" Ghost yells, and I hear a gun beside me go off. I scream as Ghost tackles me to the ground. I fall hard, Ghost's body wrapped around me. I can't see anything, Ghost has me completely hidden but I hear guns going off. I cry, sobs wracking my body as I think of Marcum dying.

He looked so lost the last time he looked at me. So lost and... hopeless. It wasn't supposed to happen like this. We were going to have a life together. I was supposed to have his baby, we were going to raise Harley and Desi together, we're supposed to have time.

I wail in misery, the sound torn from my very soul, sounding like an animal trapped in a cage.

I existed, just wanting to break free, before Marcum stormed into my life. He was all wrong for me—but he became everything right... everything good. I don't want to live without him.

I claw at Ghost, needing to break free from him, needing to

get to Marcum. Eventually Ghost lifts off of me. I don't notice that all around me the gunfire has lessened. Nothing matters but Marcum who is lying on the ground—not moving.

Oh God... is he dead?

I take off running, needing him. I slide the last few feet to him, my fear so great that I can't remain standing. Marcum's still not moving. I don't even think he's breathing and there's a pool of blood around him. I pull at him, dragging his head into my lap and turning his body so I can see him. He's so pale, his face looking almost gray.

"Marcum, honey," I whisper, my voice raw from a mixture of overuse and tears, but I have to reach him. "Marcum, I need you to open your eyes now."

All around us are men working. Ride is tearing open Marcum's blood soaked sleeve and trying to stem the bleeding. Alvaro is dead. I don't know who did it, but I wish it could have been me. I hear Max yelling in the background. I hear Harley crying, and I hear the sound of sirens way off in the distance. Yet it all fades away. Nothing exists but me and Marcum and I need him to fight. I need him to...

Live.

❧ 74 ❧

MARCUM

"THAT'S IT, DRAGONFLY, BRING ME TO HEAVEN," I URGE HER AS she continues riding me. Her body moves above me and she smiles down, her eyes dancing with joy. She's everything, my world. I move my hands up her waist, her heated skin seeming to warm me from the inside first, and then spreading outward.

"Honey, I need you to open your eyes."

I don't understand. I'm looking up at her. My hands reach up to grab her breasts.

"Marcum. Come back to me now," Toi says and I shake my head because her body blurs. My hands move through her as she slowly dissipates. "Come back to me, honey," I hear as she finishes fading before my eyes.

It's that moment pain slams through me. I want to scream at how intense it is, but my mouth is dry and I can't get sound out. I end up coughing.

"Oh God! He's alive!" I hear Toi cry. There are others talking, but I can't make out what they're saying or even differentiate their voices.

"Toi..." I cough as reality slams back to me. I try to lift my arms to protect her and look around to find Alvaro, but I can't move my arms; they feel like solid stone.

"Marcum, oh thank God! I thought you were dead. You can't leave me, sweetheart. You can't leave me," she cries, and she lays her head on me. I feel her body jerking as she sobs. I close my eyes, trying to fight the pain back. My eyes are so heavy, the need to just let it all go and fade out is strong, but I try to push it away. I need to talk to Toi...

I need to say goodbye.

"Hush, Dragonfly. Hush for me," I groan. The words rip through me, but I doubt they're loud.

"I love you, Marcum, I love you so much." She murmurs the words against my skin as she kisses my face. Her fingers curl into my beard and it's that connection that gives me the strength I need.

I ignore the pain and my hand slides into her hair, leaving a trail of blood in the blond strands. It looks wrong—the sight of it destroys me. I did the one thing I never wanted, I pulled her down into my filth. I wanted to protect her... I just wanted to... *love her.*

I bring her head down to mine, my cold hand holding her neck, feeling the rapid beating of her pulse. I hold Toi in my arms, with death howling at my back. I know my time is limited and that knowledge burns.

"I don't have much time... need you to listen."

"No, that's not true. We have time, Marcum. You just need to fight. We have a lifetime to share with each other," she says, but she knows better. I see the truth in her eyes and I hear the fear in her words. She's practically rocking in my arms, and her nails bite into my sides.

"It's not in the cards for us," I tell her and the words hurt to even give voice to. I wanted a life with Toi. She was it, everything I wanted in life—but never knew existed.

"You have to keep living. You promised me babies. You promised..."

"We've run out of time, Toi."

"No! Please..." she cries, and I'm crying with her. I feel the tears running down my face, but I don't have shame in them. How can I? I'm saying goodbye to my world, to my... forever. "You can't die..." she says her voice cracking. "This is my fault. You can't die because of me."

"Do you remember? In our bed, when you opened to me, gave me your body... You gave me your innocence. You bled for me and I swore from that moment I'd bleed for you, die for you if that's what it took to keep you safe."

"No! I don't want this. Marcum, I don't want this. I can't live without you."

"You have to, Dragonfly. You have to live. Harley and Desi will need you. I need you to be happy. To live and love, to go on..."

"Marcum, please, baby," she cries, the sobs coming quicker now, her body quivering, one shuddering breath after another, her face scrunching as she cries, no longer able to breathe in between the waves of sadness. I know... because I feel the same.

"I love you, Toi. I never knew... it existed. I saw it, with Max... but I never... not until you, Toi. I love you, Dragonfly," I tell her, giving her the words that I hadn't before. Words I should have given her every day.

Regrets... more regrets. That's what I have. I should have given them to her every day.

"If you love me you'll fight to survive..." she cries. "You'll fight for me, for us!"

She's right, but I can't make my eyes stay open. I'm sinking into the darkness and as it overtakes me, her whispered "I love you," reaches my ears and her lips touch mine as she kisses me.

Letting her go is nothing I want to do. I just don't have a choice.

Regrets... the taste of them nearly destroys me.

❧ 75 ❧

TOI

THE WAITING IS TAKING FOREVER. I'M SITTING IN THE SURGERY waiting room. I have Harley's head in my lap. He should be home, but he was there today and he's not willing to leave my side. I push my hair out of my face, feeling so tired it hurts to move. I look down at my pants and see blood on them...

Marcum's blood.

You bled for me, I'll bleed for you...

I'm paraphrasing, but the craziness of what Marcum said to justify dying for me makes me angry. I want to push through those double doors, find his surgery room and scream at him. How dare he make the decisions he made! How dare he tell me goodbye!

How dare he think it's okay for him to leave me...

It's not okay. *It's not.*

I motion over to Babs, because I know I'm close to losing it and I can't do that—not in front of Harley.

I point to Harley, trying to get my message across without talking. She nods her head in understanding. Unfortunately, Harley wasn't really asleep and jerks up as I try to move so Babs can take my place.

"Where are you going?" Harley cries, fear thick in his voice. I swallow down my panic. I kneel down in front of his chair and ruffle my fingers through his soft hair. My voice is gone. Between the crying, the pain, overusing and not taking my medication... Still, I take a breath and I try.

"I..." my voice cracks and the only sound I can make is that of a wheeze.

"You're mad at me. I didn't know Toi, I swear. Cherry said you were going to make Dad send me away. She said you wouldn't want me anymore now that you had a new baby, because I had been mean to you."

"Harley." I try to push through my limitations. I say his name, but it's so quiet that I doubt even Harley could hear it.

"It's my fault. It's all my fault, Toi. I killed Daddy," he cries and my heart breaks all over again. I fall to my ass on the floor and pull Harley into my lap. I hold him so close that I'm probably squeezing him too tight. I put my lips at his ear, because I need him to hear me.

"You are not the reason Daddy is hurt and Daddy is strong. He's going to survive Harley. He's going to survive," I tell him and I'm praying I'm right. "It's going to be okay," I whisper over and over, rocking Harley in my arms. While, in my head, I'm begging Marcum to hear me and fight to come back to his family.

We need him.

I need him.

❧ 76 ❧

TOI

I STARE AT THE CASKET, EERILY CALM. I FEEL SO COLD. THERE'S nothing left inside of me. It's all gone, everything. Around me are Marcum's men; Desi and Harley are with Max. They're all remembering Marcum, smiling and quietly subdued.

I'm sitting here staring at the casket, unable to move. Above the casket is a monitor and it's going through pictures of Marcum. Some I've never seen. Some from when he was young. He looked like he was about to defy the world. Picture after picture pages through his life. Pictures of him with Max, some with his other kids, pictures with Harley and Desi, and with all of his men. In each, he's smiling that cocky smile that says, *"I got it under control."*

The one thing that's not on the screen... not once... are pictures of me and him together. That's because we don't have any. I loved him with all my heart and now it's like... like we were never a part of one another's life. Like Marcum led this happy, beautiful life... without ever having met me.

I was no one.

I've watched the pictures cycle through over and over. I've lost count as to how many times and each time... it hurts more.

There are no pictures of me.

There are no pictures of our marriage.

There are no pictures of the children we would have had.

No pictures of the life we would have had... because we didn't get that.

We'll never get that.

That's when the sobs start. Huge, uncontrollable sobs that rock through my body, leaving destruction in their wake.

"Hush for me, Dragonfly. Hush for me."

I look up at the casket and Marcum is sitting up looking at me, telling me to stop crying.

I scream.

~

"Toi, honey, wake up."

I'm jerked back to reality by Max's arms as he shakes me. I look up at him, blinking—tears still falling down my face.

I look around the room frantically searching for Marcum. But I'm not at his funeral. There is no casket and the only people in the small private hospital room are me and Max—and he just got here. I was alone in here all night.

I rub the back of my hand over my face, drying my eyes.

"Sorry... I was..." I trail off, not sure how to explain the nightmare I just had.

"I understand," he says, patting my shoulder gently. "I thought you could use this," he says handing me a coffee.

"Thanks. Where's Tess?"

"She wasn't feeling great this morning and Maddie needed snuggles."

"You should be with them," I tell him, bringing my hand down to Marcum's. I squeeze it, hoping he knows I'm here—but mostly I do it to reassure myself he's still here. His touch is still warm, though his color is still gray. There's so much equipment hooked up to him, the mechanical noises and beepers are slowly destroying me.

"You need to go home and rest, Toi. You've been here nonstop for a week."

I blink. I hadn't realized it had been that long. One week since my world was destroyed. I look up at Marcum and sigh.

"I'm not leaving."

"Sweetheart, Marcum is a stubborn asshole. He will kick my ass when he wakes up and finds you've been here the whole time and not taking care of yourself."

"No offense, but I don't care as long as he wakes up."

Max sighs and sits down beside me. He takes a drink from his own cup and looks up at me.

"Has there been any change?"

"Not much. The latest test results were encouraging—at least that's what they're telling me."

"Still no movement?" Max asks and my hand goes to Marcum's by reflex.

"None...."

"Toi maybe—"

"He'll come around, Max. He will. He's just resting his body right now. He'll come back to me," I reassure him.

He has to...

MARCUM

"MARCUM, ENOUGH IS ENOUGH. IT'S BEEN THREE WEEKS. YOU promised me a life together. You promised me babies. Are you just going to break that promise? I started my period today you know. The last thing I need is to be in this damn hospital room. I need to be back home, in bed, while you rub my stomach and feed me chocolate. Instead, I'm here putting lotion on you and hurting."

Toi...

"I hate having my period. You promised me a baby and I want that... I deserve that. And why did we never take pictures of the two of us? I know life has been hectic, but you have pictures of everyone in your life but me. Do you know how that makes me feel? You told me you loved me, did you lie? Of course you also told Ghost to take care of me apparently. It's so nice of you to give me away. You arrogant asshole."

Pictures...

"Is that what you want? To see me move on to another man? Have another man father my children? Live life with another man? You think it's okay for you to just give me away?"

No!

I can't get the words out. Fuck, it's still black, I can't even manage to open my eyes. I feel like I'm in the ocean and the undertow is dragging me down.

"Fine. If that's what you want, Marcum Kincaid. That's what you'll have. In fact, there's a doctor here that's been giving me the eye every day. I think I'll talk to him. He can give me babies and a white picket fence and pictures! I deserve fucking pictures!"

That's it. I don't know exactly what's going on, but hearing Toi talking about another man is more than I can handle. I fight to open my eyes—and it is a fight. I open my eyes and immediately close them again. The light is too bright—too harsh. I blink several times, trying my best to adjust. Finally, I squint to look through the room.

Toi is standing at the foot of my bed. Her blond hair is pulled up on top of her head, she doesn't have any make up on, and even though my vision pretty much sucks—I can see dark circles under her eyes. She's rubbing something on my feet and she's talking the entire time, but now I can't seem to grasp what she's saying. All of my attention is just on looking at her. I watch as she tucks a blanket back on my feet. I moved my toes, but I don't think she even noticed. She walks back to the side of the bed and is washing her hands with some sanitizer, drying them on her jeans. Jeans that are hugging her body closely, accenting every damn curve she has. I may feel like death, but when she turns around to put a paper in the trash and I see the way the denim caresses against her ass, my dick still jerks.

That's when I notice the pain.

Pain everywhere, and damn it, I feel like someone has taken a sledgehammer to my head.

"I've been here every day and night for three weeks, Marcum. *Three weeks*. I've waited on you long enough. It's time you hold up to your promises. You're not the youngest man on the block you know. You're wasting time and it's time we don't have."

Damn.

"You're going to be married to me for at least fifty years. Do you hear me? Fifty. I won't accept anything less. You're going to hold my hand when we're both old and gray. You're going to give me babies. I need them, and Harley and Desi need them. They have an army of older brothers and sisters, they need to enjoy getting to be the older ones for a change," she huffs and then she sits down. That's when I see the sadness on her face.

Toi...

I can't get my throat to work. I can't make her hear me.

"Harley needs you, Marcum. All of us do, sweetheart—but he really does. Cherry did so much to him, things I'm just finding out. He's having nightmare after nightmare... He needs you to pull through this. He's blaming himself and it doesn't matter how much I reassure him... He thinks you don't love him anymore. At first I thought that was because of me, but last night he told me you weren't his father. Cherry told him that he and Desi weren't really yours. I swear if that bitch wasn't already rotting in hell, I'd hunt her down and send her there myself. I hope her and Alvaro are keeping each other company."

Toi...

I try again, still unable to say the word, though I think I at least managed a squeak this time.

Toi lays her head on my chest, her arm reaching out to hug me.

"I miss you so much, Marcum," she whispers, and it sounds like she's crying. "I was just lying about the doctor. I don't want anyone else. Just you... I just... need you. I want the life we're supposed to have together ... I want our babies... and I want pictures... I want so many pictures of us together, of our lives together, that we barely have room to store them all. I want our life together, Marcum..." She keeps whispering and this time I know she's crying because her body shakes against me.

She's hurting and it's my fault.

"Hush for me, Dragonfly."

I manage to get the words out... or maybe just one of them. I don't know, but it's there. Toi's body goes completely still and then she turns to look at me.

"You're awake!" she squeals. She sits up immediately and both her hands go to frame my face. "You're awake!" There's so much joy on her face. It's beautiful and then she brings her lips to mine and gives me some of that beauty in just her touch.

❧ 78 ❧

MARCUM

"IF THIS ISN'T REAL, DON'T WAKE ME UP," TOI WHISPERS WHEN I walk in from the bathroom.

I was released from the hospital this morning and it's been an exhausting day—but beautiful, because I made Toi my wife today. I had Maxwell set it up and when we got to the club the preacher was here, there were decorations everywhere and on each table was a fucking camera. I'm still not a hundred percent, but after being in the hospital and then rehabilitation for almost four months, I'm a fuck of a lot better.

She's sitting on my bed—*our bed*. She's wearing one of my T-shirts and nothing else and all around her are polaroid pictures from our wedding. Pictures our friends took, pictures of our cere-mony, of our dancing... *of us*. The joy on her face feeds that need inside of me to give her everything good I can. To feed it, because it needs to grow. I give her that. I give her joy and I want to make sure that's all she gets from now on.

"You're not dreaming, Dragonfly. I told you, I'm giving you nothing but good now. I'm going to bust my ass to give you every-thing you want."

"You already have, Marcum. You gave me you. That's all I

need," she says, standing up, and she wraps her arms around my neck, my shirt riding up on her thighs as she stretches. I grab her ass and pull her against me, holding her there, and take her kiss.

"And pictures," I remind her, grinning down at her when we break apart.

"Beautiful pictures, though I'm afraid you overdid it today," she says and she turns around, gathering the mountains of pictures on the bed, putting them back in the basket she has them in.

I watch her for a few minutes, teasing me with that ass, my shirt just skirting the curves of her cheeks. I haven't had her in six fucking months and while my body might not have been in the shape to have her, that doesn't mean it didn't ache for her just the same.

I came close to dying... too fucking close. Toi's love brought me through. I tell her that all the time, but she doesn't believe me. It's true, just the same. I fought to come back to her and to be the man she needs. I fought even though my body was tired of the fight.

This is my reward—Toi.

I never knew women like her existed, especially not for an asshole like me. Toi was everything good and innocent in the world and maybe I should have never touched her. Maybe I was reaching too high—but she's mine now. Mine, and I'm not letting go because I now have one final rule to add to all of my unwritten ones that clutter my brain.

A good woman seeps down inside of you. Feeds the soul. Brings you peace.

When you find her, you hold on and you never stop fighting to give her joy... because she deserves it. She deserves all that and more.

"It's real, Dragonfly," I whisper, squeezing her ass gently.

"Marcum," she says softly turning around to face me. "I love you."

"I love you too, honey."

"You have no idea how empty this bed has been without you," she whispers, lying her head on my chest.

"I know how empty I've been, not having you with me," I tell her, and I pull my shirt up over her body.

"Marcum, I... don't think this is a good idea."

"It's the best fucking idea I've ever had. Besides, I've given you a wedding, now I need to give you babies."

"But you're not completely healed..." she complains, but she helps me get her shirt off, and pulls the towel loose from around my hips.

"You can do all the work," I tell her with a smile, nipping at her lips as I turn us so I can sit on the bed and bring her down with me.

"I can?" she questions when our lips break apart. She's standing while I slide back on the bed and lie down with my hands behind my head.

"Ride me, honey. Come ride your man and bring me to heaven."

EPILOGUE

TOI

Two Years Later

"Did you see that hit?" Harley asks excitedly, walking from the ballpark, his dad beside him. Desi and I are sitting on the bleachers. It's February, but Florida being Florida it's humid as heck out here and I feel like I'm melting. It's more than worth it though, to be here to watch Harley bat his very first homerun.

"Of course we did! Didn't you hear me and Desi yelling?" I laugh. I know he did, he kept looking over here, smiling.

"Yeah," he says almost shyly as he and Marcum make it to us. Marcum has his hand on Harley's shoulder and sweet Jesus... Marcum is always hot, but seeing my tattooed biker, with his leather cut, next to his little boy, holding him close and smiling ear to ear... all my female bits want to heat up and explode.

"You were a star out there, Bub," I tell him, ruffling his hair.

"Mom," Harley complains, but he's laughing.

"Who's ready for ice cream?" Marcum asks and my laugh is drowned out by the screams of joy from Desi and Harley.

"Is this a private party, or can anyone join?" Max laughs as he and Ride stand up behind me.

"Shouldn't you be in a hurry to get back to Tess, boy?" Marcum asks, shaking his head.

"Please. She has Maddie and Bella on a playdate today, which means she's napping. I'm not about to interrupt that," Max answers naming his newest baby girl, Bella. I think they were hoping for a boy at first, but are completely in love with their two daughters. Max likes to joke he's surrounding himself with beautiful women so he will look good in his old age.

"Then you help the kids load up Harley's crap in the SUV and I'll help Toi up," Marcum agrees.

"Jesus, I'm heading out. All this baby shit and kid life is making me old before my time," Ride says with a wink. "Later people. Catch you next time, Dawg," he adds with a wave.

Once everyone heads out, Marcum reaches down to pull me up.

"I'm not that fat, you know. I could have got up on my own," I tell him, and I probably could, but I'm so fat and round it would have been a struggle.

Marcum places his hand on my stomach. I look down at his ink-covered hand with heavy rings adorning each finger, holding my stomach where inside our little boy is resting, and I wonder if a woman could die from happiness.

In the last two years, life has become as perfect as humanly possible. Every single day with Marcum just gets better and better. He's still Marcum but he's happy now. You can see it written all over his face. I feel the same. I've grown so close to Desi and Harley, as well as Marcum's other kids, and now we're finally going to have our own child.

We both decided to wait until Harley felt more secure. In the end, I had Marcum do a DNA test to confirm he was the their biological father. If I'd been wrong, we would have never told either of them, but I was right. Seeing the proof in writing that Marcum was truly his father healed Harley's fears completely. If there was any doubt left inside of him, it disappeared when I officially adopted the twins as my own. I didn't offer to adopt the other kids; they didn't need that from me. But, a few call me their mom and I'm completely happy with that.

I even got up the nerve to have surgery on my throat. It kept getting better, and the doctor said some of my issues were psychological, and I was slowly healing that part on my own because I felt safe now. Still, since the surgery I'm good now. I still have days where my voice is off, but they are few and far between.

"I just wanted a moment with my woman. Is that so bad?" Marcum whispers, bringing my attention back to him. He's looking up at me with his beautiful dark eyes.

"Not at all. I missed you, though I have to admit it was kind of hot watching you coach Harley out there."

"Did you get pictures?" he asks. He's always asking that and each time he does, my heart flips in my chest.

"A million of them," I tell him.

"That's my girl," he laughs and then he pulls me up in his arms and carries me toward the vehicle.

I'd argue that I'm too heavy, but it never does any good and honestly, I love being in his arms.

"I love you, Marcum."

"I love you too, Dragonfly. I love you too," he says and if hearts could smile... mine would definitely be smiling right now.

EPILOGUE

MARCUM

FIVE MONTHS LATER

I open the door slowly. I'm late getting home. The boys and I have been on the road all day. It was a long ride and one we probably would have stayed overnight for, but I couldn't. I needed to get home.

Home to my family.

Toi left a light on by the bedside and it bathes the room in a quiet glow. I stop by the crib first and look down on our little boy.

Matthew is officially one month old today and somehow he gets more precious with each day. He's got a head full of dark hair like his old man, but his eyes are blue like his mom's. He's already sleeping through the night for the most part and seems to have his mother's personality rather than his old man's—and that's probably a good thing. I look over at a sleeping Toi, her long blond hair spread out over her pillow, and once again it hits me just how fucking lucky I am.

My gaze travels through the room and I take in all of the pictures Toi has strewn around. Pictures of us with the boys and women in the club, pictures of us riding my bike, pictures of us on our wedding day, pictures of the day we found out she was pregnant, pictures of all of our kids, pictures of Desi cheering and Harley playing ball and pictures of Matthew—they're all here. So many pictures you would think she would run out of wall space, but she never does, and each one is a day I remember as clear as the Florida morning sky.

I've given her a wedding, I've given her a baby and I'm doing my best to make sure she has pictures of every day we're together. I won't stop either. I'll keep giving her everything, because she deserves it. Because she's everything to me. And if I have anything to say about it, I'll keep doing that for fifty years and even longer if I get the chance. And when we travel into the next world together? I'll keep doing it there.

Because when you find a good woman, you hold on tight and you never fucking let her go.

EXCLUSIVE EXCERPT OF TAKING IT SLOW

CHAPTER 1
Faith

I WHIMPER WHEN THE DAMN PING OF MY PHONE WON'T HUSH. I squint, opening one eye—and one eye only.

Sweet Jesus on a turnip truck, I drank way too much last night. I warned Hope I didn't do weddings. I hate them. She was in Vegas, everyone knows you do the deed at a quicky drive-thru chapel somewhere and get it done—if you are ever crazy enough to say I do.

I won't... ever.

Slowly the room begins to come into a focus... it's a blurry focus, but still.

The first thing I notice is everything hurts.

Even my hair.

Definitely had too much to drink. The second thing I notice is I'm not in my one room apartment, lying on my broken down, never comfortable, probably ruining my back forever, futon.

I'm in a bed. A *really* soft bed. I'm also in what appears to be a very fancy room. A room with entirely too much sunshine coming in through the windows. My gaze immediately goes to the opened glass doors that lead out to a balcony. When I look around I can see I'm not only in a strange hotel room, I'm in one that costs bank.

Lots of bank.

Then, I just happen to notice the crumpled wedding dress on the concrete floor of the balcony.

That's when panic begins, as memories flood through my mind.

Memories of the night before.

Of course, it might not be the crumpled dress that brings those back quite as much as the huge leg—*not that leg*—wrapped over mine, the arm currently wrapped across my stomach and the third leg—*yes, that leg*—pushing against my ass.

I look down at the milk chocolate beast of an arm and I swear the female bits between my legs tingle as memories of the night before flood through me. Memories of... *Titan.* I have the strongest urge to wiggle against the semi-aroused cock, pressing against my ass, but I don't. I hold myself really still.

Because, I'm in the middle of the biggest panic attack ever.

I can't remember all of what I did last night. It's a blur of devil's juice, eating the worm—disgusting by the way, and I may never drink tequila again—and sex... so much sex.

Sex everywhere. Bed, floor, shower, closet—don't ask—and against the wall. Sex against the floor to ceiling window with my ass mooning the strip, but... sex on that balcony after I was stripped of my wedding dress is the one that sticks in my mind. Sex where I hung over the concrete balcony screaming, *"Fuck me, harder, Big Daddy,"* while Titan did indeed fuck me harder for everyone and anyone to see. There are other balconies close by. I can't be entirely sure who saw us... or who we may have scarred forever.

Because, let's face it sex in real life is never like the porn movies.

I slide out of the bed, an inch at a time—panic making my

heart slam against my chest so loud I want to cry, because my head hurts like hell. Titan grumbles but flops over on his back, still asleep. I stand there looking down at him and I can't move.

He's that beautiful.

His arms are slung out on each side of him, his head turned to the side, his well-trimmed goatee and beautiful, thick lips making my knees weak. The sheet is tangled in his feet and his dick is obviously alert, even if the rest of him isn't.

The sight of his dick makes me glad I was drunk last night.

Lord have mercy on me, a poor sinner girl... he's fucking huge. I take a step toward it, before I can stop myself. It's bobbing up in the air like it's nodding at me. It's wide, as in—thick as hell. How many women has this man sent running from the room in fear —*that kind of thick*. I've seen a few dicks, I'm not a whore or anything—*not counting last night*—but I have, and this one is in a class all by itself and he's long. I don't have a tape measure on hand, and I wouldn't risk waking Titan up for it, but this man could be the pink unicorn of dicks. He could actually be a foot long. He might not be, but it would not surprise me. I back away when Titan grunts in his sleep. Each step I take hurts, only adding credence to Titan's dick. Damn, I might not walk right for a month.

I run bare-ass naked to the balcony. It's early, the sun is shining, but the Vegas heat hasn't raised its evil head yet. I'm definitely going to have to soak my poor abused body soon, however. I can feel where Titan has drilled—*so to speak*—with each step. I grab the wedding dress and step into it, trying to remain bent over so I cover my body. I might not have been shy last night in my tequila haze, but I don't have that luxury today. I shove my hands through the dress, rising up so I can zip it—when I hear a throat clearing. I look behind me and see a man standing there, grinning at me.

He's older, as in probably Uncle Jansen's age and he's wearing a cowboy hat. He's sexy, but not my style.

"Morning," he smirks, his Texan accent strong.

I give him a tight smile over my shoulder and then reach

behind me to zip up the dress and hide my ass from the guy—even if it is a little too late. Walking back into the room, I look around for my shoes. I see some empty condom wrappers—*thank you Jesus!* I also see an empty bottle of tequila and Titan's clothes.

Titan Marsh... pro football player, a hell of a goodtime in bed, and ... my husband.

That last part makes me cringe. I don't want a husband. He didn't want a wife. We discussed that numerous times while drinking tequila and gambling the night away. How we ended up in that all night Elvis wedding chapel, I don't remember exactly. But, I clearly remember saying I do and twirling my hips like Elvis when he proclaimed us husband and wife. I also remember turning to Titan and demanding—in my best Meg Ryan voice—to take me to bed or lose me forever.

He did take me to bed, but he didn't get the whole Top Gun reference. I get the feeling Titan isn't a big movie buff.

I look around for a few more minutes and pick up my veil, I look at the white converse tennis shoes and frown. I wore tennis shoes to my wedding?

Whatever.

I put them on, lace them up quickly. Just as I'm heading out the door, I find a blue flowered garter. It's on the entry table. I pick it up and start to stuff it into my pocket, but the dress doesn't have pockets.

I look back at Titan and then down to the gold band on my hand. I walk back toward him, still feeling him between my legs with each step I make. I clutch the garter tightly in my hand. As I look down at the sleeping man, with the dick that apparently never sleeps, I only know one thing. *I don't want to be married.*

He damn good in bed, though. Maybe if he finds me we can start over and be friends and take it slowly.

Decision made I hold out toss out my garter, toward his dick. It snags on the wide head, and lands at an angle. Titan's hand comes down and he cups his balls, before scratching them. I watch and my mouth falls open and my eyes widen in shock.

When the garter decides to fall down the long shaft of his dick I have to fight back a giggle. Then I hightail it out of the room. I don't stop to think, I don't stop to take in the strange stares I'm getting from the people in the elevator, or in the lobby. I head straight for the door.

Preorder Your Copy today: TAKING IT SLOW

READ MORE JORDAN

WITH THESE TITLES:

Doing Bad Things Series
Going Down Hard (Free On All Markets)
In Too Deep
Taking It Slow (Preorder- Releasing March 13, 2018)

Savage Brothers MC
Breaking Dragon
Saving Dancer
Loving Nicole
Claiming Crusher
Trusting Bull
Needing Carrie

Devil's Blaze MC
Captured
Burned
Released
Shafted
Beast
Beauty

Lucas Brothers Series
Perfect Stroke
Raging Heart On
Happy Trail

Pen Name Baylee Rose & Re-released
Filthy Florida Alphas Series
Unlawful Seizure
Unjustified Demands
Unwritten Rules

LINKS:

Here are my social media links! Make sure you sign up for my newsletter. I give things away there and you get to see things before others! I also have a blog on my webpage you can subscribe to and besides my strange ramblings I'll update you on my work in progress.

Webpage Subscriber's Link:
https://www.jordanmarieromance.com/subscribe
Facebook Page:
https://www.facebook.com/JordanMarieAuthor
Twitter:
https://twitter.com/Author_JordanM
Webpage
http://jordanmarieromance.com
Bookbub:
https://www.bookbub.com/authors/jordan-marie
Instagram:
https://www.instagram.com/jordan_marie_author/

CPSIA information can be obtained
at www.ICGtesting.com
Printed in the USA
FSHW011616170120
66197FS